tilt

Also by Ellen Hopkins

Crank

Burned

Impulse

Glass

Identical

Tricks

Fallout

Perfect

Margaret K. McElderry Books

Ellen Hopkins

Margaret K. McElderry Books
NEW YORK LONDON TORONTO SYDNEY NEW DELHI

This book is dedicated to all families
dealing with chronic illness.

Walk bravely.

MARGARET K. McELDERRY BOOKS • An imprint of Simon & Schuster Children's Publishing Division • 1230 Avenue of the Americas, New York, New York 10020 • This book is a work of fiction. Any references to historical events, real people, or real locales are used fictitiously. Other names, characters, places, and incidents are products of the author's imagination, and any resemblance to actual events or locales or persons, living or dead, is entirely coincidental. • Copyright © 2012 by Ellen Hopkins • All rights reserved, including the right of reproduction in whole or in part in any form. • MARGARET K. McELDERRY BOOKS is a trademark of Simon & Schuster, Inc. • For information about special discounts for bulk purchases, please contact Simon & Schuster Special Sales at 1-866-506-1949 or business@simonand schuster.com. • The Simon & Schuster Speakers Bureau can bring authors to your live event. For more information or to book an event, contact the Simon & Schuster Speakers Bureau at 1-866-248-3049 or visit our website at www.simonspeakers.com. • Book design by Mike Rosamilia • Book edited by Emma D. Dryden • The text for this book is set in Trade Gothic Condensed No. 18. • Manufactured in the United States of America • 10 9 8 7 6 5 4 3 2 1 • Library of Congress Cataloging-in-Publication Data • Hopkins, Ellen. • Tilt / Ellen Hopkins.—1st ed. • p. cm. • Summary: Three teens, connected by their parents' bad choices, tell in their own voices of their lives and loves as Shane finds his first boy-friend, Mikayla discovers that love can be pushed too far, and Harley loses herself in her quest for new experiences. • ISBN 978-1-4169-8330-9 (hardcover) • ISBN 978-1-4424-2359-6 (eBook) • [1. Novels in verse. 2. Dating (Social customs)—Fiction. 3. Love—Fiction. 4. Family problems—Fiction. 5. Family life—Nevada—Fiction. 6. Nevada—Fiction.] I. Title. • PZ7.5.H67Til 2012 • [Fic]—dc23 • 2011040867

FIRST
EDITION

Tilt

Should the sun beat
summer too fiercely
through your afternoon
window, you can

                      slant

the blinds to temper
heat and scatter light,
sifting shadows this way
and that with a

                             lean

of slats. And if candor
strikes too forcefully,
step back, draw careful
breath and consider the

                                        angle

your words must take
before you open
your mouth, let them leak
out. Because once you

                                                    tilt the truth,

it becomes a lie.

My World Tilted

Completely off its axis the night
I hooked up with Dylan Douglas.
It was New Year's Eve—five

months ago—so maybe part of that
earth-sway had something to do with
the downers, weed and cheap beer,

a dizzying combo on an empty stomach.
What I know for sure is, when he came
slinking up like a cougar—all tawny

and temperamental—something inside
me shifted. Something elemental.
I, probably the oldest prude in my whole

junior class, transformed into vamp.
When he smiled at me—me!—I knew
I had to make him mine. I would

have done anything. Turned out, all
I had to do was smile back. Just like
that, we belonged to each other.

Love at First Smile

That's what it was. He says so,
        and I agree. What kind of girlfriend
                would I be if I argued about something

like that? Not only that, but we
        fell in love as a new year began.
                Symbolism there. And I didn't need

a resolution when a result had
        just occurred. All the hurt of
                losing my last boyfriend—who was

at the same party, slobbering
        all over my ex–good friend,
                Tricia—dissolved, shaved ice in

a cup of hot tea. Dylan is a hundred
        times the guy Josiah is. Thank
                God I didn't give my virginity

to *him*. I didn't give it to Dylan
        right away, either. Unlike Josiah,
                he never pressured me to. But after

a couple of months, love spoke
        louder than fear. One night
                we were mostly naked and

all knotted up in each other's
        arms. And the time just seemed
                right to say, "I want to. Please."

        Dylan was just so cute. *Are you*
                sure? He said it right before
                        I stripped off my panties. And

he confirmed, *You're positive?*
        just as I pushed him inside me.
                I think I wanted it more than he did.

And all that hype about awful
        pain? Well, that may be true
                for some people. But, except for

a couple of seconds of intense
        pressure, it didn't hurt at all.
                But it made our connection steel.

Loving Someone

That much—so much he means
more to you than anything—changes
things. You lose friends, because
you'd rather be with him than with them.

I've always been popular. Cheerleader.
Junior class president. Homecoming
princess. All the girls wanted to hang
with me. One was even a stalker.

Now, they still smile and say hello,
but the only ones who I'm really close
to are Audrey and Emily. Both of them
have sleepover boyfriends, at least when

their parents aren't home. That's another
thing love changes—your relationship
with your parental units. It becomes
them versus you, as if they're afraid

of losing you. Jealous of the person
who can make that happen. News flash,
Mom and Dad. I'll be eighteen in a few
months. You've already lost me.

Now It's Summer Vacation

Definition: sleeping in. Lazy days
        at Tahoe. Parties. And that leads me to
        deception. Because here's the thing
about parents. Mostly, they don't want

their kids to have fun, at least not
        if it involves underage drinking,
        illegal substances and the possibility
of sex. This is the first party of

the summer. I plan on an all-nighter.
        Which means I can't say I'm going
        out with Dylan. So I invented a sleep-
over at Emily's. "Hey, Mom," I call

toward her bedroom. "I'm leaving
        now." I grab my backpack and keys,
        start toward the door. I'm almost there
when my brother comes out of the kitchen,

        yacking down a sandwich. *Emily's,*
            huh? Trace checks out my shorts,
            the scoop of my tank. *God, man,*
        you look like a Fourth Street hooker.

"When were you on Fourth Street?
        Anyway, know what they call a guy
        who looks at his sister's attributes
like that? Pervert." His face turns

the color of ripe watermelon flesh.
        Ka-ching! Got him. Trace is fifteen
        and never been kissed. At least, I'm pretty
sure he hasn't been. It's not like I follow him

around, and it's not like he'd go
        bragging about it if he had. Trace is
        the so-quiet-you-have-to-wonder-what-
he's-hiding type. Except, that is, when

it comes to ragging on me. "Tell
        Mom I said bye, okay?" I escape into
        the gentle warmth of late afternoon
June. The party won't start until after

dark. But I don't have to wait that long
        to see Dylan. He's picking me up at
        Em's. I see it as a French vanilla lie.
Not totally white. But close enough.

Emily's Parents Aren't Home

So I don't bother with the doorbell. "Hello?"
No response but a meow from Monster Cat.

Ah, now I hear giggling behind her bedroom
door. She's either on the phone or not alone.

I probably shouldn't barge in. Tyler's probably
in there, too. Instead, I text Dylan. HEY, BABY.

COME GET ME. Just as he says he's on his way,
Emily comes out of her room, adjusting clothes,

hair mussed and makeup smeared. Good call.
"I take it Ty's here?" They've been going

>out for almost a year. Serious love.
>*Uh, no, actually. It's not Tyler. It's Clay.*

The look she gives me is half challenge,
half plea. Last time I looked, Clay happened

to be going out with our mutual friend,
Audrey. "Hey, I won't tell." But I can't

believe she'd cheat on Tyler. "Did you and
Ty have a fight or something?"

>She smiles. *Nothing like that. I just
>wanted to try something different is all.*

Something Different?

God, I'm glad Dylan is everything
I need. Two horn blasts tell me he's outside,
waiting. "Are you coming to the party later?"
I don't ask, "Are you coming with Tyler or Clay?"

> *Probably.* She grins. *Depending.*

Whatever. All I really care about
right now is Dylan. My pulse picks
up speed as I hurry down the walk
to his shiny green Jeep. He always

keeps the Wrangler spotless. When
he sees me, he gets out and waits,
and his perfect smile spreads across
his incredible face. God, he's amazing—

bronze skin beneath too-long blond
hair that makes him look like a little boy.
Well, except for the fact that he's six
foot two and buff as hell. He opens

his arms. I give a little jump, and
he's holding me and we're kissing.
His lips are smooth and he tastes like
peppermint. And I never want to stop.

> But he does. And he says, *I love you.*

Three Words

And everything bad in my life
        melts away. I look into the turquoise
        deep of his eyes. "I love you, too."

I tangle my hands into his hair,
        pull his face into mine for another
        kiss, this one hotter than the last.

        A passing car beeps going by.
            Dylan draws back, laughing.
            Maybe we should get a room?

"Maybe." We could probably
        get one inside. But then Dylan
        would find out about Clay.

He and Tyler are friends.
        "Let's get something to eat.
        Not good to drink on an empty

stomach." Experience has
        taught me that. Dylan agrees.
        But before he detaches himself

        totally from me, he slips a hand
            down the scoop of my tank.
            Can't wait to kiss these, too.

Dylan

Can't Wait

To get her all alone,
pull her nakedness into
me, silk skin slick against
my own, eliciting
the proper reaction.

She
smells like summer
wildflowers, as if
they were woven into
her hair and crushed
by the weight of our love.

Tastes
like strawberry pie,
thick drizzles of whipped
cream melting down over
luscious ripe fruit.
I could lick her all day.

Of
all the girls to inhabit
my dreams, she is the one
I want to stay there,
a shimmer of winter
beneath the heat of

summer.

Thank God It's Summer

I thought I'd never drag myself
through the last few weeks of school.
It wasn't the work or the struggle
to pull exceptional grades.
It wasn't even the gay-bashing.

I got used to that in grade school,
before I even knew for sure I was
gay. Somehow, a few other people
sensed it, like coyotes sniffing out
a pack misfit. Something weak.

Something that needs culling.
Coyotes hunt in packs, and so do
assholes. There's safety in numbers,
especially when attacking prey
that's bigger. I'm pretty big, and

one-on-one I can hold my own,
queer or no. But facing down
a posse of pricks requires charisma.
Intelligence. The ability to redirect
negative energy toward something

more deserving—the fast approach
of a teacher, or a cheerleader's barely-
there skirt. I am an expert bad mojo
shifter. But that has nothing to do
with why I'm glad it's summer.

What's Got My Tightie Whities

All bunched up is my sixteenth birthday
in two weeks. Give me a car, everything
about my life will move into the plus column.

I'm sick of bumming rides with my own pack
of losers and freaks. Not that I mind the perks—
a regular supply of weed and the occasional snort.

But I need a reliable way out of this house,
which reeks of rubbing alcohol and dirty diapers.
The stink permeates everything, despite the incense

I keep burning behind my bedroom door. Cherry.
Vanilla. Sandalwood. A thick combination. None
of it can disguise the smell of Shelby. My sister

is four, and though her doctor says it's a miracle
a kid with Type I SMA has lived this long, I don't
see it that way. She will never walk. Never even

sit up on her own. Her muscles are wasting away.
And the most vicious thing of all about spinal
muscular atrophy is the disease lets her think.

Lets her feel. Lets her attempt communication,
though the best she can manage is pigeonlike coos.
Trapped inside that useless body is a beautiful spirit,

one that deserves to fly, untethered. Instead,
it is earthbound, jailed by flesh. Fed by tubes.
Lungs pumped free of snot. Miracle? In hell,

maybe. Then again, this house is a lot like hell.
My parents despise each other, but don't dare
divorce. I mean, what would the neighbors think?

Mom is so hung up on caring for Shelby
that she has lost all her friends. No one calls.
No one comes over, not even Aunt Andrea.

Dad spends all his time at work. And when
he actually has to come home, he makes sure
to get in very late and sleep in the guest room.

He hardly ever talks to Mom. And when he
wastes a few words on me, it's almost always
some snarky remark about queers. Dad hates

me, too. At least Mom accepts who I am,
or claims to. I don't know if she's really that
open-minded, or just can't stand the thought

of losing her other kid. Shelby doesn't have
a lot more time here. Despite its omnipresent
proximity, her death will devastate Mom.

And So

My desire for regular escape.
My best friend, Tara, usually

provides it. But her parents
are touring Europe. Without her.

So she's spending the summer
with her aunt Dee in San Francisco.

Tara and I have been friends since
before I outed, and she was the first

> person I told. *Well, duh*, was what
> she said. *I've known that forever.*

"Really? How come you still hang
out with me? I don't embarrass you?"

> *It's who you are. And I love who
> you are. Just the way you are.*

Tara is a big reason I am proud
of who I am. She's smart. Pretty.

If she can love me, other people
can, too. Exactly the way I am.

I Actually Met Tara

In Sunday school. When I was a kid,
Dad was a decent Christian. I'd say
it's funny his name is Christian, except
his parents were hard-core Methodists,
who named him that for a reason.

Tara and I were drawn to each other
right away, like we knew we were
destined to be friends, even though
we were only eight. That was B.S.,
of course — Before Shelby. Mom

> was all about having a little girl,
> something I didn't understand. *All*
> *women want daughters,* Tara counseled,
> as if she could know that in second grade.
> *Don't be jealous. You'll always have me.*

Except for today. And there are things
I want to tell her. Developments.
I text her: INTERESTING STUFF GOING
ON. CALL ME WHEN YOU GET UP, OKAY?
I don't say I think I've met someone great.

I Want Her Opinion

And I really want out of here.
　　　　Later, I'll call someone for a ride.
　　　　　　　Somewhere. Anywhere. For now,

I'll distract myself with some
　　　　fine medicinal green and a little
　　　　　　　porn of the guy-on-guy variety.

You can get anything you
　　　　want online. It's crazy, really.
　　　　　　　All you have to do is lie and say

you're eighteen. Well, you need
　　　　a credit card, but I borrowed one
　　　　　　　of Dad's once when he passed

out, totally drunk, before lunch.
　　　　That's not a rare occurrence.
　　　　　　　This time, I managed to store

the numbers from one of his Visa
　　　　cards on my computer. Pretty
　　　　　　　sure it wasn't one of his company

expense account cards, or I'd
        have heard about it by now.
                Then again, maybe Dad has

a porn allowance. Don't most
        mega-corporation vice presidents?
                Whatever. So far, I've had no

problem at all satisfying
        my sleaze curiosity. These
                guys have freaking amazing

bodies, especially Mr. Top. God!
        If I ever have *that* kind of sex,
                I hope it's with someone like him.

Okay, kind of unrealistic, but
        still. So far, I haven't had any
                kind of sex, with any kind of guy.

Nothing but fantasy boinking.
        I'm saving myself for true love.
                And that's never easy to find.

Till Cupid Comes Calling

I'll make do with this. I finish
off a fat blunt and am almost ready
to finish myself off when I hear
footsteps come down the hallway.

Clip-clip. Clip-clip. They pause
at my door. Shit. Not now, Mom.
My window is cracked, but it reeks
in here and I really don't need grief.

> *Shane!* A fist volley tests the wood.
> *Open up right this minute!* I stay quiet.
> *I'm not leaving until you open the door.*
> Quiet. *I know how to unlock it, you know.*

What the hell. If she insists on
being privy to my every move,
fine. I don't even turn off the movie.
"Yes, Mother? What can I do for you?"

> She blows through the door, stomps
> to my desk, double-takes the roach,
> still leaking a thin stream of stink.
> *What, exactly, do you think you're doing?*

It's comical how she stands there,
hands on hips, pretending to be
tough. I try to hold the laughter
back, but it snorts from my mouth.

"I would think that's obvious, Mom.
I'm smoking weed and checking out
a little guy-on-guy action." She never
even noticed! Her eyes go wide at

> Mr. Top drilling Mr. Bottom. *God,*
> *Shane!* She clicks the mouse and
> the screensaver pops up as she launches
> a rant about how am I paying for porn

and pot and now she's onto Grandma's
good china, which I remind her she
never uses anyway. But when I joke
about hooking her up with my connection,

she rails about not smoking in the house
and asks if I want to kill my sister.
"No, Mom. I don't want to kill her."
Deep breath. "But I wish God would."

Too Far

I pushed too far. Mom's face goes
white and she folds up into herself.

>   *I know you don't mean that*
>   is all she says, before leaving

me listing in a wake of sadness.
I wish I didn't mean it. But I do.

I love my sister. Wish her inner
light could somehow make her whole.

But her only chance at perfection
is on the far side of death. And until

that door opens for her, those of us left
on this side can't get on with living again.

Instead, we stumble through our days,
barely connecting, and when we do,

it's often with misplaced anger.
Happiness seems just out of view.

I won't find it here. But that doesn't
stop me from searching elsewhere.

Lately I've Been Searching Online

It's not like I can reasonably look
        for a boyfriend at school. Same-sex
        hand-holding is frowned upon at Reno

High. And while I don't exactly
        hide my queerness, I don't flaunt
        it, either. Anyway, if heteros can

find love on the web, I don't
        know why I can't, too. I've cyber-
        met several, weeded out the total

pervs and ding-your-warning-
        bell creepsters. That left a few
        possibilities, which I've narrowed

down to one incredible boy.
        Alex is seventeen, smart as hell,
        and his webcam shows him Goth-hot.

I hope when we meet in person
        that he likes me as much for real
        as he seems to like me online.

Alex

When We Finally Meet

How much do I confess?
Our bond is tenuous.
Frail as a drift of moon-
light on open sea.

                    Would

the truth crash us
apart? Some secrets
can't be kept too long.
No matter how hard

                    you

try to hide them, sooner
or later, they scurry out
from your cupboards,
cockroaches on the

                    run.

No way to grow closer
with deceit wedged
between us. Should I tell?
Or should I hide it

                    away?

I Hide Hurt

Behind a fake smile. I wear
       it all the time. Everyone says how
I always look so cheerful.
       Shows what they know, I guess.

Not that things are so bad.
       When I think of little kids starving
in Africa, or old people freezing
       to death, my life seems pretty good.

Mom's got a decent job at DMV.
       There's plenty of food in the fridge.
I wear semi-nice clothes, and I've got
       stuff—a cell, an iPod, a laptop.

School is okay, at least up till
       now. I start high school end of
August. I have good friends,
       including my excellent BFF, Bri.

Which leaves one thing missing.
       My dad. I hardly ever get to see
him, even though he only lives
       fifty miles away in stupid Fallon.

So This Weekend Visit

Was a surprise. When Dad called,
I swear I went all fan girl. (Can you
go fan girl over your father? Dumb.)

> *Hey there, Sugar, he said. I sure
> have missed you. Want to come
> out to the sticks for a couple of days?*

My heart started hammering and,
for once, my smile turned real.
After I said, "Sure," I added, "Daddy."

I like to try and guilt-trip him that way,
not that it works. As far as I can tell,
he's totally guilt free. The highway from

Carson to Fallon is flat and plain.
"I wish you didn't live so far away
so I could see you more often."

> Dad keeps both hands on the steering
> wheel and his eyes on the road. *Glad
> you said that. Looks like I'm moving*

*back to Reno. Cass . . . uh . . . my new
girl has a house there. And I landed
a job at Terrible's. So I'll be closer.*

I'm all jumbled up. Happy, because
he's going to live closer. A little scared,
because I don't know what that means.

And a lot jealous. Dad has a girlfriend,
and this time it sounds serious. "You're
moving in with her? How long have

you been seeing each other?" I ask, even
though it doesn't matter at all. I stare out
the window as the power poles zip by

and try not to scrunch my nose at
Dad's obnoxious cigarette-and-sweat
smell. *I guess it's been about six months*

*now. We met just before Christmas.
You'll like her. She's funny and sweet
and really cute. Not as cute as you, though.*

Usually

I like when people say I'm cute.
　　　But not when it feels tacked on.
　　　　　And not when comparing me
　　　　　　　to someone else. And especially

not when the someone doing
　　　the comparing is my dad,
　　　　　stacking my cuteness against
　　　　　　　his new, serious girlfriend's.

Anyway, cute is okay. But I'd
　　　rather be pretty. Beautiful.
　　　　　Hot. (Okay, not in my father's
　　　　　　　opinion. That's just gross.)

I want boys to look at me like
　　　they look at Brianna. It's hard
　　　　　having a best friend who draws
　　　　　　　everyone's attention when you

never do. I keep hoping some
　　　of Bri will rub off on me, but
　　　　　so far, no. Mom says I'm a late
　　　　　　　bloomer. But it's summer already.

Well, Officially

Summer is still two weeks away.
Maybe I'll bloom by then.
Dad turns off the highway, zigs and
then zags and we pull onto a cracked
cement driveway. He doesn't live

like a king, that's for sure. The house
is a prefab, and an old one. The beige
siding is chipped and brown paint
peels from the eaves like scabs
leaving skin. Eww. Disgusting.

Bent chain link surrounds a yard
that looks like it once had grass.
A few green patches remain midst
the crusty brown stuff. "You should
water the lawn once in a while."

> But Dad is already out of the car
> and headed toward the house.
> He turns long enough to say,
> *Grab your stuff and come on.*
> *Cassie is anxious to meet you.*

She Stands in the Doorway

Tall and too thin and melon-boobed,
with long wavy hair the color
of fall scarlet maples. She
isn't cute. She's pretty.
She reaches for Dad
and they're kissing
like people do in
the movies. I
can see their
tongues
moving
from here.

That part
grosses me
out. What's
worse is how it
looks like they're in
love. It's not fair. How
can he love someone else
when he can't find enough love
for me to keep me solidly in his life?
Mom's right. He is one selfish bastard.

I Stuff All That Inside

Find my phony grin and go to meet
Dad's new girl. As I get out of the car,

they stop the tongue dance. Thank goodness.
At least I don't have to see it up close.

> *Hi!* (Her voice is all breathy.) *You must
> be Harley.* (Duh.) *I'm Cassie. Well,*
>
> *really Cassandra, but Cassie for short.*
> (Double duh.) She does have a nice

smile, though. What do I say that
she hasn't already said? "Uh . . . hey."

> Cassie pokes Dad's shoulder. *You
> didn't tell me how gorgeous Harley is.*

Gorgeous. A bit over the top, but I
have to admit it thaws me a little.

> *Come on inside and meet my son.*
> (Great. She probably wants me to babysit.)

Cassie holds out her hand and I don't
know what else to do but take it. Her skin

is softer than I expected and when her
hair moves it smells like cinnamon over

tobacco. She tugs me gently across
the threshold. The place looks like a tornado

blew through, depositing clothes and
fast-food wrappers everywhere.

> *Sorry about the mess. Your dad isn't*
> *so good about picking up after himself.*
>
> *That will have to change when he moves*
> *in with me. Chad! Come say hi to Harley.*

It takes a few seconds, but eventually
footsteps clomp down the hall. Heavy

footsteps. Either he's a really big little kid
or Cassie is older than I thought. OMG!

Chad is maybe sixteen, tall like his mom,
and amazing, with hair the color of a shiny

new penny and superdark eyes that check
me out and make me feel all hot and weird.

They Also Make Me Feel

Not good enough. Like they're
measuring me and I'm sure to
come up short, the way I always do.

I struggle to find my best real
smile and hiss an awkward, "H-hi."
Cassie notices my stupid stammer

      and crazy embarrassing blush.
      She slides her arm around my
      shoulder. *Harley says she really*

      wants to learn how to ace World
      of War. I told her you're the best
      gamer I know. You'll teach her, right?

            Now Chad smiles back at me.
            Why not? That little bedroom
            was getting claustrophobic.

He goes to turn on the PlayStation
and TV. Cassie winks and nudges
me toward the sofa. The gaming begins.

Chad

Gaming

Master the controller,
conquer the rules and
perhaps for the very first
time in your life, you savor
power. The learning curve

teaches

the value of patience.
Practice. Self-restraint,
when external discipline
has too often forced

you

down on your knees.
Virtual killing is safe passage
to the pleasure of revenge
when you don't know

how to

get it any other way.
And when you too often
hear people shouting,
"You're a loser," kicking
cyber-butt convinces you
that you can

win.

Mikayla
No-Win Situation

That's pretty much where you find
yourself when your uncle is the cop
who busts you at a party, stoned
out of your head. Okay, in a way

you win, because he hauls your butt
home instead of taking you to juvie.
But in lieu of institutionalized
lockup, you end up jailed at home.

I should be at Tahoe with Dylan
today. But, no. Dad grounded me
with no set release date. I'm not
even allowed to use my computer

or cell phone. Cut off completely
from the outside world, exiled to
my stupid house, what am I supposed
to do for entertainment? School

would be better than this. I could
pick a fight with Trace, but all that
would do is irritate Mom, who I'm
pretty sure has a hangover. Mom

is my only ally here. She acted all
put out about the party, but I could
tell it was mostly for Dad's benefit.
She gave me a one-question quiz

about my drug use (deny, deny, deny).
Accepted my lame answer (win, win,
win). And the only thing she said
about my crooked clothes, smeared

makeup and obvious sex perfume
was to take a shower. Okay, she said
it twice. So I'm pretty sure she knew.
We've never had that mother-daughter

heart-to-heart you imagine is coming.
I guess, since they start teaching sex
stuff in, like, fourth grade, she figures
she doesn't need to worry about details.

Of course, Mom is so wrapped up in
herself lately (not to mention pretty
buzzed when she walked in on the scene),
maybe she didn't notice anything at all.

God, I Miss Dylan

Okay, it's only been a couple
       of days, but it feels like forever.
He's everything, and all I can think
       about right now is how we made love

that night. We had messed around
       lots of times before, but it had never
seemed quite like this—much more
       about making each other feel good, less

about just having sex. Maybe it was
       the Southern Comfort, or the weed
(green and so stony!), or the two
       together. But when we took off our clothes

in the back of his Wrangler, skin
       raked by cool claws of moonlight,
insane, hot need grabbed hold
       of me. All I wanted was his mouth

and tongue kissing me all over
       my body. I was wild for it, really.
And that was very new. I think
       it kind of scared him, although

he liked the things it made me do.
        Things you don't learn. Things
you just intuit, like you're born
         to do them. Threads in the silk

of womanhood. I feel like a woman
        now. It's weird, because when you
read about sex, or see it in movies,
        they work so hard to make it seem

great that it sort of feels like fiction.
        But this was not playacting or words
lifted off a page. This was real,
        and when we reached that ultimate

peak, it was nothing I'd ever
        experienced before. We seriously
both went, "Wow," in unison.
        And then we both laughed. Together.

Afterward, I wasn't in a hurry to
        get dressed. Which explains why,
when the cops showed up, I think
        Uncle Stan caught a glimpse of my boobs.

If I Keep Reliving

That night, I'm going to go apeshit.
I'd watch TV, but Brianna has got
some god-awful baseball game on.

What kind of thirteen-year-old girl
is in love with the San Francisco Giants?
When they won the World Series,

after all those dreadful years, I swear
I thought she'd totally cry. She's
cheering now, so they must have scored.

I guess I could read, but I don't have
a book I'm currently interested in.
Looks like it's solitaire or . . .

My eyes settle on a magazine, lying
on the kitchen table. On the cover
is a collage of pictures—kids, adults. Families.

The caption says: *Technological Tools
for Birth Family Searches.* I flip to
the article, which is all about how social

networking is reuniting adoptees
with their birth parents. Mom is adopted,
and over the years, she has made half-

hearted attempts to connect with
the people who created her. Each
time, she has come away disappointed.

But I'm betting she never tried Facebook.
As I read, she shuffles into the kitchen.
Usually by now she's run five miles

and showered, which is why I'm thinking
she had a little too much to drink last
night. Whatever. Everyone needs to party

once in a while. "Have you ever thought
about trying this?" I hold out the magazine.
"I mean, c'mon, Mom. No-brainer."

She skims the article. Shakes her head.
I barely know how to update my status.
I'd have no idea how to start.

"You want to know where you came
from, right?" She shrugs. Looks kind
of confused. "I'll help, Mom." At least

I won't croak from boredom. "Tell me
what you know about your birth parents.
No names, right?" She shakes her head.

> *Your grandma told me they were from*
> *Elko and my mother got pregnant*
> *in high school.* Grandma, meaning

Mom's adopted mother, who kind of
defined the word *bitch*. "So you were
born in . . ." Some quick calculations

net a scary fact. "God, Mom, you're
going to be forty." In less than two
months, my mother will officially be

> over the hill, no matter how good
> she looks for her age. *Don't remind me.*
> *I can almost see the Grim Reaper.*

So Not Funny!

"Mom! Don't say that!" The idea gives
        me goose bumps. "You are not allowed

to die. Ever!" She reminds me of
        a lioness, with tawny skin and golden

eyes. I wish I looked more like her
        and less like Dad, though I'm pretty

sure I don't have to worry about
        going bald and he definitely does.

"Okay, I think I know what to do
        first. . . ." Mom lets me use my laptop

to start my research. I'm looking
        for Elko High's Facebook page when

Dad barrels through the door, all pissy
        about one of his clients. Oh, shit. He sees

        me. Goes off. *What the hell are you*
                doing online? Shut that down.

Mom Jumps to My Defense

Which only makes him madder still.
Now he's yelling about how stupid
Mom is to take a chance on hurting
herself with another pointless search,

and how she doesn't need anyone
but us to love her, anyway. I can see
her struggle not to turn this into
a major fight. Why should it be

> an argument at all? Mom defuses
> his anger a little, but as he stalks off,
> griping about his day, she tells me to log
> off. *No use irritating your father more.*

"Fine! But it's so not fair. Why does
he have to be such a jerk?" Her eyes
go all sympathetic, so I ask, "Can I call
Dylan? Just to say hello?" She almost

says no, but when I prod her with
a question about remembering love,
she capitulates. I'm feeling smug.
Until I notice my brother eavesdropping.

Trace

Smug

That's the expression stamped
into my sister's face. But
here's the thing about

                                          feeling

like you've got the world by
the tail. Grab hold and tug,
sometimes you get bitten. A

                                          superior

intellect than my sister's
is at work here—my own.
The information I've just learned

                                          might

offer me some advantage
in the future. Or, play the cards
much differently, it could

                                          result in

a shitload of current fun.
Choosing the "now" might
very well bring

                                          disappointment.

But waiting for the "later"
stokes my impatience.
Decisions. Decisions.

I Hate Decisions

Especially the little ones, like what to wear
for a first date. Weird, in a way, to call it that.

But that's what it is—a boy date. Alex and I
are finally going to meet in person. If we don't

hate each other at initial sight, we'll have dinner
and go to a concert. Okay, since he bought

the tickets already, we'll probably go even if
we decide we can't stand each other. Don't think

that will happen, though. We've been Skyping,
and every conversation has been salted

with revealing factoids, peppered with laughter.
A seasoned relationship, if a fairly short one.

Ha ha. Anyway, what *should* I wear? He'll be
all Goth. So I guess I'll settle for regular jeans

and my Nirvana T-shirt. We're going to see
Stone Temple Pilots. I should get in the mood.

I Shave

Shower, using the gingerbread-scented
soap Gram and Gramps gave me
for Christmas. Another holiday, steeped

in melancholy, with Shelby all dressed
up in green velvet and Dad passed out
drunk before dinner. Mom and I ate

prepackaged turkey slices, Stove Top
stuffing and canned corn while Shelby
hummed along with carols. Tubes feed

her. One day, I swear, I'll host big, fancy
feasts and have ceiling-high evergreens,
decked out in colored glass ornaments,

with tons of presents swirled under
them. Everyone will be happy, and
no one will be drunk or pissed or dying.

But that won't be this year or next,
so I dry myself off, spike my hair
and go dig up some clean underwear.

By the Time

I've located my folded laundry,
beneath a pile of dirty stuff,
nerves are jittering in my belly.
I know I smell great. But is how

I look good enough for someone
like Alex? What if . . . ? Ah, screw
it. This is the best I can do. Mom
has taken Shelby to swim therapy

and Dad is who-knows-where?
I leave a simple note: *Gone out
with a friend.* Stand by the window,
waiting for Alex to pick me up,

and as the clock approaches four,
the nerve dance has quieted some.
At least, until I see the dark-blue
Honda cruise slowly into view,

searching for the address. When
it pulls against the curb, I almost
want to puke. But that would give
me nasty breath. Instead, I go say hi.

What I Know About Him

As I open the passenger door,
bend to say hello, is this:

> He is almost eighteen and
> > goes to Manogue, the local
> > > Catholic high school, where
> > > > it's even less copacetic

> to be gay than it is at
> > Reno High. He's on track
> > > to graduate a semester
> > > > early and he's grateful for

> that. He lives west of the city
> > in Verdi, with both parents,
> > > three sisters and one brother,
> > > > all of whom are straight.

> He likes big dogs, little cats,
> > action movies and reality
> > > TV. His favorite foods are
> > > > pizza, burritos and mangoes.

Mangoes Make Me Itch

So I don't like them much, but
      I'm good with the rest of his likes.
      I wish we could have a dog, big
or small, but pet dander and Shelby

would be a disastrous combo.
      Alex knows all about my sister.
      I thought it might gross him out,
but he was totally sympathetic.

We won't talk about her today,
      though. When I open the door
      and duck my head, our eyes connect
for real. "Hey." It's all I can think

      to say. Stupid. My face flares.
         But he smiles. *Get in. Wow, dude.*
         Awesome digs. I've always liked
Caughlin Ranch. Verdi is a hole.

Most of it is a pretty nice hole,
      but it is a low-lying valley. Still,
      "A great view does not a decent
home make. But it will do, I guess."

Not to mention, when the ice
    caps melt, y'all will keep your
    feet dry. One other thing about
Alex. He moved here from Texas

just three years ago. His voice
    still carries a hint of honeyed
    twang. It's sexy as hell, in fact.
Jeez, who knew I liked "cowboy"?

I do know I like Alex, so I guess
    it isn't hate at first sight, at least
    not on this end. I'm completely
speechless, unusual for me.

    Alex breaks the cloying silence.
        The concert starts at seven. I hear
        the opening act is pretty good,
    so we should get there on time.

It's, like, a little after four.
    Dinner shouldn't take more
    than an hour. What else does
he have planned? "Sounds good."

Turns Out

What he's got in mind is talking.
We drive to this little tucked-away
park beside the Truckee River.

It's shaded by big old cottonwoods,
and totally deserted. We sit in the car
with the windows down, listening

to the soft heave of slow-moving water.
"I've lived in Reno forever, and have
never been here. How did you find it?"

> *My best girlfriend, Dianne, brought*
> *me here one time when I was feeling*
> *really down. I love this place.*

I get what he means by girlfriend.
Lots of women like hanging with
gay guys. I have a best girlfriend, too.

This is the perfect location to toke
a fatty. I know he smokes weed,
want to share. "This shit is stony."

I torch the blunt, inhale deeply,
and despite the dropped windows,
skunk-flavored smoke envelops us.

> I hold out my offering, sure he'll
> accept. Instead, he says, *Smells good.*
> *Before I take it, I have to tell you*
>
> *something you won't want to hear.*
> *But if you don't, we can never share*
> *anything even approaching intimacy.*

He looks at me steadily, cat-green
colored eyes filled with anxiety.
I hold his gaze. "Sounds serious."

> *It is.* He takes a deep breath. Starts
> to say something. Sucks it back in.
> Finally spits out, *I have HIV.*

A pound of dread just tumbled into
my gut. "What?" I watch the joint
go out. "Why didn't you tell me?"

He Struggles

To find the right words.

> *Look. When we were just talking*
> *online, it didn't matter, you know?*
>
> *But then I started to like you. To*
> *really like you a lot. I wanted us to*
>
> *be more than web buddies. For that*
> *to happen, I had to be honest with*
>
> *you. I lost my last boyfriend because*
> *I didn't tell him soon enough and . . .*

His voice trails out the window.

> *And I don't want that to happen*
> *with you. I know HIV is scary. It*
>
> *scares the hell out of me. But I started*
> *antiretrovirals very early. It will be*
>
> *many, many years before the virus*
> *turns to AIDS, and with new drugs*

> on the horizon, that might never be
> a concern. For now, it's under control.

He pulls himself up straight.

> Obviously, I don't want you to become
> infected. Common sense will prevent that.
>
> You can't get HIV from saliva, so swapping
> spit doesn't pose a danger. Blood and, um . . .
>
> semen do. I mean, we could, like, share
> a smoke or a drink or even a kiss without . . .
>
> Ah, God. I sound desperate, don't I?
> I'm sorry. Just, so fucking sorry.

The weight in my gut sinks deeper.

> Listen. You can tell me to screw myself
> if you want. But before you decide,
>
> let's have dinner and go to the concert,
> okay? You can't catch it like that for sure.

Bitch-Slapped

All the way down on my knees.
What happened to a fun first date?
Still, he's right. You can't contract
HIV from sitting next to someone.

I know because when I decided I was gay,
I got myself tested, just in case my one
close encounter was dirty. The doctor
fed me the latest theories about infection.

Never thought I'd actually have to put
them to the test, however. Especially not
the one about saliva. I realize Alex is waiting
for me to say something. Anything.

What the hell. He's still hot, and science
is only wrong once in a while. I torch
the blunt, take a deep drag, offer it
to him once again, this time with

knowledge. He was right. He had
to be honest with me up front. And
since he's being straight with me,
I ask, "How did you get infected?"

Alex

Straight

I

never felt like that term
applied to me, at least not
once I realized there

was

another way to be. But homo, hetero
or somewhere in between, *no*
should mean absolutely not, and

never

did I say okay to my stepfather's prick
brother, Stu. I was ten when he came
creeping. Claimed it was the way I shook
my pretty ass. I might not have said

anything

about the bleeding or the chokehold
welts around my neck—I wept over
his promise to kill my sister if I told—

but

a blood test for mono turned up
something we couldn't ignore. Stu
passed on his HIV to his completely

queer,

but up-until-then-virgin step-nephew,
me. And I didn't ask for it. Not at all.

I Didn't Ask

To come from a split family.
Especially not one where the two
halves are so totally pushed apart.

I'm pretty sure Mom doesn't
think I should love my dad.
But she's the one who left him.

Just because she stopped
loving him, does that mean
I should, too? Okay, I do kind

of remember all the fights
they had. I was in first grade
when Mom decided she'd had

enough. And then there were
a lot of years where he hardly
ever even called to say hello.

He totally missed my birthday
a couple of times, and yeah,
that made me cry. So I sort of get

why Mom is irritated with him
        wanting to step back into my life
                like none of that ever happened.

She wants to protect me from
        getting hurt again and I'm cool
                with that. What I really can't take,

though, is having her come
        storming in and embarrass me
                in front of Chad. Of any boy,

really, but especially him
        because he's, like, the only
                guy even close to my age who

has ever paid me the thinnest
        sliver of attention. Mom says
                I'm too young to worry about

being one of the few geeky girls
        left in my class who have never
                been kissed. But I so do not agree.

I'd Say

It's because I'm too fat—I pretty
much resemble a pot-bellied piglet—
but that can't be it. Bri looks great
in skinny jeans, and guys always

check her out. But so far none
of them have kissed her, not even
at boy-girl parties because whenever
we play Truth or Dare she always

chooses truth. I always choose dare,
but the wildest thing anyone has
dared me to do to a boy was to lick
his big toe. Everyone else was making

out like crazy, though. Bri and I sat
there watching, half-fascinated, half-
grossed-out that people could tongue-jab
so obviously in public. I don't know

what it makes me, but I really want
to try it. And I really want guys to
stare at me the way they stare at Bri.
So even though I'm mad at Mom

for pretty much yelling at me in
front of Chad, I need her help.
"How do I lose weight, Mom?"
She could shed a few pounds, too,

> but I don't say that, and I'm pretty
> sure she doesn't think so. *Fewer
> calories, more exercise.* Too basic
> to work, right? I look into the skinny

visor mirror. I think what I need
are laxatives or diet pills, but I'm very
sure she won't go for that. Exercise?
"Would you help me? Please?"

> She chances taking her eyes off
> the highway to give me a concerned
> look. *Of course. But why are you
> worried about it, all of a sudden?*

I can't tell her it's about wanting
Chad to like me, but I can admit,
"I want to wear skinny jeans, like
Brianna does. They're the style."

Which Somehow Launches Us

Into a whole conversation about
Chad, anyway. It's like she knew.

I try not to mention too much
about Dad and Cassie, because

I can see how just saying their names
and talking about Dad moving back

to Reno makes her feel bad. I mostly
think it's awesome because when

I go visit Dad, Chad will be there,
too. And he's just so cute and he's

really nice. And he doesn't have
a girlfriend. I didn't ask him, of course.

Cassie told me. I thought I was going
to hate her, but she's pretty sweet.

I don't mention that, either. "I'm on
a diet as of today. Can we stop at the store

and get healthy food? 'Cause you buy
too much junk food, and you know me.

I can't say no to chips and soda.
And I really think we ought to go

organic because I read something
about how additives can cause you

to gain weight. . . ." I glance over
at Mom, who's nodding her head,

but I'm not really sure she's listening.
I love Mom, but I swear sometimes

she lives on another planet, or maybe
a comet—all ice and gas and deserted

except for her and me. Doesn't she get
lonely? I mean, I can't always be there

for her. "Hey, Mom?" I wait for the words
to slice through the silence. "Don't you ever

get lonely? For a boyfriend, I mean." After
a long second or two, she responds,

> *Harley, honey, for the most part men*
> *are more trouble than they're worth.*

Lame

Not only cliché, but it can't be
          the truth, or why would every
girl in the world (okay, except
          for lesbians) work so hard

to attract guys? There must be
          something to all the hype.
"But what about sex? Don't
          you like it? Are you . . ."

What's the word I'm looking
          for? The one that means cold?
Oh, yeah. "Are you frigid?"
          Ha. That got her attention!

          She kind of sputters. *Wha-wha?*
                    Did your father tell you that?
          Because I am most definitely
                    not *frigid, missy! I like sex*

          just fine, only not with some
                    selfish prick who is all about
          pleasing himself and not worried
                    at all about satisfying his partner!

Way TMI!

"Whoa! Wait a second, Mom.
Dad never said anything like that.
He doesn't really talk about you.

I was just wondering. And I'm sort
of worried about you. Pretty much
all you do is work." Her shoulders

> slump and she sighs. *That's not
> exactly true. I go out once in a while.
> And I do lots of stuff with you.*

"Big whoop. Doing things with me
or Brianna's mom isn't like hooking
up with someone you're in love with."

> *Believe it or not, it hasn't been all
> that long. You don't know everything,
> munchkin. And the problem with falling*
>
> *in love is falling back out of it again,
> usually because you've fallen in love
> with a lie. That happens as often as not.*

Munchkin!

She hasn't called me that since
        I was a little girl. I hated it then,
        and I hate it worse now. Why not
just call me *Oompa Loompa*?

I think about what she said
        and how bitter she sounded.
        What don't I know? Has she
fallen in love recently, and

back out again? No. I'd know.
        She couldn't keep something
        that big from me, right? Darn it.
That's going to bug me now.

"Hey, Mom. If you *did* fall
        in love, you'd tell me, wouldn't
        you?" She says of course, but
not with much conviction.

I am totally bothered the whole
        time we shop for healthy food.
        And as soon as we get home,
I call my best friend to discuss.

Brianna

A Best Friend

Listens when you rant
about the bad, the blah,
the totally stupid.

A best friend

comments when you want
her to, shuts her mouth
when you don't. She

is

the one who laughs at your
jokes, no matter how idiotic.
She can interpret the tone of

your voice,

cries if she hears pain,
smiles at each hint of joy.
She will tell you to stop

when you

don't see danger or twist
toward wrongdoing. She is
your conscience when you

can't find it.

Mikayla

A Conscience

Can be an annoying thing.
Especially when considering
a major deception, like sneaking
out to meet your boyfriend.

Tonight won't be the first time
I've done it since I've been
grounded. I've mostly given
up on listening to that stupid

little nag inside my head. Every
now and then it insists I'll be
sorry, and maybe I will. But if
Mom and Dad won't lighten up,

I don't have much choice but
the covert route to Dylan. So I wait
for all the lights in the house
to extinguish. For every voice

to quiet way beyond whispers.
And then I wait just a little bit
longer before texting Dylan to come
pick me up. The tiny voice complains,

"You even pilfered Brianna's cell
to send the TM." And I argue right
back, "Yeah, but she never uses it,
except to call Harley, who's busy

helping her dad move. And I couldn't
exactly 'borrow' mine from off Mom
and Dad's dresser, now could I?"
Anyway, I didn't really steal it.

I'll put it back in Bri's backpack first
thing in the morning. She won't miss
it at all. I check my makeup, lotion
my hands so when they touch Dylan

they'll be satin-soft. Spritz perfume—
just a little. Don't want to smell, as Trace
would say, like a Fourth Street hooker.
Luckily, his bedroom is on the other

side of the house. I'm pretty sure
if he heard my window creak open
this time of night, he'd be sure to let
someone (like Dad) know immediately.

So I'm Very, Very Quiet

As I urge the window open,
        slip through the gap, holding tight
        to the sill. The house is built into

the hill, but it's still a drop from
        my upstairs room to the ground.
        Getting back in is harder, but I've

figured out how to shimmy
        up the rough siding, using the family
        room window frame as a boost.

It's a perfect June night, warm
        with a soft sigh of breeze and
        star spatters splashed across

the blue-black sky. My heart
        skips as the neighbor's old dog
        yaps. Trying to bust my escape.

I hurry down the driveway,
        turn toward the main road through
        the valley. Dylan's headlights find

me before I reach it, though.
Just seeing his face, illuminated
through the windshield, fills me

with happiness. I jump through
the passenger door. "Let's go!"
He gives me a quick kiss, then

guns the Wrangler. *Ty's parents
are out of town. He said we can
hang out there if it's okay with you.*

I consider our limited options.
The back of the Jeep isn't very
comfortable, and who knows when

a nosy cop might decide to
check out the usual summer night
party spots. The last thing I need

is my uncle or one of his buddies
eyeing my boobs again. Tyler's is
safer, and it's close. "Sounds good."

Out of the Loop

For a couple of weeks, communications
limited to a covert phone call or six,
I have not been privy to gossip concerning

my posse. Turns out, Ty walked in on
Emily and Clay. Caught them mid-dirty.
Dylan informs me of this so I'll know what

> to say, or what not to say, when we get
> there. And then he makes the comment,
> *I didn't know your friend was such a slut.*

Em and I have been tight since third
grade. My first reaction is to jump in
and defend. But then I remember the last

time I saw her, how she told me she just
wanted to try something new. I look at Dylan,
all iron-jawed in his conviction. "Neither did I."

Now I'm torn between asserting a semi-
warped sense of morality and standing up
for a friend. My best friend, really. If the Ugg

were on the other foot, would she react
differently? Ack. Relationships are so
complicated. I'll think about it later.

> Meanwhile, until we get to Tyler's, I let
> my hand crawl up Dylan's thigh, all the way
> to the burgeoning bulge. *Quit,* he says.

> *God, girl, don't you have any idea how much*
> *I've missed being with you? I'm desperate*
> *to show you. Just not here. Five minutes, okay?*

It takes three to reach Tyler's. Thirty
seconds to get through the door, kissing
each other like we've never done it before.

The house smells like skunk. Green weed.
Now I know the source. Ty is sitting on
the couch watching TV with Caitlin Bowers.

They barely look our way and suddenly
I hear the canned moans that can only mean
they're watching cable porn. Disgusting.

Guess he's not really missing Em. *Make
yourselves at home*, he says, patting the sofa
beside him. Orgy? Don't think so. Thank

God Dylan is on the same page as me.
*Uh. Not now, thanks. Mik and I would
appreciate a little alone time, you know?*

Ty waves us down the hall. *You can have
my parents' room. Just be sure to clean
up after yourselves, okay?* His bluntness

stings, but not enough to keep me from
following Dylan, feeling like I'm about
to do something really filthy in a stranger's

bed. Which sort of makes me wonder
what has gone on in that bed before we
got there. Dylan pulls me through the door,

and his kisses are filled with intent. "Wait,"
I say, going into the bathroom to get
a big clean-looking towel. I put it over

the pretty paisley spread and as we start
taking off our clothes, it comes to me that
we've barely said a dozen words to each

other tonight. That's plenty for Dylan, who
pulls me down on top of him. I look into
his eyes. "I love you." Does he know how

>very much? *I love you, too. Totally.*
>We are kissing. Licking. Biting. Moaning
>louder than the TV in the other room.

He's ready. Wants inside me. But
there's something important missing.
"Not yet. Where's the condom?"

>*I forgot it. But it's okay. I'll pull
>out. Don't worry.* Don't worry?
>We didn't use one last time. It was

right after my last period. But now
it's been a couple of weeks. "Dylan.
This is dangerous. I can't get pregnant."

He Rolls Me onto My Back

Strong. Sure of himself. Then he smiles
down at me. *I know what I'm doing.*

Promise. I won't get you pregnant.
And I have to have you right now.

He hesitates, waiting for my answer.
Everything about me is shouting yes,

so I nod and lose myself in the moment.
Making love with him is so beautiful.

We rock together, in rhythm. One.
As he starts to tense, I remind him with

a subtle lift of his hips. He withdraws just
in time, slicking my belly. *See? All good.*

I am happy for the towel beneath us.
Happier to lie together, bathed in sweat

and the sticky proof of our love. It is, for sure,
all good. At least, until I get home.

Tyler

He Takes Mikayla Home

Dylan, my almost brother.
The top of my list of best

buddies

and yet I have never once
confessed that I loved Mikki
before he did. Why that fact

should

bother me now, I have no idea.
I mean, he and she are superglued.
Maybe it's because Emily and I are

not

inseparable anymore. Caitlin
is a diversion, that's all.
I will never

covet

time with her, like I did with Em.
Like I once hoped to with Mik.
Dylan and I have been

each other's

sounding boards. But when it
comes to what really counts
to us, and between us,

things

border on secretive.

Some Secrets

Should never be admitted outside
a confessional. Should be written
on scraps of paper. Shredded. Burned,
their ashes allowed to lift upon the wind
toward heaven. Whispered apologies
to the only One capable of forgiveness.

Other secrets should be shouted long
before they ever are. Should be sung,
solos in front of the choir. Given voice
and melody. Arias, swelling to fill
the dead, empty space around deception
with the unbearable lightness of truth.

And then there are those that can only
be whispered. Shared between trustworthy
friends, if only to lighten their weight
in the telling. Secrets meant to be kept
like treasure—secured in a concealed
lockbox, tucked away inside your heart.

Why?

That's the question I keep asking myself.
       Why did I have to fall in love with someone

destined to die early? Impending death
       hangs thick around here already. I'm steeped

in it and its cologne does not wash off
       easily. Okay, I know Alex isn't, like, even

close to checking out. His HIV is under
       control for now. He's not even sick, not really.

I've researched the virus in the past—
       just needed to know the facts, man, before

ever expecting to tumble for some guy
       who was actually infected. I get that he isn't

going to croak any time soon. Understand
       that there are ways to be together without

catching it myself, even if our relationship
       grows beyond chastity, all the way to passion.

I'm Tired

Of living chaste. Damn it, today
I'm sixteen years old. And I know
that isn't exactly over the hill, but
I want to see what sex is all about.

Most of me wants to find out with
Alex. But the little piece that's afraid
is completely paranoid. The kind of
paranoid love struggles to conquer.

I've smoked weed with him. Held
his hand. And I've kissed him—
full-on making out, so much better
than anything I expected or could have

invented in my warped imagination.
But when I get home, I take massive
doses of vitamin C and zinc. Stupid,
I know. Like Airborne could ward off

HIV. Still, it's a start. Anyway, I don't
have a choice. Though I haven't admitted
it to him yet, wrong, right, dangerous or harmless,
I am totally in love—and lust—with Alex.

Later, We're Going Out

To celebrate my birthday. Not
like anyone here at home is planning
a party. I mean, what a surprise

it would be if one of my parents
actually acknowledged the occasion.
As usual, Dad was out the door before

I even got up this morning. And when
I sat across from Mom, drinking coffee
as she read the newspaper (complete

with the date and everything!), she barely
looked up. "Hey, Mom," I said. "Any
plans for the *day?*" But she just kept

skimming the pages. *Nope. Nothing
special. How about you?* Articulated
like she actually gave a half damn.

"Having dinner at La Strada, with
my b—my friend, Alex." It's one
of the fanciest restaurants in Reno.

A date restaurant. But all she said was,
That's nice. Wherever her head was at,
it was certainly not thinking back to

the day she had me. I've heard it
was a tough labor. Maybe she'd rather
not retrograde to the delivery room.

I gave up. Went and called Lucas, who
is an asshole, but his brother scores
awesome weed. He picked me up and

we're on our way to get Chad,
who is almost as big an asshole as Lucas.
But beggars (of weed, that is) can't choose

the company their suppliers keep. "Where
does Clay get this stuff?" I try not to exhale
too much smoke around my words.

Lucas shrugs. *Some guy he knows
has a Humboldt connect. Clay buys it.
I borrow it. Hope he never catches me.*

No Shit

Clay is huge. If I were Lucas, I'd be wary
about "borrowing" anything from him.

We pull into the driveway of a cute little
house with perfect paint and a pretty yard.

"Chad lives *here*?" The house so misrepresents
him. "Are his parents clean freaks, or what?"

> Lucas laughs. *Don't know about that,*
> *but his mom is, like, hot. Not that you'd*
>
> *care. And I think she's divorced, although*
> *last time I was here, some creepy guy*
>
> *was hanging all over her. Guess he's moving*
> *in. Chad's not happy about that at all.*

Lucas beeps and Chad comes slinking
out the door—a lizard on two legs.

Behind him is his mom—a tall, skinny
redhead with impossible breasts. Plastic.

Even if I were straight, I wouldn't find
her hot. But the dude grabbing her from

behind obviously does. Wait. Holy shit.
I think it's Harley's dad. I haven't seen

him in a really long time, but . . . yeah.
Pretty sure it's him. Chad ignores both

of them, though I can see his mom saying
something to him. He waves her off.

Then he notices me and if scowls could kill,
I'd be a corpse. He settles into the backseat.

Gets straight to the point. *Why you hang
with fags, dude?* Lucas's face goes red,

but he keeps quiet, so I answer, "As friends
go, fags are totally nonthreatening, unless

you happen to be questioning your own
sexuality. Are you, uh, worried, Chad?"

That was a lot more fun than admitting Lucas
is not really my friend and only consorts

with me because of the money I give him
for weed that he steals from his brother.

Chad Sputters a Denial

And that's all good. Just wanted
to make him squirm. "You can take
me home," I tell Lucas. Let the boys
play without me. Who needs them?
I got my weed, and it's my birthday,

and in just a few hours, when I see
Alex, this upside-down place I find
myself in will right itself. I mean,
I'm the queer here. So why do I feel
like I'm the only normal one in this

piece of crap stinking car? But I'll
want to score again sometime, so
I don't say that, nor do I say that
the reason gay guys prefer girls for
friends is because they're not hung

up on dick size. (Well, not personal
dick size, anyway.) When we park
in front of my house, Chad draws
a needle-sharp breath and I take sick
satisfaction in his obvious envy.

Of Course, He Doesn't Know

That all the money in the world couldn't
fill this beautiful big old house with
happiness. That the expensive furniture

and art were bought with loneliness.
Mom's. Mine. Can't say for sure Shelby
is lonely. Maybe she's content, adrift

in bed, Barney and Dora and the Playhouse
Disney gang for company. Maybe she is,
in fact, happy. But Mom wears sadness

like skin—tight and irreversible. Dad?
I'd say he was born pissed, but if I dig
way deep into memory, I can see him

playing with me. Laughing with Mom.
Now, all he wants is to be away from
the home he works so hard to pay for.

I slip through the front door. No balloons.
No presents. No party. No surprise.
Only silence. Happy birthday to me.

Chad

Surprises

I hate surprises.
Nothing good ever
comes from them. There

are

little ones, like finding
a spider all limp and wet in
the bottom of your glass
after you've gulped

the

soda. There are medium
ones, like your buddy pulling
up with a fag in his car and
it's obvious that the

source of

the smell inside is the blunt
they've been sharing. Gay spit.
Creepy. And then there are giant
surprises, the ones that give you

nightmares.

Like when your mom moves
a new guy into your house
and the asshole wants to play
substitute father.

I Can't Believe

Almost a month of summer
        is gone already. Fourth of July
                is in just a few days. Fireworks!

Mom doesn't know it yet,
        but we're going to watch them
                with Dad and Cassie. And Chad.

At least I hope he'll come, too.
        I'm going to wear my new blue
                short shorts and red-and-white

striped tank top. I can't believe
        how good I look in them. If I
                keep up the dieting and exercise,

by the time school starts I'll be
        hot. Maybe I'll even make
                the cheerleading squad, except

I think you have to be stuck-up.
        I wonder if I was stuck-up,
                would Chad like me better?

Seems Like Guys

Go for the conceited girls.
Don't ask me why. Seems weird
to me. It's not just because they're
pretty. Some of them aren't all that much
to look at. Cassie says it's the way they present
themselves, like you'd have to be dense not to notice
how incredible they are. Maybe I should practice thinking

too much of myself. Maybe I already do. I mean, I know
Chad is way out of my league. But still, this little part
of me believes I can make him like me if I just can
figure out how to please him. Losing weight is
a good start. But there has to be something
more. He's nice enough when Cassie
makes him do stuff with me. But

otherwise, he barely notices I'm there.
Dad says he's sulky. I think he's sultry.
Mom says I need to quit obsessing. I think
it's better to be obsessed than to be depressed.
Brianna says things happen in their own time. (Has
she been listening to my mother?) I think pushing to get
what you want can't be so awful. I think it's key to success.

Maybe I'll Talk to Gram

About it. Mom and Bri and I are going
camping with Gram and Gramps tonight.

I've got awesome grandparents. I mean, they're
weird and all, but that's why they're awesome.

I watch Bri carefully folding clothes, just
to stuff them into a backpack. Talk about

obsessive. "Are you OCD or something?
All that stuff is gonna get messed up."

> She smiles. *I know. But at least it won't
> be wrinkled when it gets messed up.*

"Don't forget sunscreen. It's gonna be
hot at Prosser. Hopefully Gramps found

a campsite in the trees. Closer to the water
there isn't any shade." Bri nods, goes to

> the bathroom, returns with SPF 30.
> *Hope this is strong enough. And I also*

> *hope there will be boys at the lake.*
> *My new swimsuit is really cute. See?*

She holds up a flouncy bikini,
in a tropical print. "Really cute,"

I agree. "I'm waiting to lose a few
more pounds before I get a new one."

> *I've been meaning to tell you how*
> *great you look. Is it hard? Dieting?*

"Only when I smell french fries.
It's harder for Mom. She sneaks

M&Ms and thinks I don't notice.
But she walks with me every morning."

> *Pretty soon you'll be running, like*
> *my mom. Just don't get crazy about it.*

"Don't worry. That's not gonna happen
in a million years. Running is not my style."

> *Hey, you guys!* It's Trace, calling
> down the hall. *Time to hit the road!*

Mom Plays Chauffeur

For the hour drive to Truckee
      and beyond, to Prosser Reservoir.

Bri and I sit in back, watching
      the landscape morph from high desert

scrub to mountain evergreen.
      When I start talking about Chad,

I notice how Mom turns up
      the volume on her soft rock station.

I don't care. That way she doesn't
      hear me tell Bri, "I think he really

likes me. At least, a little. I mean,
      he doesn't completely ignore me.

That's a good sign, right?" Like
      either of us would have a clue.

      She shrugs. *I think I'd have to*
        see how he acts around you.

"You could tell? How?" Maybe
      I'll have to invite her over to Dad's.

Bri shrugs. *I know how ridiculous*
        Trace looks when he's all hung

up on a girl. And Mikki? When
        she even talks about Dylan,

she goes zombie-eyed. Mom
        chuckles at that, so I guess she's

been listening after all. *I have*
        to make a quick Starbucks stop,

she says. *I promised Gramps*
        I'd bring him some real coffee.

No drive-through here, she runs
        inside, and I take the opportunity

to tell Bri, "Next time I go to Dad's,
        I'll ask Cassie if you can come, too."

No use upsetting Mom. And no use
        asking Dad when Cassie's in charge.

Prosser Reservoir

Is an exposed expanse of water—
snowmelt, run down the Truckee River
from Tahoe, then stored for Reno use.

This being a holiday weekend, its shores
are crowded with RVs and tents and boats.
And people. Gramps was lucky to have

found a spot beneath the big trees.
Their shade, and the breeze whispers
disturbing it, make the heat tolerable.

It is midafternoon by the time we arrive
and manage to track down my grandparents,
who live a nomadic life in the big fifth-wheel

trailer they tow around the country. Bri
has been my friend since we were still
in diapers, so she's met them before.

Good thing, or she might just disown
me, seeing Gram in her mini muumuu,
and Gramps, with his long gray braid

hanging most of the way down his naked
back. Remnants of their hippie days.
Mom doesn't talk about it much, but

before moving to Reno, she grew up on
an Oregon commune. Not sure exactly
what that is except a lot of people living

together and pooling their stuff. *Commie-
style,* Dad told me once, *with plenty
of sex, drugs and rock 'n' roll tossed in.*

Don't know how accurate that was,
and don't really care. Gram and Gramps
are awesome. We get out of the car

and I run to give them hugs. *It's so
good to see you!* says Gram. Then
she stands back. *Let me look at you.*

Gramps actually whistles. *Wowzers.
What happened to you? Grew up
and slimmed down. What a beauty!*

Beauty?

Whatever, Gramps. Lots of gossip
and settling in later, Bri and I slip
on our swimsuits and sunscreen up.
"We're gonna take a dip before dinner,"

I tell Mom. She's busy yakking with
Gram, but warns us to be careful,
and back in an hour. The sun starts
a slow slide behind the western hills.

> *Guess we didn't need to worry*
> *about the sunscreen,* says Bri. *Oh,*
> *well. At least we smell really good.*
> True. Like coconut. But we're also

greasy. We hit a little beach covered
with people. It's a diverse crowd—too
young to walk. Too old to swim.
Too shy to take off their cover-ups.

Too proud of their assets to hide
them. I mean, some of these girls
are showing off just about everything.
So why are guys checking out Bri?

Brianna

Showing Off

Is so not my style. Maybe
that comes from too many
years watching my sister

                              exposing

more than she should, all
to win the attention of guys
I wouldn't want to look at me.
Her taste leans way

                              too much

toward creepy. And then,
there's my mom, who loses
weight and all of a sudden

                              flaunts

her assets like no mother
should. I mean, she's almost
forty! Even if she has

                              the inner

desire to stay youthful
and feel attractive, why
must she dress less like
a mom and more like a

                              slut?

Three-Day Weekends Suck

At least, summer three-day weekends.
I like the ones that get me out of school
for an extended period. But the long
July Fourth weekend means two things.

One—Alex has to work extra hours.
And Dad doesn't. He's home, which
is pretty much keeping me sequestered
in my bedroom. I don't even want to

go to the kitchen. Running into Dad
almost always leads to an argument.
When I was little, we got along pretty
well. But that was before I came out.

Before his mother got smashed
into the asphalt by a drunk driver.
Before Shelby. After that, Dad gave
up on just about everything except

his career, which has become his entire focus.
As for the rest—his home, his church,
his wife, his kids—well, we really don't
exist, except maybe as thorns in his side.

When I Really Stop

And think about it,
        it makes me more
                sad than angry at him.
Used to be he had
        faith, and it made
                him strong. Vibrant.
When he lost God
        he lost the way to
                self-forgiveness and
lacking that, he will
        remain broken. Crushed.
                Scrubbed of hope or
dreams. Poor Dad,
        like many so-called
                Christians, believes
I'm the one in need
        of salvation. But I never
                turned my back on faith,
and I know God hasn't
        written me off, either.
                He's too damn tenacious.

One of the Guys

I was talking to online for a while—Jess—
lives in some Bible Belt hellhole.
Once, we started talking about jacking

ourselves out of the closet. I told him
my mom took a day or two to accept
my declaration, but that my dad pretty

much slammed the figurative door
in my face. "He doesn't want to talk
about it," I said. "Or talk to me at all."

> Jess said, *When I crumbled and "confessed*
> *my unnatural sin," as my daddy called*
> *it, Mama claimed it was Satan*
>
> *who "put the homosexual inside of me,"*
> *and if I only prayed hard enough,*
> *God would most certainly cure me.*

Okay, Nevada Methodists have
nothing on Mississippi Southern
Baptists. Dad might think being gay

is a sin, but he sees it more as a sign
of human weakness, not Satanic
interference. At least, I don't think

he does. I figure it's between me
and the Big Guy upstairs. We used
to go to church a lot, and I never heard

one word to make me think I'm some
sort of abomination. If God is in fact
responsible for creating me, He made

me just how He wants me. And if He
loves every bit of his handiwork, He loves
me. And if all that is nothing more than

mythology, what harm is there in
believing the stories, anyway? When
I pray—or meditate, or consider

the universe, whatever you want to call
it—I find comfort. Self-acceptance.
Understanding, at least in some world.

One Thing

God might prefer I do without
        is porn. It presents a warped
            view of sex. That's what I've

            realized post–plenty of viewing.
        Weirdly, after a while, porn actually
gets kind of boring. Ditto jerking

off. I think I'm ready to take
        the plunge and go for the real deal.
            With Alex. Because another thing

            I've decided through a lot of
        meditation, in fact, is that life
is all about chances. You might

be safer not taking any. But
        playing it totally safe means
            you're only existing. Not living.

            I want to live. Want to emerge
        from the virtual hell of my room,
into the heaven just outside my door.

Okay, More Like

Just outside my front door, as opposed
to my bedroom door—the one that leads

into the hallway that is currently
a conduit into my parents' own hell.

They are fighting, a relatively rare thing,
mostly because Dad isn't around enough

to make it common. Their voices keep
lifting higher. Louder. Sharper. I tune in.

> *Stop it! Just stop, Marissa. Every fucking*
> *time some new treatment comes along,*
>
> *you get your hopes up. I used to let you*
> *get mine up too, but not anymore.*

Arguing about Shelby. Wonderful.
Does Dad even get that if I can hear

him, she can, too? I can tell Mom is
trying to defuse his anger, talking about

> maintaining hope. But he is steadfast
> in his hopelessness. *Look, even if that*

new drug turns out to be a cure,
Shelby's not a good candidate for

treatment. You know that as well as
I do. If it's still experimental, they'll

look for kids with the best chances
of improvement. They need poster

children, to keep the funding coming.
All true. But why destroy Mom's hope?

A short pause, and I hear her now.
That's not going to make things better.

Oh, shit. I bet he's drinking. I step
into the hall, smell alcohol, hanging

thick as incense. God, it's not even ten a.m.
Dad disappears into the kitchen. Mom

follows as far as the doorway. *Did you*
fucking hear me? I said—

Enough!

I slam my bedroom door behind
me. "Everyone between here and
Reno can hear you, Mom. If the two
of you have to fight, can you keep

it between you?" I move her to one
side, look into the kitchen to see
Dad pour a big, deep tumbler of amber
liquid. Whiskey of some kind.

"Seriously, Dad. Mom's right. What's
wrong with you?" He mutters an inane
reply about burdens too heavy to bear.
"Yeah, well, life pretty much sucks

and then you d—" Stop, man. Don't
make it any more real than it already is.
I move closer to Mom. "What's the point
of arguing? He wants to wallow."

I don't understand why he—

"Not so hard to figure out. It's all
about guilt." I pull her into the living
room, lower my voice. "He's a coward,
and he hates being one. That's all."

In a Ten-Second Span

She goes from being taut with anger
        to whipping-cream-soft from sadness.
        I wish I could see her happy for once.
Would it make her happy to know

I think I've fallen in love? "Hey, Mom.
        Guess what. I met someone, and . . ."
        What the hell am I thinking? Even if
she was okay with me talking about

        hooking up with a guy, she has other
           stuff on her mind, as evidenced by
           her empty-eyed stare. Still, she tries,
What? Sorry. I was a million miles away.

"I know. Never mind. It's not important."
        She nods, returns her gaze to the window.
        I back away, leave her lost in her worry.
As soon as I'm out of earshot, I call Alex.

He's working. Incommunicado until
        six. I leave him a message. "I've been
        thinking about you. About us. Can we
get together tonight? I really need you."

Alex

Messages

Are like secrets. Sometimes
you totally don't want to hear
them. Don't want to discern
the razor-edged meaning they

can

slice you with. Sometimes
the number attached to
a voice-mail warning will

make

your breath turn thick
as marshmallow because
you know a single sentence
could make you smile

or
break

your heart, and so you hesitate
to retrieve it. Some messages infuse
personal shadow with light.
Others will annihilate

your
day.

Ruining My Day

Seems to be my dad's summer
       hobby this year. Okay, maybe—
       just maybe—I deserved getting

grounded again for sneaking
       out. Or maybe—just maybe—
       I deserved it for getting caught

sneaking out. On the other hand,
       I'm just shy of eighteen. Pretty
       soon my parents won't be able

to control my every move. Maybe
       Dad should consider that before
       he tries to rein me in so tightly.

Anyway, it's not like I'm out
       robbing banks or stealing cars.
       (Well, technically I guess I'm

stealing my own, since I'm not
       allowed to drive it when I'm
       grounded.) All I want is to see

Dylan. God, three days away
from him and I freaking climb
the walls. Tonight, at least, is

Fourth of July. My family's new
tradition is to combine fireworks
with a minor league baseball game.

The Reno Aces play at a stadium
right on the Truckee River, and
they shoot off giant sky sparklers

post-play. Dad got his usual
seats behind home plate, but
general admission people can

sit on the grassy hills above
the outfield. Dylan is a GA kind
of guy. My cell has been confiscated,

and I had to give back Bri's when
I got busted with it, so I'm on the land
line, jelling things with Dylan. "See

you around six." Just as I'm about
                to hang up, I notice the phone status:
                conference call. "Bri? Is that you?"

        But it is not my sister who answers
                me. It's my pain-in-the-ass brother.
                Nope. Not Bri. Oh, shit. Trace's

interference has caused me to
                get busted more than once. And
                now I can hear him call down

        the stairs, toward the family room,
                *Hey, Dad. Did you know Dylan
                is coming to the game with us?*

That brat needs to die. Now what
                do I do? The best defense is a solid
                offense, right? The plan was *not*

for Dylan to come to the game
                with us (as my brother knows).
                But maybe if I say it was, it will

defuse what just might be
                an ugly situation. One day soon,
                Trace will be very, very sorry.

I Plaster On

My most innocent, contrite face
and go see what I can do. Dad catches

> me coming down the stairs. *What's
> this about Dylan? He is most definitely*
>
> not *coming with us to the game tonight.
> What would make you think he was?*

"I want you and Mom to get to know
him. I thought it would be a good way

to do that. Maybe then you wouldn't be
so suspicious of him—or of us. We love

each other, Dad. And you'd like him,
too, if you'd just give him a chance."

If I didn't care about trying to make
this work, I might have to smile at the way

> anger creeps, red, all the way up my dad's
> neck, igniting his face. *I have absolutely no*
>
> *desire to spend my day off getting to know
> your derelict druggie boyfriend.* He is yelling,

so I respond in similar fashion. "Dylan
is not a derelict. How can you call him

that when you haven't ever even met
him? You are completely unfair!"

Suddenly, Mom slams in through the door,
dripping sweat from her morning run.

What is going on? she huffs. *Do you
two know any other way to communicate?*

Play it up! "Dad says Dylan can't
come to the game with us tonight."

You're still grounded! Dad screams.
Grounded means no proximity to your

*boyfriend, who, just by the way, is
the reason you're grounded in the first*

place. Why is this even an argument?
He looks at Mom for support and she has to

*give it. Honey, this was supposed to be
a family evening. Dylan probably has plans.*

"He does! He planned on hanging out
with me. Please, Mom. I haven't seen

him in weeks. . . ." Slight exaggeration,
but still. "He'll buy his own ticket

and everything. Don't you get it? I have
to see him. I . . . I . . . am in love with him."

> *You don't know the first thing about
> love!* Dad is totally freaking out, leaking

> spit like a lunatic. *And if you believe
> Dylan is in love with you, you're crazy.*

"Shut up, Dad. You think you know
everything." Who the hell does he think

he is? "Why are you so fucking mean?"
God, that felt good. Almost as good as

seeing the crazy mad look on Dad's face
right now. But, of course, Mom brings me

back to reality. Convinces me to apologize.
"Sorry. I shouldn't have said 'fucking.'"

Bizarrely

That makes him laugh. I mean,
like lock-him-up-in-an-asylum
hysterical laughter. Mom asks
what's so funny, and he says,

> *She just reminds me of me is all.*
> *I once said something similar to my*
> *dad. The main difference being,*
> *he kicked my ass. I don't guess*

> *I feel the need to kick your ass,*
> *Mikayla. But regarding Dylan*
> *and the game, my answer is still*
> *the same. And until you show us*

> *a little respect, as far as I'm*
> *concerned, you're still grounded.*
> God! He pisses me off. I want to say
> more, but he turns on one heel

and leaves the room. Mom tries
to soothe my raw-edged nerves
by telling me she'll see what she
can do about ungrounding me.

She's So Playable!

Which works out well for me
            when we get to the game. Dad
                    and my jerk-off brother go for
                            hot dogs. I give Trace a look
that lets him know without
            a doubt if he says a word
                    about me, I'll shove that foot-
                            long down his throat whole.
We're early enough that the team
            is signing autographs. My weird
                    little baseball-loving sister begs
                            to stand in the signing line, so
Mom goes along. Which offers
            the perfect opportunity to go
                    find Dylan, who is waiting for
                            me on the right field walkway.
He stands out from the crowd—
            tall and strong-muscled in his
                    shorts and tank top. Suddenly
                            I really wish we were somewhere
a lot more private than a ball
            game on Fourth of July. But,
                    as my grandma often says,
                            half a loaf is better than none.

Turns Out

All we'll get is a couple of stale
crusts. I am in Dylan's arms,
kissing him for the first time in

> way too many days, when all of
> a sudden he goes completely stiff.
> *Uh, looks like we've got company.*

I peel myself off him, turn to find
Mom glaring at me. Shit. Damn.
My first thought is to grab Dylan,

push him through the crowd to
the nearest gate. But then what?
Mom's familiar "come hither" head

bob turns me to concrete. Flee?
Screw that. I have nowhere to go
but home. "Sorry. I love you."

> *I love you, too,* he says, all mopey
> and cute. I kiss him goodbye like
> they do in the movies. Dirty movies.

Dylan

Dirty Movies

Are the best I'm gonna do
tonight. Again. I never thought
whacking off would get old, but
after you've had the real deal,
all warm and creamy,

calloused

skin, too cool with lotion,
can't measure up. And once
you've experienced the low
growl of building passion,

dubbed

moans and groans get annoying
really fast. And after you've
tasted authentic nipples, all sweet
with strawberry shower gel,

fake

boobs, no matter how giant
and airbrushed, kind of seem
like letdowns. No, once you've
made love with your amazing
girlfriend, getting off solo is

bullshit.

Making Love

For the first time is probably scary
        for everyone. I'm totally terrified.

It's been two days since I told
        Alex that I think I'm ready.

He insisted I wait, to be sure.
        Tonight is the Fourth of July.

Independence Day might seem
        like a strange occasion to celebrate

my growing dependence on
        Alex. Sex will bind us even tighter.

That isn't what frightens me.
        Neither does leaping so far into

adulthood. No, what scares
        me is actually doing it. The act.

I've seen it done plenty in movies.
        But they always get straight down

to business. It never looks
        what you might call romantic.

I want Alex and me to be all about
        romance. So okay, we start with

a sweet, long kiss. Let the sweet
        melt like brown sugar from heating

desire. But once the ol' heart starts
        the kettle drum beating, then what?

Do I rip off my clothes? Rip off
        Alex's clothes? Do I let him do

the ripping, or expect they'll find
        a way to fall off on their own?

I guess I'm overthinking things,
        but the little details worry the hell

out of me. And then, there are
        the big ones—the ones they show

in the movies that don't look very
        romantic. God, I'm so confused.

The Closest I've Come

To doing any of this was an "almost"
with Marlon Dufrena—a hulking dude
with hands the size of baseball mitts.
Hands that scared the crap out of me.

I was fourteen and he was twenty,
and I understood his interest had nothing
to do with romance. I also knew
there was something not quite right

about a guy that old wanting to get
off with me. But I was curious. Hungry
for knowledge and for identity.
He was mostly hungry for ejaculation.

There were no dinners. No concerts.
Definitely no kissing. Just those
awful hands, grasping. Pushing.
Pulling. Insisting, after I'd said no.

He was bigger. I was quicker.
One kick, well-placed, slowed him
down long enough for me to run.
After, I almost decided to try straight.

Of Course, Going Straight

When you're totally, unabashedly
        born perfectly gay isn't possible.
As much as I wanted to hide in
        my closet, uh . . . not going to happen.
Which explains my online outlet.

The only hands I had to contend
        with were my own. I trusted them
completely. But, like any red-
        blooded human being, I wanted to
fall in love. Finally, I figured out

that love and sex don't have to be
        intertwined. But maybe, just maybe,
they can be. I'm damn sure willing
        to give it a try, so I'll work on not
overthinking the details, give up

all thought of control, see where
        love will carry me tonight. Alex.
Damn. Why you? Okay, I know
        there's no such thing as forever.
So what can we be, in the now?

While Waiting

For Alex to pick me up, I go see
what Mom's up to. Pass Dad, snoring
on the couch. God, does being home

always have to equal being drunk
for him? His liver must be pickling.
I mean, it's only seven, and as far as

I can tell, he's been dead to the world
for about three hours. Okay, maybe
I shouldn't talk about bad habits.

But at least mine don't make me
emotionally sterile. Hmm. Interesting
thought. Wonder if his venom

is some feeble attempt to feel. I hear
Mom futzing around in the kitchen.
Dinner for one, with me going out

and Dad asleep and Shelby noshing
from tubes. I clomp past the almost
corpse of my father. No need to tiptoe.

"Hey, Mom," I say, watching her slide
a Lean Pocket into the microwave.
"That doesn't look too appetizing."

She turns, offers a lukewarm smile.
You're kidding, right? This is gourmet.
Said with a not-silent *t* at the end.

"You gonna watch the fireworks?"
Our deck overlooks downtown Reno,
where they lob them skyward from casino

rooftops. When I was little, we used
to have July Fourth parties here. Back
BS— Before Shelby, whose lungs can't

handle the slightest whisper of pollen-
heavy evening breeze. "Not much wind
tonight. And it's warm." I leave the hint

hanging. Shelby should see fireworks
at least once before . . . "Oh. There's Alex."
I give her a quick hug, duck out the door.

It Is, in Fact

A perfect evening, the wind hushed as the sun sinks
low to the west. I suck in a deep breath of jasmine-
scented air to quiet the chatter of nerves. When I open
the passenger door, peek in to say, "Hey . . . ," I am struck

for about the billionth time by Alex's Irish beauty—
black coffee hair over unblemished white skin. And
when he smiles, his emerald eyes glow. *Hey back
at you. Get in.* Excitement shades his voice. *I've got*

a surprise for you. When I ask—ridiculously—what
it is, all he says is, *If you want to smoke, light up now.*
Of course I want to smoke. Weed is the only thing
that will calm the churn in my gut. I share the blunt

without hesitation. Swapping spit doesn't worry
me anymore. I researched again. Found out
what I needed to know. We end up downtown.
Alex stops in front of Harrah's valet, pulls

a small suitcase from his trunk, hands the attendant
his keys and a five-dollar bill. He looks at me
expectantly. *Come on. Wait until you see this!*
We take the elevator to the twelfth floor,

and he tugs me down the hall, into a room.
He stops long enough to kiss me sweetly, then
gushes, *Our first time should be memorable.*
Look. We'll be able to see the fireworks!

The big windows face toward the city's heart.
"But how did you manage to get a room here
on the Fourth of July?" Not an easy thing. "And
how did you ever afford this?" I shake my head.

My aunt Katie has worked here forever.
She pulled some strings. And all those extra
hours I was working? For you. For us.
He kisses me again. This time, the sweet

segues quickly to thrilling. His hands
wind into my hair in a most primal way.
My heart beats crazy fast. Blood whooshes
in my ears and I cry out, "I love you."

I regret the words for about two seconds.
But then he claims, *Oh, God, I love you, too.*
And we're kissing again. And we're halfway
to naked as we fall, tangled, on the bed.

Any Small Sense of Fear

Vanishes as logic dissolves in desire
        heightened by declarations of love.
                I love him. And he says he loves me.

        Alex slows forward movement.
             I don't want to hurry. I want to
                    commit every second to memory.

We lie on our sides, looking into
        each other's eyes as our hands
                begin slow, mutual exploration.

There is no top, no bottom here.
        There is only the web of us. Outside
                the big window, the sky grows dark,

except for the far distant stars
        I can see, fighting the garish
                lit neon. I don't have to think

about what to do. Mouth. Tongue.
        Hands. Skin. All in perfect order.
                And now, there are fireworks.

Alex

Fireworks

I have been in love before—
snared by emotion so intense,
deception by omission was easy.
But lies smother love. And in the wake
of my cónfession came a white-hot

sizzle

of anger. I deserved every hateful
word. Lying here, inhaling new love,
hope swells inside me. Skin against
skin, I lose myself within the sharp

crackle

of passion, freed by embracing
the truth I cannot change.
I find slender rays of fear
in his eyes, yet he places his trust
in me and I will not

shatter

that. I blanket his body with mine.
Tattoo him with pleasure.
Lead him to the edge of the cliff,
push him over, feel him fly,
wings beating softly in the promise of

this night.

This Night

Is probably the best one ever
in my entire life. Mom and I have
done fireworks in Sparks (yeah,
I get the irony) since I was a little

kid. We hang out in the big plaza,
waiting for the sun to go down
and the sky to grow really dark.
There is live music. Food. Craft

booths. People pitch sunshades,
put down blankets. Grown-ups
drink too much alcohol, which
is sometimes entertaining.

Usually it's just Mom and me,
and maybe one of my friends.
But tonight we're hanging with
Dad and Cassie and Chad, too.

Mom looks kind of pissy because
Dad is pretty drunk and Cassie
isn't far behind. Mom says she has
to play chaperone, so she's sober.

Oh, well. Liquor is fattening.
Mom is starting to look good.
Our diet is working. The shorts
I'm wearing are a whole size

smaller than the ones I wore
last year. I swear, I think guys
are checking me out. Maybe
it's good Bri didn't come along.

For once, I'm getting the attention.
Some of that is from girls, too.
Mostly because every time I ask
to go get a drink or check out

the band, Cassie tells Chad he has
to go with me. *Lots of crazies out
there, you know. We have to keep
our Harley girl safe.* She's sort of

slurring now—*ourharleey girlshafe.*
But that's okay. It only makes Chad
want to walk around more. And I can
find plenty of excuses to go along.

There Are Couples Everywhere

Holding hands. Making out.
Dancing real, real close. I wish
Chad would hold my hand, but

the closest he's come to that is
propping an arm on my shoulder.
Whatever! He actually touched me!

We slice through the crowd.
For some reason, people get out
of Chad's way. He doesn't seem

to notice. "What's it like, having
my dad live with you? My mom
thinks he's a jerk. Do you?"

> He doesn't even hesitate. *Totally.*
> *That's all Mom ever hooks up with.*
> *But as jerks go, he's low voltage.*

Should I be mad he thinks Dad's
a jerk? Probably not. Lots of people
do, including Gram and Gramps.

"What do you mean, 'low voltage'?"
We keep walking, aiming nowhere
in particular. But he stops in front

of the antique steam train taking
up space on a downtown sidewalk.
He watches the kids crawling over

> the engine like ants. *Low voltage*
> *means nothing he does shocks*
> *me. Mom has had worse losers*
>
> *hanging on. Including my asshole*
> *dad. Now, he was high voltage.*
> *Bastard beat Mom black and blue.*
>
> *Almost killed me once. They locked*
> *him up for twenty-five years, and*
> *that isn't even close to long enough.*
>
> *I hope he rots there. And before*
> *he does, I hope some con with a giant*
> *dick makes him his little bitch.*

Subzero Cold

That's what that was, and little
        shivers work their way up my spine,

despite the warmth of the evening.
        I really don't know what to say,

except for the lamest thing ever.
        "I'm sorry." The look he gives lets

        me know he concurs with my lame
            assessment. *What are you sorry about?*

I shrug. "I'm sorry he hurt you.
        At least my dad's a nonviolent jerk."

        Chad's turn to shrug. *I was in*
            the hospital for a while, but I was little

        and barely remember it. What
            I do remember is how much I hate him.

That explains why Chad is frozen.
        I want to be the one who thaws him.

But I don't know where to start.
        Don't know what he likes in a girl.

"Did you ever have a girlfriend?"
   Okay, that must have been a dumb

   question because he bayonets me
      with his eyes. *Of course I've had*

   a girlfriend. What do you think
      I am, a eunuch or something?

My face is on fire. "No. That's not . . .
   I mean, will you tell me about her?"

   What do you want to know?
      She was hot as hell and a total

   skank, and I really kind of loved
      her that way. He smiles at my

obvious discomfort. "Oh. Why
   aren't you together anymore?"

   She dumped me for another guy.
      Girls are impossible to satisfy.

"Not every girl." Not me. I'd be
   happy if he'd just like me a little.

Suddenly, Someone Yells

Chad's name. He waves at a guy
cutting through the crowd. *Stay here,*
he tells me. *I'll be right back.*

I watch him go meet his friend,
a kind of cute guy with dark blond
hair. They talk for a few, leaving me

to wonder what about. Me? Not
me? Is Chad ashamed to be seen
with me? How can I change that?

How can I get him to like me
a little? Or, better yet, to like me
a lot. He said he loved his ex-girlfriend

because she was skanky. Does that
mean because she dressed like a sleaze,
or because she put out like one?

These shorts are about as sleazy
as I know how to get. Chad did lean
his arm on my shoulder today.

Could my shorts be the reason why?

Now He Waves Me Over

To where he's standing with
        his friend. Awesome. He must
        not be ashamed of me after all.
I hurry toward them, arrive just

        a little bit breathless. Chad says,
            Hey, sweetheart. Would you please
            get me a Coke? Here's a five-spot.
        Lucas and I will wait right here.

Sweetheart! Oh. My. God.
        "S-sure," I manage to sputter around
        the giant lump that has formed in my
throat. Before I go find a snack stand,

I give him the prettiest smile
        I know how to—the one I practice
        in the mirror. The concession line
is kind of long and the whole time

I stand in it, one word keeps
        repeating in my head. *Sweetheart.*
        Finally, I get the soda, pocket
the change so I don't lose it.

But When I Turn Around

I can't see Chad anywhere. No Chad.
No Lucas. I look everywhere, but no sign
of them. Maybe they needed a restroom.

I wait at our designated meeting spot.
Wait. And wait. It's getting really dark
now. They'll shoot off the fireworks

any second. Maybe I'd better go on
back to Mom. Did he ditch me? No
way. That can't be. He called me

sweetheart. I reach our blanket just
as the first gigantic sparkler paints
the sky red. Mom is pacing, worried.

> *Where have you been? And where
> is Chad?* She turns dagger eyes on
> Cassie and Dad, who are too drunk

to notice. "I, uh . . . I guess he ditched
me." Mom hugs me to her and I watch
the rainbow explosions, blurred by

traitor tears. He called me sweetheart.

Lucas
Traitor

When Chad wanted to
ditch his little girlfriend
in favor of a fat, stinky blunt,
I asked if he felt like

                              a traitor.

I mean, he did desert her,
and considering the way she
looked at him — like he was a god
or something — she's probably
feeling like shit. But Chad

                              has no

connection with her except
his mom hooking up with
her dad, at least that's what
he says. Considering, like me,
the dude lacks any sort of

                              moral

filters, that girl is in for
a world of hurt, unless
she follows the unwritten

                              code

of unrequited love: When
it all gets too heavy for comfort,
scream bloody murder and run.

I Wanted to Scream

When Mom caught me with Dylan
at the baseball game. I wanted to

grab his hand and run until we had
to stop or risk bursting lungs. But

I had nowhere to run to. So I stole
another kiss, tucked my tail and

followed my mother back to our seats.
Watched the game and fireworks in

silence, knowing I would not be
ungrounded for some time. Turns out

that was a wise move, because Mom
talked Dad into letting me off the hook

> early. *We have to give her a chance
> to earn back our trust,* she told him.

I'm pretty damn sure I'm not worthy
of that. But, hey, at least I'm free.

So When Emily Called

And said she needed a ride
somewhere, I said I'd be right
over. As much as I want to see

Dylan, he is in Stockton right now,
helping his big sister move into
a place near the University of the Pacific,

where she'll be a freshman in
the fall. Dylan is such a sweetheart.
I'll see him later. Right now, I'm

just happy to be out of my house,
on my own. I pull up in front of Em's
house, text her that I'm here. Don't want

to chance running into yet another
boyfriend. She and Clay didn't last long.
Mostly because he never broke up with

Audrey, who still happens to be a friend
of mine (if not Em's!), further complicating
things. Can't people commit anymore?

Em Comes Straight Out

So there must not be a guy stashed
in her bedroom. "Hey, girl," I say
as she slides into the passenger seat.
"What's wrong with your car?"

>	She smiles. *Nothing. I just didn't*
>	*want to take it where we're going.*

Say what? "Where are we going?
Montebello?" The heart of Reno
gangbanger turf. If she says yes,
I'm seriously changing my mind.

>	*No, silly. Planned Parenthood. I have*
>	*a checkup so I can get on a new pill.*

Unbelievable! This girl has nerve.
"Great. So now *my* car will be parked
there for all of Reno to see? I swear,
Em, if you weren't my best friend . . ."

>	*But I am, so it's cool, right? Anyway,*
>	*your car isn't as noticeable as mine.*

That part is true. She drives a lemon-
yellow Camaro—a *sorry I'm never*
around, but this proves I love you
car, as she puts it. "Okay, fine.

But don't say you don't owe me."
I aim my unnoticeable silver Nissan
toward Planned Parenthood. While
I'm there I should make an appointment

for myself. I need to get on the pill.
But the idea of some strange doctor
touching me there creeps me out.
"So isn't the gynecologist thing gross?"

> *Kind of, yeah. But . . . wait. You haven't*
> *done it yet? You don't use birth control?*

"Well, yeah, but you know . . .
rubbers and whatnot." It's the whatnot that's kind of scary. But I don't
feel like giving her the dirty details.

> *Better than nothing, I guess. But*
> *God, be careful. Preggers would suck.*

No Freaking Kidding

The parking lot is jam-packed.
        I pull into a space next to another
                little silver car, not much different

from mine. Unless people have
        my license plate memorized,
                we're pretty much incognito.

Emily goes to check in, then sits
        next to me in an ugly orange plastic
                chair. There must be two dozen

women, waiting to be called in
        for checkups, HIV screenings,
                and other services. This is the kind

of place where you don't look
        other people in the eye. I watch
                little kids run back and forth,

or play with puzzles that have
        seen better days. The building
                smells old so I spritz perfume.

Finally, a nurse calls Em's name.
This shouldn't take too long unless
I get the cute doctor. She winks.

Disgusting and funny, all at
the same time. I pull out my
cell and text something totally

suggestive to Dylan, then start
playing SmackShot. I'm so
absorbed in just missing bull's-

eyes that I barely notice someone
sit down next to me. *Hey, Mikki.*
Long time no see. It's Audrey,

and she looks pretty awful. Pale.
Shaky. "Yeah, I guess it has been
a while. How's your summer?"

Not wonderful. I, uh . . . She looks
around. Clears her throat. Drops her
voice to a whisper. *Was pregnant.*

Past Tense

Was pregnant. The words drop
like stones, into a pond: *plunk, plunk.*
First the "pregnant." What a horrible
thing to deal with. Then the "was,"

which means, what? Considering
where we are, I have a pretty good
idea. "Wow, Audrey, I don't know
what to say. Did you . . . uh . . . ?"

> She draws her eyes level with mine,
> and though she keeps her voice low,
> it is thick with anger. *What else*
> *could I do? Everyone told me I had*
>
> *no choice—Mom, Dad, Clay.* "What
> about senior year? What about college?"
> Mocking. *No choice. How ironic, you*
> *know?* Now she looks down into her lap.
>
> *I—I can't stop thinking about the baby.*
> *Was it a girl? A boy? It already had*
> *a heartbeat. I realize it would have been*
> *hard to keep it. But . . . what if . . . ?*

The Sentence Remains Unfinished

Because apparently Emily's doctor
wasn't the cute one. She's already
finished, prescription in hand. She

comes bouncing along the corridor,
slows when she sees who's sitting
next to me. I can feel Audrey tense.

> *I didn't know she was here. You
> can't tell her, Mikki, okay? I'll die
> if she finds out.* Considering the dirty

chalk color of Audrey's face, Em will
probably guess what's up. But I promise,
"I won't tell." Does this mean Audrey

knows—or, at least, suspects—Emily
and Clay hooked up? I hurry to ask,
"Are you and Clay, uh, doing okay?"

> *No.* Tears soften the fierce look she
> shoots Em's way. *Love isn't invincible.
> Some people take advantage of that.*

I Despise Being in the Middle

Of a battle between friends. I jump to
        my feet, leaving Audrey with a weak,

"If you need to talk, call me, okay?"
        She nods. Buries her face in a magazine

as Emily exits the smeared glass door.
        I follow, happy for fresh air, even if it

is tainted by city smells—hot cement,
        exhaust, a hint of Dumpster. Em waits

        until we're both in the car to query,
                So what's up with her? She's fishing,

but I'm not taking the bait. I shrug.
        "We didn't get to talk all that much."

        A caustic smile contorts her face.
        I thought she might have mentioned

        the abortion. Don't look so surprised.
                Of course I know. Clay told me everything.

What else do I really not want to know?
        Maybe being grounded isn't such a bad thing.

Audrey

A Bad Thing

Happened this summer,
and it began as something
wonderful. Something shared

between

two people awash in forever
love. Sex, not for carnal need
alone, but as an outpouring of

heaven-

born connection. I believed that.
Then, an inkling of conception,

and

in the first days, denial. Tick.
Tock. Certainty dawning, the

brimstone

of anger and blame seethed,
roiled by fear into a magma
of doubt. And what emerged from

the limbo

was a decision that he has already
forgotten because he doesn't believe
in ghosts. I do. And this one tiny
glowing will haunt every hour

of living

until my own light snuffs out.

Glowing

That's how I feel most of the time
since I've hooked up with Alex.
It's like he pours his fire inside

of me and when he leaves an ember
remains, smoldering. He thaws me.
Feeds me. Affirms me. Builds me up.

I accepted my sexual orientation
years ago, but Alex has shown me
how to embrace it. Celebrate it. Believe

with all my heart that I deserve love,
and know I am safe here, within
the "what" of me. I have undergone

some elemental transformation
that will inform my future, and it's
all because of Alex. I am in love

with him. Addicted, really, and I
am very sure that he is totally in love
with me. So why do I chase him away?

When I Think Like That

It makes me wonder if some random
grown-up has infested me, *Invasion*

of the Body Snatchers–style. Then again,
when was the last time I considered

myself a kid? Not since Shelby, for sure.
But seems to me that even before she was

born, the "child" had been excised from
my childhood. Dad was perennially absent.

Mom was always lonely, and mourning
a daughter who was at the time nothing

more than something yearned for. The only
real fun we had was when Gram and Gramps

stopped by, bringing with them their unique
brand of entertainment—hippie elitism.

That still holds true. I'm glad they've
decided to hang around a little longer

this year. It's like they bring spring-soft
sunshine into this house of shadows.

Mom needs someone to talk to, and
Gram is always ready to listen. Gramps

is just funny, in a totally crazy way.
I mean, he's all into Burning Man—that

insane Labor Day freak-out on the playa.
On the surface, he's a sixties throwback.

But inside, he's what I want to be—
smart. Intuitive. And nonjudgmental.

When I first came out and everyone else
was freaking, he was the first to support

me. I can tell him anything. So I'd really
like to ask him what's up with me.

Last night, Alex and I had an amazing time.
We went to an Aces game. Scarfed post-

game pizza. Then we stretched out on
a blanket under the black velour sky

and had long, slow, love-soaked sex,
whispering over and over again, "I love you."

It Was Like Chanting a Mantra

"I love you," into his open mouth
as I looked down into his eyes.

> *I love you,* as his tongue traced
> the outline of my lips.

"I love you," and then we full-on
kissed. Not gently. Not that time.

> *I love you,* and he circled me
> with his arms, drew me into

the heat of his body and then
the whispers built into cries of

> *I love you.* And we rocked
> against each other, into each

other. "I love you." Wet with
sweat and spit and spilled tears.

> Because we were defining
> "making love," and that's all

that it was. Making love with
each other and to each other.

> And at the pinnacle, his final
> *I love you* was a scream into

the face of the night. Afterward,
we lay there, knotted together.

> Then he said, *I wish we could
> stay exactly like this forever.*

Forever

Three syllables. Piercing me.
Daggers. And suddenly I was pissed.
Okay, in retrospect, it makes no sense,

but last night, anger surged, hot.
I rolled away, slipped into my jeans.
"We should go before we get busted."

> *What's wrong? What did I say?*
> His voice was small. Hurt. He watched
> me slide my T-shirt over my head.

"Nothing. It's just me. I'm weird,
you know." As he started to dress,
I added, "I think maybe I'm bipolar."

I tried to keep it light as he drove me
home. But when he asked if I wanted
to go to Tahoe today, I found an excuse

to say no. Which doesn't exactly explain
why I'm in the backseat of Lucas's stinking
car toking with his brother Clay, Kurt

the turd, and Tobias, the odd. Dopers
are strange, which says something about
me. Lucas turns up Caughlin Parkway. "Dude.

This is kinda close to home. Don't speed,
okay?" He slows, but not much. We're
cruising maybe ten over the limit, skunk

> smoke streaming. *Look at that,* says
> Clay, who's riding shotgun. Now Lucas
> slows a whole lot more. What's

the big deal? I lift up in my seat to
see. Oh my God. It's Mom, pushing
Shelby in her stander. Clay sticks

> his head out the window. *Holy shit.*
> *Check out the retard. Or maybe it's*
> *an alien from the planet Ugly-As-Uranus.*
>
> *Hey, do aliens dig weed?* He exhales
> a big drag out the window. Lucas punches
> it and I duck down, but not before I see

Mom's certain recognition. I think
I hear her yell my name, but we're gone.

Everyone's Laughing

Everyone except me. "What the hell
is so damn funny?" My right hand lashes

out, almost involuntarily, pops the back
of that fucktard Clay's head. Probably not

a great idea. I'm not small, but he's got
fifteen pounds of pure muscle on me.

> He whips around. *What's your mother-*
> *fucking problem? You looking to die?*

"You could try. But I swear it won't be
easy." I push really hard not to sound

> gay. Don't think it worked, though.
> *Listen here, you queerbait. I'll kick*

> *your ass and not feel a thing. Pull over,*
> he commands, and Lucas does as he's told.

Suddenly, everyone is out of the car.
Kurt and Tobias stand back, but Lucas

holds on to his front-row seat. I take my
best defensive stance. "You think talking

crap about some poor crippled kid
makes you tough? Dude, you're nothing

but a shit-leaking asshole." Bam!
His fist connects with my left eye.

Ooh. That's gonna be ugly. I reply, but
he ducks and I barely graze his cheek.

> *Nice. Just like a girl.* But before
> he can gloat too much, I send another

one, a roundhouse to the gut. *Omph!*
goes his air. Which only pisses him off.

He comes up swinging and I do my
best, but he's good with his hands

and now my nose is dripping thick, red
snot and my upper lip splits wide when

> my teeth drill through. Then, strangely,
> he draws back. Asks, *What was it to you?*

Blood gushing, I admit, "That alien was
my little sister. She's not ugly, jerkwad."

Believe It or Not

That ends it. *Let's go,* says Clay, and
his parting look is nothing but sympathetic.
Something there, but I'm not sure what.

They jump in the car, leave me geysering
crimson on the sidewalk. Home is only
a few blocks away, though. I feel beaten.

Bloodied. Uglified. But vindicated.
I limp home, wishing I would have said
yes to Tahoe. I need an Alex fix.

I take four or five heavy steps beyond
the front door and Mom comes rushing
down the hallway. *Shane! What in the hell—*

Now she sees me, in all my dignified
glory. I tell her I'm fine. Swear I stuck
up for my sister, not an alien but an angel.

By the time I get to, "I think I might need stitches,"
Mom is my mommy. She may have forgotten
my birthday. But today she remembers me.

Clay

Wish I Could Forget

My mother. Our mother—
mine and Lucas's and our
little sister, Jenny Leigh's.
How Mom looked just fine

some

mornings before she died.
Like the cancer had up
and skittered off in the night.
If that had been fact,

things

would be different now.
Dad wouldn't be a pitiful
drunk. Jenny Leigh would
still be someone

you

want to know, not an eighth-
grade slut. Lucas would have
a heart, and I'd be college-bound,
like Mom wanted. But you

can't

gamble on college when you
know construction pays.
Pipe dreams of law school
are something I'll just have to

forget.

Harley
It Pays

To be patient. That's what Mom
        always says when I ask her why

she doesn't have a boyfriend.
             I'm waiting for the right guy,

she says. *Someone really special.*
             But for now, you're all I need.

I kind of like that she thinks so,
        but I'm afraid she's missing out

on something everyone needs—
        someone to gather you in, hold

you close. Someone to make
        every day a little brighter.

On Fourth of July, when Chad
        took off with his friend and left

me alone, I asked Mom how
        to make him like me. She told

me to be patient, too. *You can't*
make someone like you. It has

to happen organically. Maybe
Chad isn't the right guy for you.

She doesn't understand how
much I like him. I might even

love him. I can barely breathe
when I'm close to him, and when

he smiles, my stomach does flips
until it starts to ache. Sometimes

he touches me—our legs brush
or our fingers collide. Once in

a while, he'll rest his arm on my
shoulder, and then I totally die.

He doesn't ignore me. But he
doesn't give me what I'm craving.

I Want Him

To call me "sweetheart" and mean it.
I want him to glance at me and not
be able to tear his gaze away.

I want him to be helpless when I part
my lips, touch them lightly with
my tongue, like in movies.

It may never happen organically.
There must be a way to force
it. To make a power play.

I've lost ten pounds. Dieted my butt off,
literally. Plus, I've still got boobs.
If it's not my body, it must be

my face. Tonight, Cassie is showing
Bri and me how to do makeup.
Dad's working. Chad's out.

Hopefully, by the time he gets home
I'll be transformed. Not good with
"skank." Vamp will have to do.

Speaking of Vamps

Now that we're done with the eyeliner,
mascara and blush session, we're having
a girls' movie night, and we're making
it a *Twilight* saga marathon. Bri and I

have seen them all, numerous times,
but Cassie has, so far, resisted. "Wait
until you see Robert Pattinson. You'll
love him. He's, like, totally dreamy."

> Cassie pops the first movie into
> the player. *I've never been much
> of a vampire fan. Bloodsucking
> kind of reminds me of leeches.*

> Bri snorts. *Don't worry. There isn't
> a lot of bloodsucking. It's mostly
> a romance. Like, the best romance
> ever.* We watch Bella arrive in Forks

and start her new school, complete
with these perfectly beautiful
brother-(pretend) sister vampires.
And I fall in love—again—with Edward.

If He Can Love Bella

Chad can love me. I want him

    to be my Edward—taking

        care of me, always. Watching

           over me, day or night, unsleeping.

        Keeping me safe, by his side.

      Caring for me with a passion

so pure it can't be corrupted

    by time or distance or seduction.

      I know Edward is only fiction.

        But that doesn't have to mean

      love like his can only be found

    in books and movies or rooted

in the misty world of dreams.

The Movie Ends

And Bri and I sigh at exactly
the same time, which makes

> Cassie giggle. *Robert Pattinson
> is pretty cute. But I expected*
>
> *a little more action or gore
> or something. It wasn't even scary.*

"Now you sound like Gram.
I loaned her my book last summer.

She said it was boring. That
nothing happened, and that boy

vampires shouldn't sparkle
because it makes them girly."

> That makes Cassie spit her beer.
> *She kind of has a point. But hey,*
>
> *I've heard the werewolf is pretty
> hot. Popcorn and* New Moon?

It's After One A.M.

By the time we finish *Eclipse.*
Dad came in from work halfway through, but that didn't
make Cassie quit watching, so

I guess werewolves are definitely
more her style. Looking at Dad,
sitting in the kitchen, hair too
long and stringy and disheveled,

I guess I shouldn't be surprised.
Bri and I are putting our sticky,
Coke-smeared glasses into
the dishwasher when Chad semi-

> stumbles through the door.
> He's wasted. But still adorable.
> *Hey! Am I missing a party or*
> *what? Kinda late for . . .*

> His eyes crawl up and down
> Bri, then turn toward me. Do
> the same. *Wow. What happened*
> *to you?* It takes a few seconds

for me to figure out he's talking
about the makeup. Awesome.
But I have to play dumb. "What
do you mean?" I smile through the lip

> gloss. *It's just, you look great.*
> *And you, too,* he says to Bri.
> *Whoever you are.* Kind of snotty
> and totally Chad. Then again,

I didn't introduce them. "This
is my friend Brianna." Who
is staring at him with smoky eyes.
I give her a nudge. "I'm tired."

> *Don't forget to wash your faces,*
> says Cassie. *Nothing worse for*
> *your skin than sleeping in makeup.*
> She gestures toward the bathroom.

I go, and Bri follows me. Once
the door shuts behind us, I turn on
the water and whisper, "He's cute, huh?"
Maybe cuter than Robert Pattinson.

Faces Washed and Teeth Brushed

We head outside. Usually, I sleep on
the couch, but tonight Bri and I are camping
under a big maple tree in the backyard.
We scoot into sleeping bags, looking
up at the big canopy of branches.

When the breeze blows the leaves,
I can see stars. We talk for a while.
Then she drifts off—silent, but for
the steady in-out of her breathing. I listen
to her soft snore, and the occasional

growl of a passing car—who is
driving around at two a.m.? I close
my eyes. The next thing I know,
it's morning, and late morning,
by the sun's height in the sky.

"Bri?" She's not here, so I go inside
to find her sitting next to Chad on
the sofa. And just as I come through
the door, she turns her face into
his, and the two of them are kissing.

Brianna

Kissing

I can't believe it, but that's
what I'm doing—kissing
a boy for the very

first

time. I know it's wrong
that it's *this* guy, but when
he looked at me with

hunger

in his eyes—hungry for me!—
kissing him seemed like
the right thing to do.

And

my inner voice doesn't say
one word as I close my eyes,
lean into him. But

then,

when it all turns into a wet,
sloppy mess, my conscience
laughs out loud at my

disappointment.

And now, hearing my best
friend gasp, I yank away
and toss a Hail Mary

apology

I know she won't accept.

Apologies Are Useless

To my dad.

I mean, okay, I came in three
hours past my midnight curfew.
But Dylan's Jeep got a flat, and
his spare was flat, too, and it
took us forever to fix them
especially since pretty much
everything is closed at twelve a.m.

To my mom.

Who I went off on when Dad
wouldn't listen about the flats
and all. True, I mentioned her
state of dress—too slutty for forty,
with a thigh-high skirt and boob-
baring neckline. But I was angry.
And anyway, she deserved it.

To Dylan.

Who is really very tired of me
being grounded, and I can't blame
him. This summer was supposed
to be fun, but we haven't even
made it to Tahoe. The only thing
we've managed to do is have sex
a few absolutely amazing times.

I've Said I'm Sorry

So many times this summer, it's starting
to sound like a ringtone. At this point,

no one believes it. Not even me. But I
think I found a way to escape the house

today. Mom is taking Trace and Brianna
to Wild Waters. It's an absurdly disguised

plot to get Bri and Harley speaking again.
I know because I overheard Mom and Andrea

hatching their evil-moms plan. I could probably
go along, but I'd rather spend some stolen

hours with Dylan. Just not here, in case
Dad happens to come home. So, as Mom

squeezes into a little pink bikini and slips
a cover-up over her head, I ask, all innocently,

"Can I ride my bike? I need some exercise."
Surely the Workout Nazi can't say no to that.

> She looks at me with a fair amount of
> suspicion. *Bike riding and what else?*

"Nothing else." Wide-eyed and wounded.
"Jeez, Mom, if I don't do something I'm

going to start school in size-twenty clothes.
Please?" That was pretty good, I think.

> Okay. But don't stay gone too long.
> And don't ride East Lake. Too dangerous.

I cross my heart, even though East Lake
Boulevard is the only way to get to Washoe

Lake State Park, where I'm meeting
Dylan. Reno and Wild Waters are in

the opposite direction, so I'll wait until
after they're gone. It doesn't take long.

> The doorbell rings and Mom calls,
> Trace! Bri! Grab your stuff and let's go.

I open the door for Andrea. God, I wish
I had a camera. The look on Bri's face

is priceless. *What are* they *doing here?*
she snaps. *I'm not going if* she's *going.*

> *Oh, yes you are,* says Mom, pushing
> Bri toward the door. *This is getting old.*

Andrea laughs and Trace smirks and
Bri's body language shouts *whatever.*

Out the window, I watch Bri shove
Trace into the backseat ahead of her

and right up against Harley, who is
hunkered against the far side of the seat,

refusing to acknowledge any of this
is happening. Kids. Sometimes I wish

I could go back a few years, to when
school was still fun and friendships

were easy and relationships with boys
were only inventions of imagination.

I Let Dylan Know I Can Escape

It will take him a while to get out here, so I sway
away from the rules again, check my email.
When I see the one that just arrived, I get a little
rush of excitement. It's from Leon Driscoll, who

I found through his ex-wife on Facebook and
who just might be Mom's biological uncle.

It says: HELLO, MIKAYLA. IT WAS A SURPRISE
             TO HEAR FROM YOU. MY EX SHOULDN'T HAVE
             GIVEN YOU MY NAME. BUT I'VE ALWAYS
             BELIEVED MY BROTHER, PAUL, SHOULD

             HAVE MADE HIMSELF AVAILABLE TO HIS CHILD,
             SO I FORWARDED YOUR EMAIL TO HIM. IT IS
             MY OPINION THAT HE IS, IN FACT, YOUR
             GRANDFATHER. HOWEVER, THIS IS HIS RESPONSE:

             "PLEASE INFORM HER THAT I HAVE NEVER
             HAD SEX WITH ANYONE OTHER THAN
             MY WIFE, SO I CAN'T POSSIBLY BE RELATED
             TO HER." I'M SORRY HE SEEMS UNABLE

             TO COWBOY UP AND TAKE RESPONSIBILITY
             FOR SOMETHING THAT HAPPENED
             FORTY YEARS AGO. VERY SORRY. BEST
             I CAN DO IS GIVE YOU TWO THINGS.

I Ponder Those Two Things

As I pedal along the sweltering August
asphalt. The first was a photo of a man—
Mom's father, despite his ridiculous

declaration. What kind of wimp-ass guy
claims he's only slept with one woman—
the one he married *after* pumping enough

sperm into some other girl to get her pregnant?
That girl, in this case, is my grandmother,
Sarah Hill. Leon Driscoll's second gift

was her name. This discovery should
feel like a victory. Instead, something
very close to shame has dug a hollow

in my gut. To the west, obsidian thunder-
heads claw over the mountain. Ozone
crackles and perfumes the air. It's going to

storm something awful before the afternoon
is over. I am almost to the park entrance
when a pickup zips by, close enough to slip-

stream my bike. And he has the nerve
to honk as if it's my fault he almost hit
me. Mom's right. This road is dangerous.

And so is my mood. I flip the idiot off.
Like, already a mile or so away, he can
see me. Like he would care if he did.

I turn into the park, pedal over under
a stand of cottonwoods, sit in the grass
beneath them, cooling off in the lush

greenness. Dylan! I'll see him soon.
I close my eyes, waiting. Kind of
dozing. Smelling barbecue and . . .

       suntan lotion. *Hey, Mikayla.* Tyler.
       His voice brings me upright. Damn.
       Whatever he's been doing to work

out, he should keep doing it.
He's shirtless. And he is hot.
"Hey, Ty. What are you doing here?"

He Holds Up His Longboard

*Skating. But it's getting kinda hot
and I was just thinking about
taking a dip. Want to join me?*
He half licks his lips and I wonder

if that means something besides
they're feeling a little chapped.
"Nah. Dylan's on his way. I told
him I'd meet him right here."

I expect him to go dive into the lake.
Instead, he sits beside me, close
enough so I can smell his haze of
sweat, clinging sun-roasted skin.

I lie back in the grass again, and
he follows me, sighing at the cool.
"Sorry about you and Em," I say.
"I never thought you'd break up."

He turns onto his side, leans up
slightly over me. *Like they say, shit
happens. Anyway, you can't keep
someone who doesn't want to stay.*

I Consider That

Disagree. I'd fight to keep Dylan.
But I probably shouldn't say so.

"I guess not. So, how are you
and Caitlin doing?" I suspect

> his answer before he tells me,
> *There is no me and Caitlin.*

> *I'm flying solo for now. How
> about you and Dylan? Last time*

> *I saw him he was griping about
> you being so unavailable.*

I sit up. "Really? When did you
see him?" Ty sits up, too, looks me

> in the eye. *A couple of nights
> ago, at Kristy Lopez's party.*

Kristy Lopez is Dylan's old girlfriend. And wait just one damn

second. "Dylan went to a party
without me?" No way. He wouldn't.

> *That was my very first question*
> *when I saw him—where's Mikki?*
>
> *He said you were on house arrest.*
> *Again. And that he wasn't going*
>
> *to sit at home alone anymore,*
> *waiting for your tight-ass parents*
>
> *to let you off restriction while*
> *the summer kept ticking away.*
>
> *Of course, he was pretty buzzed*
> *by then. All worked up, really.*

Of course he was. I can't believe
he'd go out without me. That's bad.

What's really bad is partying
at Kristy's. That is unforgivable.

I'm Not Really the Jealous Type

But right this second, the evil
buzz inside my brain is a hive
of tiny green-eyed monsters
hissing *Kristy, Kristy, Kristy.*

Stop it, Mikayla. Dylan would
never cheat on you. Not with
Kristy, or anyone else. But
why did he go to that party?

> Tyler must have noticed how
> my face flushed, even though
> I'm solidly in the shade. *Sorry.*
> *Maybe I shouldn't have told you.*

"No. It's okay. Dylan should
have told me, is all." Why hadn't
he? The answer is ridiculously
obvious. He didn't want me to know.

Which makes me wonder what
else he's hiding. Before I can consider
it more, the guy in question squeals
into a parking space right in front of us.

Dylan

Uh, Question

What the fuck is Tyler doing
here, sitting so close to Mikki?
A big ol' switchblade of

jealousy

takes a stab at me. He doesn't
think I see the way he looks
at her, but I don't miss a thing,

and

there is always a blink of longing
in his eyes, friend of mine or no.
Then again, it's possible

guilt

is at play here. The other night,
Kristy flirted mercilessly and I
didn't exactly chase her away. What

could

that mean? Nothing. That's what.
One glimpse of my Mik, and
I know my heart could never

be linked

with anyone's but hers. But now I see
the look on her face. What did he tell
her? How much does she know?

Distraction

Is not what I need right now.
        Alex is letting me drive his car.
                I need to practice parallel parking.

Once I get this down, all I have
        to do is talk Dad into going to the
                DMV with me. "All" I have to do.

"Stop talking to me for a minute,
        okay? You're distracting me, and—"
                Bump! The back tire finds the curb.

        Alex laughs. *Sorry. Try again,*
                and cut the wheel a little harder.
                        Then I want to hear about the concert.

I pull forward and even with
        the Prius parked in front of
                the space I'm aiming for. And just

        as I start to turn the steering wheel,
                Alex says, *By the way. Have I told*
                        you that little scar on your lip is hot?

"If you don't stop talking, I'll
      never get this right. Do I have
           to make you get out of the car?"

      Ooh. Survive one little fight,
           and now you're a tough guy?
                Cool. I kind of like tough guys.

That cracks me up completely.
      But somehow I manage to slide
           in next to the curb, pretty much

spot on. "Let me try a couple
      more times. In silence, okay?"
           I kind of get the hang of it before

putting the Honda in drive and
      aiming it toward the freeway.
           I want to practice merging, too.

      And once I do, Alex reminds me,
           Now can I hear about Bob Dylan?
                He's kinda getting up there, isn't he?

So Is His Audience

At least, some of them. "The concert
was pretty great, really. More for
entertainment value than the music.
There were, like, hundreds of old hippies. . . ."

Including my gram and gramps, but he
already knows that. "I mean, like, guys
with long, gray hair and beards, smoking
weed. It was weird." I'm pretty sure Gramps

took a hit or two off a blunt going
around, although he tried to hide it
from Harley and me. I don't share that,
either. "And then Dylan comes onstage,

and his voice is all scratchy and everything.
This one obnoxious drunk dude sitting in
front of me kept yelling, 'That's not Bob
Dylan,' until finally security hauled him off."

Gram told him to shut up and when he refused,
she went in search of a uniform. "And then,
there was my cousin, Harley. She's only
thirteen. And boy, was she vamped

out in a really short skirt and really
tall heels and a really tight tank top
that made her boobs look really big.
I've never seen her dressed like that

before. She was even wearing makeup."
Heavy makeup. Not quite trampy,
but close. "Some of those old guys
were checking her out. Perverts."

> *Takes one to know one, sweetie.*
> *I really like your grandparents,*
> *by the way. Wish mine were more*
> *like them. They hate me being queer.*

"Mine are pretty cool, okay. Wish
they'd stick around more. Mom
could use their support." They took
off for California. They'll be back in

a couple of weeks. But then, who
knows? "Okay, parallel parking?
Check. Freeway merging? Check.
Now if I can just get that parent signature . . ."

The Last Time I Asked

Things didn't go so well. I give
Alex the highlights now:

Me: "I've been old enough for
over a month." Forgotten birthday.

> Dad: *You can have it. When I find
> the time to take you to the DMV.*

Me: "You never have time for me.
And you pretty much suck as a dad."

> Dad: *You're not exactly my idea
> of a noteworthy son, either.*

At which point, Mom jumped in,
trying to avert catastrophe. She said

she'd try to take me. I told her to chill.
She worries too much already.

Me: "All you have to do, Dad, is sign
the papers. I can use Alex's car."

> Dad: *Alex. Perfect.* Said as he poured
> himself another drink at ten a.m.

I watched the Irish whiskey glurg
into his coffee. Couldn't let it go.

Me: "No wonder you don't want
to take me to the DMV. You'd get busted

for drunk driving. Do you drink
at work too, Dad?" Which somehow

segued to him beating me down
over my sexual orientation.

> Dad: *Do you screw your boyfriend
> at school?* How one thing led to

another, I'm really not sure. But
suddenly, it wasn't about my wanting

a driver's license. It was all about
how my being gay is a sin, at least

in Dad's eyes. I asked him when my
qualifying for heaven became a priority.

> And all he could say as he slurped
> Irish coffee was, *I'll pray for you.*

A Soft Whistle

Escapes Alex. *Wow. I knew your dad*
isn't exactly accepting. But I had no
idea it's because he's religious.

"He's not. I mean, when I was a little
kid, we used to go to church all
the time. But then he started to travel

a lot. And then his mom, who was
the religious one to start with, got run
over crossing the street. After she died,

he never went to church again. If he
lost his faith, whatever. But that does
not give him the right to turn into

a no-good, nasty, loser drunk, or to try
and make me believe God hates me
because I'm some sort of an abomination. . . ."

I'm out of breath and losing steam.
But now Alex wants to know, *So, you*
believe in God? I mean, considering . . .

"Considering what? That I watch
porn and smoke weed and have
a boyfriend? Yes, as unlikely as it

might seem, I do believe in God.
See, I never felt exactly 'mainstream'
as a kid. The closest I ever got was

when we went to church and the pastor
would say stuff like we are all God's
children and He made us in His image.

Christ was all about walking with sinners,
Alex, and paving a path to heaven for
whores and homos and such. I bet his disciples

even strayed now and again, you know?
I mean, after all, they were men walking
the wilds with other men for weeks at a time."

I wink and he laughs, but then he gets
all serious and says, *And you believe
in heaven? That there's life after death?*

Death

I can't stand thinking about
that word in relation to
Alex, but he's waiting for me
to answer, and I think he needs
to hear what I've got to say.

"Yes, I believe that there is life
after death. Any physicist will
tell you that energy doesn't die,
it only changes forms. What
makes you *you*, Alex? That

hunk of gray matter inside
your skull? No way. You—all
of us—have a life force. Energy.
Some people call it a soul.
Whatever you call it, it makes

you *you*. And when your body
dies, your energy will remain.
I can't say for sure what heaven is.
But I have faith that it's a special place,
and that you will be welcome there."

Alex

Faith

Belief in unproven theory, in
what cannot be seen or heard
or touched, is something

                             I

have never known. Such
an amazing gift, to rise
above the realm of

                             wish-

ful thinking, all the way
to certainty of life beyond
the curse of early death. If

                             I

had been immersed in it
as a child, would I still carry
it with me now, and

                             could

it mute the throbbing
fear? If I reach for it now,
is there a chance that I will

                             find

it, sure as day follows night
follows day? If I hold Shane
tightly enough, can I absorb

                             faith?

If You Hold Someone

Tightly enough, can you make them stay?
Seems like everywhere I look, people

get together, only to break up again.
Especially people I care about, like Dad,

who broke up with Mom, plus a string
of girlfriends, before finding Cassie.

I hope they stay together, but sometimes
I hear them arguing. Can you argue and

still stay together? Is it worth it if you do?
Then there's Mom, who broke up with Dad,

and who just hooked up with a really cute
guy a few weeks ago. Robin is from Australia,

and has a hot Down Under accent. Mom
has had dates before, but she never really

talks about them. This time, she actually
brought him home for dinner. Not only

that, but she asked me to help her cook
it, so I knew she wanted a heart-to-heart.

I was peeling apples when she launched
it, gushing about Robin and how wonderful

he was. When I didn't say anything,
she insisted, *What? Talk to me, Harl.*

Which made me confess, "I just never
thought about you falling in love."

It was obvious that she had, and yet
she swore, *Whoa, now, wait a minute.*

I never said anything about love.
Then she stood there, hands on hips.

"I know. But since you met him,
you're . . . different. Happier, I guess."

Totally true, and when she asked why
that bothered me, I said something totally

stupid. "I want you to be happy because
of me. Not him. Not anyone else."

Totally Stupid

Because I do want her to be
happy, and she never really
seems that way. I get that
she's lonely. Feel bad that I

am not enough to change
that. But when she started
talking about Chad and how
I feel when he smiles at me

and how every woman wants
that solid rush of pleasure, even
a mom (and a single mom at that!),
I completely understood. But then

> she had to use the M word. *Anyway,*
> *I'm just having fun with Robin.*
> *We're not getting married or*
> *anything like that. You know?*

Married? She'd never do that
again, would she? "Not now,
you're not. But that might change."
I still don't get why that bothers

me, and neither did she. Her eyes
kind of glittered, angry. *Harley,
how come it doesn't piss you off
that your dad found someone new?*

I'd already thought about that, so
the answer came easily. "I never
expected anything different from
Dad. He's got personality flaws."

And it was just so accurate that
she snorted, *Ha! Ain't it the truth?
Ain't it the truth?* And that stupid
saying made me laugh and some

sort of barrier fell. Then she said,
*Honey, don't worry, okay? Robin
and I have only gone out a few times.
He's leaving for Vegas tomorrow.*

*It's a friendship, not a commitment.
I just wanted him to meet the girl
who will always be my top priority.
Let him see why I love you, okay?*

How Could I Say No?

Still, as I sliced the apples into
      a saucepan and added a little water
            (per Gram's yummy applesauce recipe),

something kept eating at me—
      the commitment thing again.
            Does love have to be temporary?

Or is that only lust? "Did you ever love
      Dad? I mean, were the two of you really
            in love?" I was little when they split

up, and I can't really picture them
      together, walking hand in hand along
            the beach at sunset, or whatever.

      She considered the question for
            a few. *I definitely thought so once.*
                  But young love doesn't always last.

But it does sometimes, like with
      Bri's mom and dad, who have
            been together for, like, forever.

When I argued that, she agreed.
         And then I really needed to know
                  something else. "Have you ever

been in love with anyone besides
         Dad?" When she said no, I asked,
                  "Then why did you get divorced?"

I said it kind of mean, and I meant
         it that way, and it stung her. First
                  she looked mad, then she looked

                  hurt and I felt bad when she said,
                           all soft and almost whispery,
                                    Sometimes love isn't enough.

Right about then the doorbell
         rang, and the way Mom smiled
                  made me know she's in love with

Robin, for whatever it's worth.
         I can't really blame her. He's
                  pretty much all that, and more.

I Didn't Want to Like Him

But I couldn't help it. From
the minute he walked through
the door, he made everything
be about me. He even asked my
opinion about stuff—like what

I think about politics and war
and immigration. When I didn't
have a good answer, I made stuff
up and he pretended every word
was valid. Then, when we sat

>   down to Mom's amazing sage-
>   and-garlic-rubbed pork roast and
>   she told him I made the applesauce,
>   it was me he complimented. *Beauty,*
>   *brains, and a fabulous chef too?*

Where have you been all my life?
And even though I knew it was
just a line, it made me feel great
that he cared enough to waste
it on me. Oh, yeah, I liked him.

So I'm Sorry

He went back to Vegas.
                Where he lives. Where
                                he works as a producer
for a major casino show,
                Rumble from Down Under.
                                Just what it sounds like—
Aussie guys with six-pack
                abs and giant deltoids taking
                                off most of their clothing,
one piece at a time. At least
                Robin isn't a stripper, and
                                Mom says his job pays really
well. And sometimes casinos
                in Reno or Tahoe bring them
                                in for special performances.
Mom says Vegas isn't so far.
                It isn't exactly close, either,
                                and she really misses him.
She pretends like she doesn't.
                Like everything's just fine.
                                But her eyes have gone hollow.

I'm Afraid Her Heart Will, Too

Especially as I happen to overhear
her talking on the phone to Bri's mom.

> *I called Robin, just to say hi.*
> *Some woman answered.*
> *She told me he was asleep,*
> *and it was obvious she had*
> *been sleeping, too. God! I can't*
> *believe I was nothing more*
> *than a three-night stand. . . .*

Now Bri's mom is saying something.
When Mom starts again, her voice is tired.

> *His sister? Yeah, right. Oh,*
> *I suppose it's possible. But*
> *likely? Don't think so. He*
> *said he isn't married, but*
> *never said he isn't attached.*
> *Anyway, if he really cared,*
> *he would have called me by now.*

I can't listen anymore. What's wrong
with Mom? Why can't she fall for
someone who will love us both?

Trace

Listening In

On adult conversations
is one of my favorite pastimes.
With much practice, I have
become a regular master of

eavesdropping

from the top of the stairs.
Somehow, the people below
never seem to know I'm here.
Amazing, how nonchalant they

can be

about secrets. Or maybe Mom
doesn't care that I know about
her friend's latest hookup, come
unhooked. I guess I do feel

bad

for Andrea. She has always
been nice to me, and a second
mom to Bri. She's close to over
the hill. Probably not easy

for

a lady her age to connect
with someone who's not
a creepster. Middle-aged
dating has got to be hard on

a person.

Mikayla

Dating

Is such a weak word.
"Going out" is an awkward
phrase, too. Neither defines
my relationship with Dylan.

We aren't exactly engaged,
but we are something like
promised to each other. That's
what the ring I'm wearing says.

"Promised." He gave it to me
after the biggest fight we've
ever had, that day at Washoe
Lake. When Dylan pulled up

and saw me with Ty, he flipped.
Not that I had done one single
thing wrong. He just assumed
the worst. And how dare he?

Dylan was the one who had been
sneaking around. Not me.
We kissed and made up days
ago. But it still makes me mad.

I would not party without him,
especially not at an old boyfriend's
house. He swears nothing happened
with Kristy, and I mostly believe

him. But there was something
like guilt in his eyes. I would ask
Ty if he knows anything more,
but Dylan would be pissed

and I love him too much to risk
another blowup. Anyway, I'm not
grounded at the moment. Tonight,
Dylan and I will make up for lost

evenings like last night, waylaid
by Mom's fortieth birthday party.
She said I could invite Dylan,
but he's scared of my parents.

Don't really blame him—he's not
their favorite person. But even if
he was, I'm kind of glad he didn't
come. It was a strange evening.

For One Thing

It was supposed to be a surprise
        party. Obviously, since Mom said
                Dylan could come, she knew about it.

Brianna and Harley planned it.
        So I guess it shouldn't be a surprise
                that it wasn't a surprise. Relentless

giggling is a surefire sign. Mom
        faked it pretty well. But I think
                the biggest shock was that Grandma

and Grandpa Carlisle came over.
        They sort of put up with Mom,
                but it's clear that they don't really

consider her family. When my
        grandmother bothers to talk
                to Mom at all, the condescension

reeks. No one thinks I've noticed
        it, but how could I not? So I was
                as startled as everyone else when

the doorbell rang, and there
        stood the elder Carlisles, birthday
                orchid in hand. Grandma knows

Mom is death to houseplants.
        But Grandma was nice enough last
                night. She even tried karaoke—

the Beatles' "Yesterday." Who
        knew she could sing? Who
                knew she knew the Beatles?

Mom sang, too. "Material Girl,"
        by Madonna. Not bad. But she
                seemed distant. Barely there

at all, like she so wanted to be
        somewhere else. And not just
                because of my grandparents.

She doesn't think I've noticed
        that, either. But something is up
                with Mom. Something disquieting.

Case in Point

Her almost non-reaction to
Paul Driscoll totally denying
the sperm donation that resulted

in a little baby Mom. I showed
her Leon Driscoll's email and,
though I could see she was, like,

> punched in the gut, all she said
> was, *I never expected anything*
> *else. But thanks for trying, Mik.*

And when I told her I wasn't
done trying, that there is someone out there named Sarah Hill,

> all she said was, *Don't worry*
> *about it. You and Trace and Bri*
> *are all the family I need.* Which

pretty much mimicked Dad's
take on the whole birth parent
search thing. And then, rather

than think things over, she made
a phone call and took off for
the evening, stumbling back home

very, very late. Yet another thing
she doesn't think I notice—later
and later evenings. More and more

often. Drunker and drunker when
she finally wanders in. Yet, somehow,
she is up early to run the next day.

I think she deserves a nod from
the *Guinness Book of World Records*
for "Distance Run on a Hangover."

Do I worry about her? Definitely.
Will I discuss it with her? No freaking
way. Because she's my mother, forty

years old and able to make decisions
for herself. But I really have to wonder.
Why hasn't my father noticed?

I Think About These Things

Lounging in bed late this morning.
Karaoke and cake kept us up late.

I don't hear a lot of movement in
the house. And it's weird, but I'm

still tired, despite eight hours of
sleep. Tired, and a little nauseous.

Hey, Bri and Harley made the cake.
Who knows if the eggs were good?

Eggs. Yuck. The very thought makes
my stomach turn. In fact, I think . . .

I throw back the covers, sprint
for the bathroom. Barely make it

to the toilet before I have to let fly.
Stomach cramping, I heave. Heave.

Heave until there's nothing left
to do but lay my head against

the chill porcelain, half hoping
it's relatively clean. Pretty sure

it's not. And that totally makes
me want to heave again. Except

there's nothing left but those awful
cramps and I don't think I can heave

those out. Food poisoning? Flu?
Cold sweat erupts on my forehead.

And, though it's way warm in here,
I shiver. Tiny spasms assault me,

and with each tremor, fear builds
inside me. No. I must be wrong.

There are lots of reasons to puke
in the morning. But my period

is overdue. At one week, I didn't
even think about it. At two, I figured

I miscounted. At three, I decided
I'm never really that regular, anyway.

But now, I'm over a month late.
And I'm really very afraid of why.

I Shower Away

The sweat and vomit.
            Towel off, still shaking.
                        Brush my teeth. Mouthwash.
                                    Body spray. Deodorant. Wrap
myself in a robe, scurry
            back to my bedroom as
                        the house begins to warm
                                    with voices. Waking up.
Heading for the kitchen,
            where the scent of
                        pancakes, usually
                                    tempting, but not today,
lifts into the morning.
            Can't do the family
                        thing. Instead, I dress
                                    quickly, find my keys
and slip out the door,
            quietly as I can. I think
                        maybe Bri sees me, but
                                    that's okay. Start my car,
point it toward town,
            nothing really new about
                        that except what I suspect
                                    a pregnancy test will confirm.

Brianna

I Suspect

Mom knew about her party
all along. Harley and I tried
our best to keep it secret, but

surprises

are hard to pull off, especially
with so many people involved.
Doesn't matter. At least I

can

say everyone had fun, even
my stuffy grandparents.
We go over to their house

sometimes

and I feel like I shouldn't sit
on their fancy furniture.
I didn't know Grandma could

be

so sociable! She was kind of
like Cinderella, only a lot
older and a little bit more

ugly.

Shane
Ugly

That was my parents' reaction
when they found out about Alex's
HIV. Okay, to be fair, at first Mom
thought it was me who was positive

when she came across the prescription
bottle Alex left in my room. It
didn't have a label, so she researched
the actual pills. Wow. She freaked.

When I came in, she was shaking
so hard I thought she might crack
like overbaked clay. She jerked
me down the hall, into my room

and over to my desk, where
the bottle sat. She picked it up
gingerly. *Do you have something
to tell me? About these, maybe?*

God, Shane . . . Her eyes filled
with tears, but she held them back.
Tell me you're not HIV positive!
I think she shrank about an inch.

When I told her they belonged
to Alex, and not to worry because
he's got the virus under control,
she only relaxed a little. "And

anyway, HIV isn't an automatic
death sentence anymore. Alex found
out early, and these antiviral drugs
will keep him from getting AIDS

for a very long time. When we're
together, we're very careful to
always use condoms. And the main
thing is, I love him, Mom. My life

would be empty without him in
it." She shrank a little more, but
it's the truth, and she knows it.
She kind of nodded, then left.

I know this only heaped more
worry on her already sagging
shoulders, and for that I'm sorry.
But it changes nothing at all.

It Might Have Ended There

But Dad happened to make a rare
      appearance at home, only to find

Mom researching HIV, the word
      flashing loudly on her computer screen.

Like her, at first he thought I
      had it. But finding out it was Alex

changed nothing for him. He had
      hit the bottle hard that morning.

      I thought he was going to kick
            my door in. *Open up!* It took me

      a minute to react. Too slow for
            Dad. *Goddamn it, you little shit.*

Open this fucking door! When
            I finally unlocked it, he pushed

      straight through, grabbed me
            by the shirt. *Are you plain stupid?*

He reeked of booze and his
      eyes carouseled, unfocused.

I could have taken him if I let
　　　　it get physical. I decided to try

humor instead. "Is there another
　　　　kind of stupid? Like, uh, fancy

stupid? Or beautiful stupid?"
　　　　Guess he didn't think it was funny.

He tore at my shirt. The motion
　　　　splashed whiskey out of the glass

　　　　　　he was holding. *Shut up. What*
　　　　　　　　the hell are you doing? Trying to

　　　　　　die? You can't mess around
　　　　　　　　with HIV. AIDS is God's way of

　　　　　　saying "gay" is a very bad choice.
　　　　　　　　God again! Plus, the word "choice."

I kept my voice low. "Do you
　　　　know how Alex contracted HIV, Dad?"

I described how Alex's uncle raped
　　　　him. "No choice in that, Dad. None at all."

His Face Flushed Beet Purple

And he let go of my shirt. And, though
he didn't say a word, something inside
him shifted. I could see it in his eyes.

He made an about-face, exited my room.
Not long after, he left the house and I fell
into a big pit of black depression.

That happens sometimes, when too much
shit gets flung at me at once. It's like
all the external pressure sucks into me,

then tries to escape again. But it can't.
So it builds. Throbs. Makes me feel
like my skin is anxious to split. I think

that feeling is why some people cut—
little slices so they don't shred completely.
I'm too much of a coward to cut.

That day, I closed my blinds. Turned off
the lights. Crawled into bed and turned
myself off, too. So I didn't rip apart.

Later, Something Happened

I don't know what, but it must
have been bad, because voices

cut through the artificial night
in my head. At first, just one.

> Mom.
> Talking to herself.
> Asking questions.

Then, silence. A second voice.

> Aunt Andrea.
> Whispering.
> Consoling?

It was weird. More like a dream
than real. And, even though Aunt

Andrea never comes over, I told
myself nothing could be that wrong.

Finally, the third, slurred voice.

> Dad.
> Denying.
> Crying?

I wasn't about to get involved,
so I convinced myself it wasn't real.

But after, Mom had changed.

She Is Distracted

Even more distant than usual.
She mutters. Throws her hands
into the air. Talks to the sky.

        Sometimes she shouts obscenities,
        mostly directed toward Dad. Like now.
        From the kitchen: *No! You fucking*

        son-of-a-whore. How could you
        do this to me? It's probably useless,
        but I so want to help her, hurry

to try. I find her, hair messed up
and red-rimmed eyes. "What happened?
What did he do?" Will it ever end?

        She shrugs. *Nothing. I'm sorry.*
        I didn't mean for you to hear
        anything. We had a fight is all.

"A fight about me." They always fight
about me, but Mom says this
time it was about Shelby and

a new SMA treatment she saw.
*Your dad doesn't think it would
be worth a try. But I do.* That's not

it. But she isn't going to tell me
what it really is. She did, however,
give me the opportunity to get

something off my chest. "Mom, you
probably don't want to hear this,
but I agree with Dad. I think you

should let the disease run its course.
Shelby deserves a dignified death.
More treatment won't stop her from

dying. But it will take away her dignity.
I don't want to watch that, and neither does
Dad. And I don't think you should, either."

There. Feelings shared. God, does it
piss her off. *I can't believe you said
that! Where did you get such ideas?*

The Answer Is So Obvious

It sinks its fangs immediately.
Is that how you feel about Alex,
should he develop AIDS? That
he deserves a dignified death?

I tell her that's exactly how
I feel. Once there is no choice,
I pray his death is dignified.
"I hope I'll be there to help him

through it, but that will probably
be many years from now." She
gives me a strange look. Kind of
like, really? "I know the odds

of us staying together that long
aren't good. I mean, we're both
young and stupid." It's enough
to saw through the tension.

We are both sort of half smiling
when Dad barrels through the door,
carrying — groceries? When was
the last time *he* went shopping?

Not only that, but it is late afternoon
and I'm pretty sure he hasn't been
drinking. It's like whatever broke
Mom down tried to fix Dad up.

Success in That Endeavor

Is highly unlikely. Dad's eyes scroll
back and forth between Mom and me.
Questioning. His mouth opens. Closes.

Mom says, *We're talking about death.*
His face creases, so she adds, *Dignified
death, actually. For people we love.*

I . . . , he tries, *uh . . . oh.* He starts
unpacking the grocery bags. *I got steaks.
Thought we could barbecue.* He turns

back to me. *I bought an extra one, in case
you wanted to invite Alex to join us.* What
the hell? *I'm sorry we fought yesterday.*

Wait just one damn minute. Was that
an apology? Not to mention acceptance
of Alex and me? "Alex and I will still both be gay."

He doesn't miss a beat. *That's what
I hear. Guess I'll have to get over
it. You're still my son, Shane. I love you.*

Invasion of the Body Snatchers

Yeah, that's it. Has to be. Alternately,
      what does this stranger want from me?
Must find out. "Actions speak louder
      than words, Dad. But steak is a good start."

          He actually smiles at me. Creeping
      me out. *And rib-eye, too. Thought*
          your mom was looking a little anemic.
      Where did he find a sense of humor?

I don't even know how to feel
      right now, because I'm pretty sure
everything will be back to "usual"
      without warning. Maybe someone

prescribed him new meds? I think
      about *not* inviting Alex. But I'm
dying to see him, and to make him
      feel something like normal while

          in the company of my family. Surreal.
      When was the last time *I* felt that way?
          I am not far toward my room when I hear
      Dad say, *You didn't tell him, did you?*

Shelby

I Hear

Nobody thinks so. But I do.
Sometimes people whisper.
Sometimes they yell.
Sometimes they say mean things.

I see

more than the TV. It's my friend.
I don't have any others, like the kids
on Barney do. Why are people afraid
of me? I don't want to hurt them.

I taste

only the sweet air, whooshed
through tubes to help me breathe.
If I'm lucky a bit of flavor comes
with the wind or skin or clothes

I smell.

I wish my mouth would let
me tell Mama I love her.
Let me tell Daddy I miss him.
Let me tell Shane how good

I feel

when I see him happy with Alex.
I like when I swim because when
I float, I am free. I like when I sleep
because I dance when

I dream.

Harley
Dancing

That's where Dad and Cassie
are going later. Which means
Chad and I will be home alone.

And I've got a plan. Formulated
from watching many episodes of
Jersey Shore, *The Bachelor* and

Desperate Housewives. Mom
would throw a regular fit if she
knew those shows have become

my sources of inspiration. It's
called the direct approach. So not
me. But what do I have to lose?

Meanwhile, I'm going school
shopping. With Cassie. I think
Mom was a little hurt that I didn't

want to go with her—the low
fashion queen. I love her. But style
is not her thing. Cassie knows

the kind of look I'm after, and
she knows where to find crazy
cool clothes that aren't too pricey.

I squish into a pair of stretchy
jeans. Tight, with back-pocket
detailing that draws attention

to my size-five butt. Size five!
It was worth walking every mile.
Next I try on a really short skirt.

Hmm. "Cassie," I call to the far
side of the dressing room door.
"I need your opinion on something."

> Mom would freak immediately,
> but Cassie takes the time to really
> check it out. *Turn around.* She kind
>
> of whistles. *It looks great, but*
> *you definitely better not bend over*
> *in it. At least, not without panties.*

Cassie Rocks

She's funny. Pretty. Smart, at least
about some things. And she always

makes time for me. Acts like she cares
about me. She even talked Dad into

contributing to this shopping excursion.
One thing Mom gripes about is how he has

never paid child support. She has a pretty
good job, but back-to-school always pinches.

This year, at least, he's kicking in a little.
Stepping up to the plate, or at least as far

as the backstop, all because of Cassie.
All stocked up on jeans, skirts and blouses,

we look for shoes. It's my lucky day.
Payless is having a two-for-one sale.

Which means I get four pairs—two athletic,
two heels. And once those are paid for,

> Cassie says, *What about that hair?*
> *Want to do something bold? My treat.*

We Are Cruising the Mall

Discussing bolder hair and sipping
        iced coffees (despite the caffeine,
which will stunt my growth, according

to my mom). We duck into Sephora,
        check out the testers. There's one flowery
one I really love—rose, violet and a hint

      of vanilla. Pricey stuff, so for now,
           the lingering reminder will have to do.
      You have a birthday coming up soon, right?

"Three weeks," I agree, and I love
        that she remembers, not to mention
the fact that I now have hope of smelling

      this way when I start school. As we
           leave the store, Cassie tenses suddenly.
      Shit. Shit. Shit. She half pushes me out

the door, steers me into a sharp right turn,
        picks up her pace till I practically have
to run to keep up, shopping bags swinging.

Quick veer down a perpendicular
          aisle, then she allows herself to
glance over her shoulder. Apparently

whatever she saw to get her all worked
          up isn't there anymore, because she slows
and I can finally breathe. "What's wrong?"

          Nothing. But she keeps walking
                    purposefully toward the exit. *I mean,*
          not nothing, exactly. I just need to get

          out of here right now, okay? It takes
                    until we're in the car, out of the parking
          lot and around the block twice, I'm

guessing so she knows "not nothing"
          isn't following us, until she thinks
about explaining. Even then, I can see

her deciding how much to tell me.
          "Jeez, Cassie, what is it? Did you see
a zombie or something?" Three beats.

And She Says

Sort of. Except, more like a vampire—
a bloodsucker that just won't die.
Look, this isn't a story I share often.
And I'd appreciate it if you don't pass
it on, especially not to your mom.

She worries about you being around
your dad enough as it is. She takes
a deep breath, then plunges in. *I was*
going to be a nurse. You didn't know
that, did you? I was studying at Western

Nevada, making good grades and
everything. And then I met this guy.
Chad's father, Damian. Typical bad
boy. Drugs. Booze. Rotten temper.
And I saw none of that. Not at first.

I never finished nursing school. I got
pregnant. Damian insisted I keep
the baby. Swore he'd take care of us,
and I had to believe him. I loved him.
That was enough. For a while.

She Turns onto McCarran Boulevard

It's the long way home, so
I'm pretty sure there's more.

      There is. We lived poor. And we lived
      rough. And Damian lived fast—crystal,
      crack, ecstasy. Anything he could get

      hold of. That made him mean. To me.
      To Chad, who was too little to know
      anything except Daddy hurt him.

      I was working one day—somebody
      had to. It was a crap casino waitress
      job, but it paid the bills, if not the drug

      tab. Anyway, Damian was supposed
      to be watching Chad, but he'd been
      on a bender, and was crashed out on

      the sofa. Chad was four. He decided
      he was hungry and was going to the store.
      So he took off walking. Alone. In a bad

      part of town. Luckily, the woman
      who found him was decent. She took
      him to her house. Called the cops.

She pauses, catches her breath.
But I have to know, "What happened?"

> By that time, I had come home,
> found him missing. After a frantic
> search, I called the cops, too.
>
> They brought him home, and when
> they tried to talk to Damian, he got
> all belligerent—first sign of a doper
>
> on the down. Next thing you know,
> he was swinging at one of them.
> They hauled him in, cooled him off
>
> for a couple of days, then let him
> out, awaiting trial. Somehow, in
> his demented mind, it was all my fault.

She stops again, and I know it's hard
for her to relive it when she says,
He beat me bloody. Broke bones. Teeth.

> Little Chad tried to stop him. Damian
> pushed him headfirst into the wall.
> We were both unconscious when he left.

As the Story Goes

A neighbor heard the ruckus.
Called 911. The paramedics found
Cassie shattered and Chad close to death,
with a subdural hematoma—rampant bleeding
in the skull, which squashes the brain. The two of
them were in the hospital for days. Damian hid
out with his brother in Red Rock. Then his
brother's wife saw the news reports and
put in a covert call to Secret Witness.

> *They threw every charge they could*
> *think of at him, including attempted*
> *murder. He got fifteen to twenty-five*
> *years. I was there when they sentenced*
>
> *him, and the look he give me clearly*
> *said, "When I get out, I'm coming for*
> *you." Well, he's out. That's who I saw.*
> *Older. Grayer. But it was definitely*
>
> *him. I don't know why I thought*
> *he'd be in for the max ride. But, no.*
> *Early release. It's weird. But in*
> *my mind, he was dead. Stupid, huh?*

I'm Kind of Speechless

But . . . "You don't really think
        he'd try to hurt you, do you?

I mean, he wouldn't want to
        take a chance on going back

to prison, right?" Jeez, I def
        can't tell Mom, or no way

would she let me come over
        to Dad's anymore, even though

I can't believe this Damian dude
        is a danger to me. Or to Cassie.

    I don't know. I would hope not,
        and I don't want to live all paranoid.

Two more burning questions.
    "Does Dad know? And does Chad

remember what happened?"
    Could explain why he's a little

    chill. *I wouldn't keep it from your*
        Dad. And how could Chad forget?

When We Get Back to Dad's

He is all cleaned up, ready to go
out to dinner, and then dancing.
Cassie doesn't want to spoil
his good mood, so she asks me

> not to say anything. *I'll tell*
> *him when the time is right.*
> *And please let me break*
> *the news to Chad, too, okay?*

I give her a hug and she goes
to get ready. I hate secrets.
Especially explosive ones.
Ones that feel ready to blow.

Dad and Cassie leave and Chad
is watching an awful Austin Powers
movie. I sit next to him, restless.
In fact, I'm almost ready to spill

> when Bri calls my cell. *Promise*
> *you won't tell,* is the first thing
> she says. *I heard Mikki talking*
> *to Dylan. She's pregnant.*

Dylan

Pregnant

The very concept strikes fear
into the hearts of young people
everywhere. In fact,

it's

right at the top of my *Do Not
Tell Me This* list, just above
"You've got cancer and are

not

a candidate for chemo."
Un-freaking-believable!
When Mik called to tell me

what

the two-blue-lines thing
meant, I thought she was
joking. Ginormous mistake—

I

laughed, and that made her
cry. Not sad tears. Pissed tears.
Then I asked her what she

wanted

to do, totally expecting her to
say abortion. She said she wasn't
sure, and that's not what I wanted

to hear.

To Abort or Not to Abort

I have asked myself that question,
over and over, for the past few days.
First I had to fight the shock of finding
out I'm pregnant. I fought the idea,

even beyond the two blue lines.
But a second test confirmed it,
and the morning sickness is very
real. I am going to have a baby.

Only, wait. Am I? Oh, God. Why
now? If I do, I won't get to finish
my senior year. No graduation. No
cap and gown. No senior prom.

Prom. Right. I can just see it now.
I waddle in, stomach big as a basketball.
Dylan and I hit the dance floor and
just as we start to slow dance,

my water breaks. (Thanks, *Teen Mom*,
for that fabulous picture.) Without
warning, my eyes burn and tears
overflow and hormones may be

to blame, but fear is the driving
force. I don't know what to do.
Dylan isn't much help. He says
he'll honor my decision but I know

he wants me to get rid of it. When
I called to tell him, his first reaction
was to laugh. He thought I was joking.
Who would joke about something

> like this? When it finally sank in
> that I was talking real, he sobered
> quickly. *Okay. Well. It's not the end
> of the world. We can fix it.* Fix it.

Like there's a patch kit. His
fix would involve ripping me
wider. Digging the wound deeper.
There are no bandages big enough

for that. How did this happen?
We always used condoms, except
for once or twice. How could
two careless times equal a baby?

I Keep Thinking of It

As a baby. I've got to stop doing that.
Right now it's just an embryo. Not

even a fetus. At least, I don't think so.
An embryo becomes a fetus eight weeks

after conception. Which time did I conceive?
It doesn't really matter, except if I decide

to have an abortion, it will have to be soon.
What happens to me if I do? If I don't? What

happens with Dylan, either way? How much
pressure can love take before it pulverizes—

marble, crushed into dust. I need him more
than ever now. But ever since I told him,

he's unreachable. Even when he's sitting
right next to me. Like now. We are on

a blanket, beneath a star-crusted sky,
and it's stifling. Not a blink of breeze

to ruffle the late-August night. Dylan
has been mostly silent. Sucked into thought.

Now he reaches for my hand. *I wish
I could make it rain,* he says softly.

Okay, that is not what I expected
him to say. Not even close. "Why?"

*Well, we need it. Don't we? And if
I could make it rain here right now,*

*I would be all-powerful. I could . . .
take things back. You know?*

I lean into him, and he gentles his arm
around my shoulder. "We can't take

anything back. It's where we go from
here that means everything."

I leave it there. No decisions. Not
tonight. No ultimatums, ever. What

he really needs to know right now is,
"I love you, Dylan. More than anything.

This doesn't change that. Nothing
can. You are all-powerful to me."

That Makes Him Smile

And this is the closest to okay
       I have felt for days. I scoot
              into his lap, straddle his legs.

Can I reach him this way? I lock
       his eyes with mine. "Kiss me."
              He hesitates, and I see a flash

of doubt, so I cover his mouth
       with mine, and there is nothing
              tentative about the way I move

my body, eel-like, against his.
       God, I've missed this amazing
              rush! I lift my shirt over my head,

wait for him to take his off, too.
       And we are skin against skin
              in the sage-scented night and I

am overwhelmed with love for
       him. He rolls me off him, onto
              my back, starts to unzip my shorts.

But Now He Stops

"Don't stop. I want to."

> *But I didn't think we would*
> *so I didn't bring a condom.*

That makes me laugh.
"And that matters, why?"

> *Good point. But I don't*
> *want to hurt you, either.*

"You won't. Pregnant
women have sex all the
time. In fact, I've heard—"

> *Stop talking. You're messing*
> *up my concentration.* He kisses
> me, softly at first, then harder.

I kiss him back even harder.
Slip out of my shorts, help
him out of his, too. And now
we are totally naked under

> a blush of summer stars. He
> kisses down the front of me,
> lifting goose bumps, even
> though the air is low oven hot.

He lifts up over me, holding
his weight with the strength
of his arms. Rocks into me with
a tenderness I didn't know he possessed.
Time blurs in a mist of making love.

When We Finish

The blanket beneath my head
        is soaked with tears. Because I know,
        as much as I want it not to be true,

nothing will ever be exactly
        the same between us. We'll grow
        closer. Or we'll be ratcheted apart.

        We lie facing each other and
                he kisses me sweetly. *Don't cry.*
                He licks the wet from my eyes,

and the gesture is at once kind
        and sensual. I flip over, draw back
        into him, loving the way I fit so well

in the harbor of his body. He sighs
        as he strokes my still-flat belly, high
        smallish breasts. I wish we could stay

just like this forever. Warm. Secure.
        Indivisible. But I'm not safe now.
        And winter always comes. "I'm scared."

I know. I'm scared, too. We need
  to decide what to do, and then it
  will get better. I . . . I've asked

around. An abortion costs about
  five hundred dollars. I've got more
  than that in my savings account.

Abortion would be the easiest
  way out. But I keep thinking about
  Audrey. I can't get her out of my head.

How could I live with that kind
  of regret? "What if I can't, Dylan?
  What if I decide I want to have it?"

Every muscle in his body tenses.
    He grows corpse-stiff. *It isn't all*
    your decision, is it? Don't I get a say?

I sit up, reach for my shirt. "Of
  course you do. But it's my body.
  And it's my . . . our . . . baby inside."

He Jolts Upright

Don't, Mikki! It's not a baby.
It's just a little glob of cells.

It never has to become a baby.
"A little glob of cells? What

is that? Internet research?"
I should know. I did it, too.

What did you expect? Total
disinterest? Sweetheart, I've been

stressing as much as you have.
He reaches for me, but I yank

away. "Really? I guess you've
been throwing up every morning?

Worrying about what to say to
your mom and dad? Thinking

about school, how friends will
gossip, or even if you'll have any

friends if someone finds out?"
Except for the throwing up, yes.

He Is So Sincere

That I smile. Almost feel sorry for him.
But not as sorry as I feel for myself.
"I've been over and over this a million

times. I know the smartest thing would
be to get rid of it. But I don't think I can.
I've seen the pictures, too. I know it

doesn't look anything like a baby yet.
But it's more than just a little glob
of cells. It's you and me, and it's alive."

> *Sounds like you've made your decision.*
> *And that I don't have a say at all. Get*
> *dressed. I'll take you home.* He is angry,

and now so am I. "Dylan, your decision
would be for some doctor to stick a tube
up inside me and vacuum our little problem

away, like dog hair and dust. I still might
choose to do exactly that. I've got a couple
of weeks. Either way, I need your support."

It's a Silent Drive Home

When we get there, he kisses
me good night, just like always.

Just like always, I say, "I love you."
And he tells me he loves me, too.

The house is quiet. I tiptoe upstairs,
use the bathroom, slip between crisp,

cool sheets, scented like detergent.
Clean. Like I can never be again.

It is one of those nights when real
sleep doesn't come, just that space

beyond true awareness. That place
where you wander through dreams,

knowing you're there. I know I'm here,
waves licking my ankles, and somewhere

beyond the breaks a baby is crying.
Floating, for the moment. The choice

is mine. Stand here and let it drown,
or dive, swim like hell to save it.

Dylan

Drowning

Can't float. Forgot how to swim.
Tired of treading water.
Going down. Down.

Down,

I have never loved her more.
Can't imagine being without her.
What will it take

to

make her see that we cannot
possibly become "three"?
What does she want from me—

the

promise of marriage?
After witnessing my parents'
freak show, that kind of

hell

is something I hope never
to suffer. Anyway, we're just kids.
No diplomas. No jobs. No hope

of

winning the lottery. Even
if our love could survive,
how would we pay for

diapers?

Shane
Paying

For mistakes is a regular bitch,
defining the word "mistake" as:

> error
> blunder
> slipup
> oversight
> gaffe.

Or things you didn't necessarily
mean to do. But when there is
intent, a clear objective to

> injure
> wound
> insult
> abuse
> harm

or sin against someone,
especially someone you've
sworn to honor, cherish and
protect, payback is likely to be

> devastating
> disturbing
> distressing
> damaging
> disastrous.

My Parents

Don't think I know what's going
on. Don't have a clue that it doesn't
exactly take over-keen observation
to comprehend the less-than-abstract

idea that Dad's been fucking off on
Mom for quite some time, and with
one person, some Skye woman, who
he works and travels with. In fact,

> they've been seeing each other for
> years. And that, as I overheard Gram
> say, *Isn't just sex. It's a relationship.*
> And what she meant by that was *love.*

Dad is in love with someone else.
Which explains why he doesn't
always come home at night. Why
he's been so distant to Mom and,

maybe, me. Bastard! I figured it
was because he couldn't deal with
Shelby. But apparently the affair
began before she was even conceived.

No, Dad's "indiscretion," which is
something of an understatement,
wasn't about "running away from."
It was all about "running to," and

that is hard to forgive. Mom didn't
want me to know, mostly because
Dad has shifted gears. Don't ask me
why, but for some reason he decided

he wanted to stay with Mom instead
of riding off into the sunset with Skye
Sheridan. One very big element in
that is his so-called change of heart

toward me. And for what purpose?
Does he really plan to be around
more now? Why do I doubt that?
And why should I care if he is?

Should I Forgive and Forget?

Be the bigger man? Luscious irony
there, I suppose. I mean, being gay

calls your manhood, not to mention
your morality, into question, at least

in some people's (including my father's) eyes.
Right up until he got busted with his pants

down around his ankles, Dad insisted
I was the sinner. But *I* wasn't fucking

off on my partner, let alone my wife.
Is infidelity—conquest—the mark of a man?

What about promises? For better or worse,
for richer or poorer, in sickness and in health?

What about the idea that genuine love
is about conquering mutual demons?

Look Up "Hypocrite"

In the dictionary. Bet you'll find
a picture of my father.
You know, I totally wish
that it wasn't so. But how
can I believe in someone
who once meant everything
to me, only to have him turn
his back, not only on me,
but also on everyone who
makes me comfortable
with who I am? Bastard!

I was almost past wanting
his acceptance. I knew, deep
down, that it couldn't happen
like switching on the air con
on a hot day. When it seemed
to, I was suspicious, prayed
for the best. Tried not to expect
the worst. And so, it stung
to discover his supposed turn-
around was all about a bid
to keep Mom hanging on.

She's Hanging On

For now, I guess. Kind of by her
      fingertips, and just barely. I hear

her talking—to Aunt Andrea,
      to her old friend, Drew, and to Gram.

Mostly to Gram, who is staying
      here for now while she and Gramps

look for a house. Gram says
      she's tired of traveling the country,

living like some Bedouin on
      wheels. I'm glad she'll be closer.

Mom needs her, even though
      she'd never admit it. Dad's taking

her to Monterey for the weekend.
      It's where they had their honeymoon,

but I'm not sure the Pacific Ocean
      will be enough to rekindle the romance.

Mom is taut as a stretched-to-the-limit
      rubber band. Hope she doesn't break.

Monterey

Is supposed to be Mom's birthday
present, so tonight we're having an early
celebration. Aunt Andrea is already here,

helping Gram in the kitchen. When
the doorbell rings, I expect it to be Alex.
I fling it open, giving little air smooches.

Nope. Not Alex. It's a woman, maybe
thirty-five, and built like a Rottweiler.
She smiles at my kissy pouts and her face

> radiates humor. *Uh. Do I have the right*
> *house? I'm looking for the Trasks.*
> *I'm Pamela Anderson.* At my dubious
>
> look, she adds, *Not* that *Pamela*
> *Anderson, obviously. I'm from the health*
> *center — a caregiver. For Shelby?*
>
> I step back to let her in. As she passes,
> she says, *How do you know her, anyway?*
> *You're too young to have been a* Baywatch *fan.*

"What's *Baywatch*? I saw her on
Dancing with the Stars. How she lasted
that long is a total mystery." I lead Pamela

into the living room. "Mom? Dad?
The caregiver is here." The doorbell
rings again. This time, it *is* Alex,

and he's holding a giant bouquet
of yellow roses. "For me? Sweetheart,
you shouldn't have!" No one's watching,

    so I kiss his amazing smile. He looks
    a little alarmed. *Um. Hi. Sorry, but
    the flowers are for your mom.*

"How come you never bring me
flowers?" I stick out my lower lip.
"Well, I guess you can come in anyway."

He is dressed in khaki pants and a Levi's
shirt, and he's wearing some exotic
cologne that makes me want to eat him.

And at This Moment

I couldn't care less about Dad's motives.
Alex is here, and welcome, and when

he gives Mom her birthday roses, her
thank-you is a kiss on his cheek, which

turns the color of ripe cherries, matching
his other cheek and the tips of his ears.

Dinner is Gram's made-from-scratch
pizza. The yeasty scent of fresh-baked

dough fills the house, and when Mom
rolls Shelby into the room, she sniffs

      the air. Grins and says, *Pri-ee.* Pretty.
      I guess it does smell pretty. I wish

she could taste it, but Shelby only
eats liquid sustenance, fed via tube.

She doesn't seem to mind, but that's
all she's ever known, and thinking about

things she's missed always makes me
more than a little sad. The heaviness

lifts quickly tonight, though. There
are no balloons, but there are yellow

roses and pizza and birthday cake.
It's a party and everyone wears

a smile, especially when Gramps
goes to the piano and starts to play

> old classic rock songs. *I once thought
> I'd be the next David Crosby,* he says.

> *But Neil Young was jealous, so they
> wouldn't let me join the group.*

Crosby, Stills, Nash and Young. Mom
used to sing their stuff when I was little.

> She harmonizes with Gramps. *Teach
> your parents well. Their children's hell . . .*

Is slowly going by. Shelby loves
the music, tries to hum along. And that

makes her cough. Mom starts toward
her, but Pamela reaches her first.

Pamela Is Efficient

Deliberate. Kind, as she instructs
Shelby to relax, not an intuitive thing
when you're hacking up a lung.

> Mom would jump in, but Dad keeps
> a hand on her arm. *Let Pamela do
> her job. That's why she's here.*

She decides the best way to do it
is to use the lung assist machine in Shelby's
room that's there to vacuum scum

> from her airways. Mom wants to
> follow her down the hall, but Pamela
> agrees with Dad. *I've got it. No worries.*

Mom has done nothing but worry
for years. This will be a learning
curve. Her nervousness grips all

> of us, though we try to get back
> into a party mood. Dad tells Gramps,
> *Can you play something slow? I want*

to dance with my wife. Mom stiffens,
and I think she's going to refuse. But
Dad persuades her to sway with some

old song I know I've heard, but
couldn't name for money. If I wasn't
privy to what's going on between

them, I'd probably find it touching.
As it is, it's pretty much creeping me
out. And, judging by Mom's zombie-ish

motion, she feels the same way. She's putting
on a show. But what's the point? It's not
like everyone here doesn't know. Well,

except for Alex. I haven't told him yet.
I kind of wanted him to believe Dad found
a soul. God, how I wish that was true.

Pamela returns solo. *Shelby's resting
comfortably, watching a DVD. I'll be
back first thing tomorrow morning.*

Mom Pulls Away

From Dad. Walks Pamela to the door,
asking questions. Giving directions.
Gram follows, listening in, because
she will be here for Shelby this weekend
when Pamela isn't. Dad goes into

the kitchen. Probably looking for booze,
although he hasn't been drinking nearly
as much as he used to. Don't know if
that's voluntary or part of whatever
deal he has forged with Mom. Either

way, he's a hell of a lot easier to deal
with when he isn't blotto. Gramps
launches a Green Day song—one Alex
knows the words to. Who knew he could
sing? Who knows what else I don't know

about him yet? How long does it take
to get to know someone totally? Does
that ever happen? How long before you
can tell when someone's keeping secrets?
Is it ever better simply not to know?

Alex

Is It Better

Not to know what's causing
a massive tide—one you happen
to be swimming in, charcoal
carbonation frothing the horizon,

              panic

likely, when limp resignation
might serve better?
You can't outswim a rip current
and an anxious sea

              swallows

what can't remember that.
Is it wiser to avoid looking over
your shoulder, intuiting a predator
is sneaking up behind

              you,

ascertaining distance? A backward
glance might cost a limb or liver,
food chain hierarchy faster
than you. A sudden shift of energy

              smothers

certainty. Disregarding it might
be preferable to overanalyzing,
if rooting out the source
of your discomfort only brings

              you

face-to-face with a monster.

Harley

A Monster

That's what Chad's dad is. No
      wonder he never talks about him.
            My dad is kind of weird and all,
                and I remember how he and Mom
argued all the time before
      they split up. But he never beat
            on Mom or me. How could a guy
                do something like that to his kid?
I haven't said a word about
      seeing that Damian ogre. Not
            to Chad. Not to Dad. Not even
                to Mom. But I'm totally dying to.
I did break down and tell Mom
      about Mikayla being pregnant,
            even though Bri asked me not to.
                That kind of secret is hard to keep.
Mom told, and everything blew
      sky-high and now Bri is pissed
            at me. I'm sorry, but I think
                her parents really needed to know.
She'll get over it. She has to.
      Mom says when I start high school
            I'll make new friends. That's all right.
                But Bri will always be my best friend.

The Worst Thing

About telling Mom about Mikayla
was having to hear, from my mother,
the dirty little details of sex. The kind
you definitely don't get in sex ed.

> *I know you're not having sex yet,*
> was how she started the conversation,
> boring into my eyes with hers, trying
> to figure out if that happens to be true.

> *And I know you got all the basics in*
> *school, so I won't go there. What I*
> *want to talk to you about is the things*
> *that might convince you to go all the way.*

Go all the way creeped me out
immediately, and things didn't get
better. First, she outlined the obvious
lines some guys use to convince

you not to use protection—how it's
not possible to get preggo the first
time you do it; how he's great at
pulling out; how he's def sterile.

That was kind of funny, actually.
But then she got into really weird
stuff, like how foreplay makes you
want to do more, only she didn't call

it foreplay, she called it "digital
penetration" and "oral stimulation."
And that really made me picture
Mom doing that stuff, and it grossed

me out totally, so I just promised to
keep it in mind whenever at some
way future date I might be in that
position. And that should have been

the end of it, except then she felt
the need to confess that foreplay
and what came after was the reason
she and Dad ended up getting married

their senior year in high school. I might
have had a big sister or brother, except
Mom lost that baby. When I asked if
that meant she never loved Dad,

she said, *I thought I did, at the time.*

I Watch Dad Now

Futzing around, trying to build
a campfire while Cassie cooks
hot dogs on a rusting barbecue.

Are they really in love? Or just
thinking they are, at this time?
Love is a fragile thing. I hope

theirs can stay in one piece.
The campground is busy—one
last reminder of summer before

school starts up again. The sun drops
down behind the western peaks,
but its warmth remains, trapped

in pine-scented evening air. Camping
with Dad means age-worn tents and
sleeping bags, and that's okay with me.

> *Dinner!* chimes Cassie, wrapping
> Polish sausages with white bread buns.
> *Ketchup and mustard are on the table.*

Dad holds out his paper plate.
Personally, I like mine naked.
He winks at Cassie, who bursts

out laughing. Chad looks at me,
rolls his eyes, then douses his own
bun with condiments. Message sent.

Wow. Some people probably think
he's a total wad. But I understand
why he's so cynical. I just wish

he'd let me break through. We scarf
down hot dogs, chips and soda. I can
feel the pounds I'm gaining tonight,

but I haven't indulged in junk food
hardly at all this summer and I'm
loving every greasy, sugary swallow.

We throw our paper plates into Dad's
pitiful fire, and when they flame
Chad tosses in some pinecones.

When those flare, he adds a chunk
of wood, which catches easily. *That's
how you build a campfire,* he says.

It's a Throw-Down

But Dad responds to the challenge
by putting his arms around Cassie

and kissing the back of her neck.
Chad bristles. The night could go bad,

and I don't want that, so I nudge
Chad's arm. "Want to take a walk?"

> He shrugs, which is his way to
> agree. *Just one second,* he says,

disappearing into his tent for
a minute or two. When he emerges,

> his hands slip out of his pockets.
> *Okay. Let's go.* As we start around

>> a long loop of asphalt, I hear
>> Cassie call, *Don't be gone long.*

>> *It's getting dark, and who knows
>> what comes out at night around here.*

Chad chuckles. *Evil things, Mom.*
She can't hear him, of course. But I can.

Evil Things

Are what I think about
as we veer off the pavement.
Dive into a thick stand of trees.
Pine needles, soft beneath our

feet, should cushion sound.
Instead, there is a gentle rustling
near the ground. "What's that?"
I ask, all paranoid. But Chad

> is unconcerned. *Nothing.*
> *The wind. Or maybe . . .*
> He looks around. *Deer. Or*
> *skunks. Too soft for bear.*

"Bear?" We don't even
have a flashlight. No bear
is going to sneak up on us,
right? I consider which

> direction to run. But Chad
> laughs and that means
> everything is okay. At least,
> until he reaches into his pocket.

Out comes a cigarette—hand-
rolled. Except when he lights
it, it doesn't smell like tobacco.
"Um. Is that marijuana?"

He takes a big puff. Holds
it in and says, around the smoke,
*Really excellent weed. Want
some?* He offers me the cigarette.

I shake my head. "No thanks."
It's not exactly a shock, I guess.
Wonder if the skunky smell
will attract skunks. Wonder if

it would scare away a bear.
*You've never smoked weed?
You should. It makes all the bad
crap kind of disappear. You know?*

Other than worrying about
bears, there isn't a lot of bad
crap bothering me. But if I took
it, would it make him like me?

I Know It's Stupid

I've got the information I need
          to make a wiser choice. I've been
raised better, and understand I have

an alcoholic father. I am programmed
          to say no. So why do I say, "Okay"?
I reach for the cigarette. But what

now? I've never smoked anything.
          Never even tried. I watched Chad
inhale and hold it. I try a little puff.

Don't want to cough and look
          even dumber than I feel. Smoke
crawls across my tongue. Creeps

down my throat. Not much taste
          at all. Good thing I didn't suck in
more. This little taste wants out.

          Chad notices my struggle. *Don't*
                    let it out yet. That's good shit.
          Don't waste it. Finally, I have no

choice but to release the tainted
         air from my lungs. Now what?
Shouldn't I feel dizzy? At least

         a little blurry? I don't feel a thing.
                  You might not feel much. Usually
         you have to do it a few times to

         catch a buzz. Chad the psychic
                  takes another drag. *But once you*
         do, you'll never go back to straight.

"You mean, you'll just stay high?"
         His frosty-eyed glare informs me
that was an idiotic thing to ask.

         Disgust weighs his sigh. *No. What*
                  I mean is that you'll want *to just*
         stay high. Wish I always could.

To make the bad crap disappear.
         He has experienced more than I.
So why do I take another puff?

Five Puffs Later

The cigarette is a tiny stump Chad
calls a roach. Each inhale got easier,

as if my throat and lungs decided
resistance was futile. I'm not sure,

but I might even feel a little fuzzy
around the edges. At the very least,

I feel a little braver. Brave enough
to walk arm-touching-arm with Chad

as we head back toward camp, soaking
up the warm August night. He doesn't

seem to mind, so I grow even bolder.
"Do you think I'm ugly or something?"

> That seems to amuse him. He snorts.
> *No. Why?* He keeps walking, so I put

a hand on his arm to stop him. "Why
haven't you ever tried to kiss me?"

> *It just wouldn't be the right thing*
> *to do. You're like my little sister.*

Chad

The Right Thing

Has never exactly been
my thing. But once in a while
something like moral fiber
threads through me, weaves

a web

around my heart. She would
be so easy. Look at the way
she tried to please me, back
there in the woods. But a rush

of affection

overtook me suddenly. I care
about her. Not that I'd confess
it. I even feel a little guilty
about the weed. How

can

I reconcile this feeling with
what I've always thought about
love—that it's really either bullshit
or lust in disguise? You can't

fix

a shattered glass with superglue.
I'd say the odds are slim that
a makeshift family can repair

a broken
childhood.

Childhood

I think childhood is something
you really don't appreciate until
it's been taken from you. When

you're really little, it's all you know.
There is good and bad, and hopefully
the former outweighs the latter.

But since adulthood looks so very
far away, there's no reason to worry
about it. As you get older, you start

to think about certain freedoms
attached to growing up. Riding
your bike solo to the store. Going

skating or to the movies with just
your friends, no parents allowed.
Sleepovers first without, then with

Truth or Dare. Still, for most, there
is an innocence in that, reflective
of lingering childhood. Then, new goal:

that magic number sixteen. Driving
can take you many places—both toward
and away from the heart of family.

Mostly, you want to come home. But
then you start considering eighteen.
No more parental intrusion. You can

be on your own. Except, I'm pretty
sure, it isn't as great as it seems.
I haven't celebrated that birthday.

Have a whole year left in high school.
But one little mistake (no, a major mistake)
has stolen my childhood from me.

You can't be a parent and still be
a child, except if you limit that term
strictly to age. Childhood is supposed

to be about fun. Pretty sure I'm not
going to have a whole lot of that
for quite some time to come.

I've Researched

Until my eyes blurred and my head
ached. Everything. Abortion. Adoption.

Teenage motherhood. I've read case
studies. Statistics. Personal stories.

I really don't think I could be more
informed. Yet I still can't seem to make

a decision. The fetus is now an embryo,
which doesn't deny a surgical solution.

But psychologically, it makes that idea
so much harder. I can't sleep. Still can't

eat much without losing it all first thing
in the morning. They say eating crackers

in bed before you move your head from
the pillow is supposed to help. But all

that does is make me puke Saltines.
Morning sickness is supposed to go

away by the start of the second trimester.
So, one way or the other, I'll get over it.

Meanwhile, I'll Keep Puking

That's how my mom found me
last week. When she knocked on
the bathroom door, I tried to flush
the evidence, wash the stench

> from my mouth. She already
> knew. I looked like crap, that's
> for sure, but I didn't think
> she'd say, *So, it's true.*

I started to deny it. "What's
true?" If she knew, I thought,
she'd be angry. But her eyes held
only certainty. "Who . . . who told you?"

> My legs got all shaky. When I
> started to fall, she caught me,
> tried to still my quaking body.
> *Doesn't matter. What's important*

> *is that you don't make any hasty
> decisions. How far along are you?
> Do you have any idea?* I nodded
> against her elevated heartbeat.

"I've missed two periods. At first
I thought no way. . . ." I told her about
the two two-blue-line tests. Halfway
through my confession, I started

to cry. Stupid. Tears. I hate being
weak. "Dylan says he'll pay for an
abortion. But I don't know if I can do
that. But I don't know what else to do. . . ."

What she said was not what I wanted
to hear. *I know the idea of an abortion
is distasteful. But you're only seventeen.
Having a baby would . . . impact your life.*

Distasteful! Impact my life? I gave
her a hard shove. "No shit! Jesus,
Mom. I'm pregnant, not stupid.
I've thought and thought about this.

Abortion is more than distasteful.
It's kind of murder. This is up to me,
not you. And anyway, when did you
decide to play mother again?"

Totally Overboard

But, you know, I have a good excuse.
        And the fact is, she has been absent
                lately. Writers' groups and extremely

late nights out with friends. Sounds
        like a regular midlife crisis to me. But
                what do I know about turning forty?

Clicking the dial to eighteen is way
        too much for me. Especially pregnant.
                Argh! Today, for a change, I'm hungry.

Maybe close to starving. Not sure if
        that shift is good or bad. Next thing
                you know I'll weigh two hundred pounds.

Whatever. I go to the kitchen, rummage
        around in the fridge for something
                that looks appetizing. What I'm craving

is fruit. But no sign of peaches or
        strawberries or watermelon. Only
                some lunch meat, a hunk of aging cheese

that has def seen better days. Yogurt.
Out of date. "Damn it, Mom. When
was the last time you went to the store?"

What's wrong? It's Bri, come to
fight me for the meager food supply.
I think there's stuff in the freezer.

She watches me wade through
frozen waffles—crusted with ice.
Meatball sandwiches—upchuck food.

Frozen Chinese. Frozen Italian.
I start tossing stuff into the sink.
Into the trash. I empty the refrigerator.

Start on the freezer. Out of control,
but so what? "Not a single fucking
edible thing! Thanks for nothing."

Bri's eyes go wide and she yells,
*Just because you're pregnant
doesn't mean you get to be a bitch!*

She Knows!

She found out somehow.
And suddenly, I'm certain.
"You're the one who told."

             Before she can say anything,
             there's a gasp at the door. Fuck.
             It's Trace. *You're pregnant?*

                          And now, Mom's here. *No
                          one knows yet, Trace. Not even
                          Dad. We want to keep it quiet.*

                          Quiet? Really? Indignant. *That's
                          going to be kind of hard to
                          do, don't you think?* Standing

there all pissed, he reminds me
of Dad lately. Bri, conversely,
looks totally slapped down.

                          And now it hits Trace. The other
                          option. *Unless . . .* Quite obviously,
                          it sinks in. He drops his head. *Oh.*

Now Mom Notices

The food in the sink, and
sticking out of the trash can.

What the hell?
says Mom.

She was going crazy,
explains Bri.

No shit, Sherlock,
adds Trace.

I'm about to defend myself,
when the phone rings.

Jace? barely
whispers Mom.

But it's not Dad. The voice
on the answering machine

is unfamiliar. *I'm trying to
reach Holly Carlisle. This is . . .*

Sarah Hill. Mom looks stunned,
especially when we hear, *Her mother.*

Trace

Stunned

What happened to my family
when I wasn't looking? Too
busy playing video games,
and apparently paying

no

attention to the weirdness.
I pride myself on my ability
to grasp the tiniest details of

news

no one wants to share.
How, then, can my sister
be pregnant and thinking
about a procedure that

is

obviously not what she wants
to do? I could see that in
her eyes. That, and fear. It's

good

that she's afraid. But, hey,
Mom promised me drivers'
training if I keep quiet
about this unhappy

news

and don't share it with Dad
for now. Booyah! Score.

First Week

Of my junior year, and everything
feels different. Incredible. I won't

see Alex at school. He's still at
Manogue, though he tried to talk

his parents into public school for
his last semester. They insisted

he finish out in college prep mode.
You'd think they would have jumped

at the idea. Catholic high school
college prep costs an arm and a leg,

or maybe even two of each. Oh, well.
Doesn't matter. Alex and I are attached,

heart to heart. Last Sunday, he came
to the door, holding a teensy white kitten.

> *Look what I found. Someone dumped
> her off in the sage next to my house.*

I'd keep her, but we already have
three cats. Can you take her?

I almost said no. We've never
had pets. Too worried about Shelby

and dander. But I swear that kitten
looked me in the eye and begged,

"Please?" Okay, it was more like *Mew*,
but she aimed that little entreaty

straight at me. "I don't have any
food or a doo-doo box, or anything."

Alex grinned. *I stopped by Petco*
on the way over. He offered the kitten

to me like the best gift ever. As
soon as I touched her silky fur,

I was hooked. I've been hiding
Gaga in my room ever since.

It's been two days. So far, so good.
It's like she knows she has to be quiet.

New Boyfriend, New Kitten

New car. Well, it's a used car,
        but it's new to me. Dad finally
                helped me get my license. Then
                        he took me to the Kia dealer

and helped me pick out
        a previously owned Sportage.
                You want an all-wheel drive
                        around here, and Kias have

a great track record, he said.
        The AWD is nice. But the car
                is really sharp. Red. Black interior,
                        neat as a pin, except for a few

fast-food wrappers—all on me.
      Even if it was a piece of junk,
              though, it's mine. If I had money
                    for gas, I could get in it and

just keep driving. Next summer,
      I think I'll do that. Take a road
             trip somewhere I've only seen
                  in pictures. The Grand Canyon.

Disneyland. Seattle, maybe.
        Wonder how Gaga would
                like riding in a car. Wonder
                        if Alex and I will still be together

then. I can't imagine us breaking
        up. But his parents are pressuring
                him to choose a college. Hopefully
                        Ivy League. I'll be here, he'll be

somewhere else. Nightmare. God!
        I've got to quit overthinking things.
                One day, one week, one month
                        at a time. Today I've got to think

about Algebra Two and chemistry.
        Talk about a nightmare! I pull into
                a student parking space, try to center
                        the Sportage as much as possible.

Door dings suck. Used to be I'd try
        to maintain a low profile to avoid
                the inevitable "there goes the gay
                        guy" looks. This year, I've found pride.

It's Only Been a Couple of Days

Since school started up again.
But I think it's working—shoulders
back, head tilted up so I can look
people straight in the eye. Even jocks.

That could backfire. When a gay guy
locks eyes with a jock, things often
go badly. But hell. I'm taking a chance.
Sick of backing down from jackasses.

I smile and wave at peeps I know.
Chin tip the ones I don't, who bother
to glance in my direction. A couple
look surprised. Others actually

chin tip back. Damn, keep this up,
I might wind up a jock, too. Heh.
Yeah, right. PE is the stuff bad
dreams are made of. I've already

fulfilled the requisite four semesters.
If I never smell locker-room sweat
again it will be much too soon.
Onward and upward, BO-free.

Algebra and Chem

Aren't so bad. Both teachers are cool,
and Tara is in chemistry with me.
We sit in the back, passing notes.

> *HEY. WHEN DO I GET A RIDE IN*
> *YOUR CAR? OR SHOULD I BE SCARED?*

"AFTER SCHOOL? I'LL DRIVE YOU
HOME. AND BE VERY, VERY SCARED."

Class is over and I've got one foot out
the door when my cell vibrates. It's Gram,
who finally broke down and got her own cell

> after years of refusing to own one.
> *Shane, honey . . .* Tension edges her voice.
> *We're taking Shelby into the ER.*
>
> *Her color is awful and your mom's*
> *worried. I was hoping you could get hold*
> *of your father. I tried calling him, but*
>
> *can't get past his voice mail. Your mom . . .*
> *well, I think she needs his support.*
> *Can you text him or something?*

I Break a Small Sweat

This isn't Shelb's first trip to Emergency,
but something about this feels different.

I text Dad: CALL MOM OR GRAM RIGHT NOW.
PLEASE, DAD. SOMETHING'S GOING ON WITH

SHELBY. SOMETHING BAD. The bell rings
and I jump from my chair. "I have to go."

        I barely hear Tara call, *What's wrong?*
        No time to answer, no time for excuses,

I run to the parking lot, search for my car.
Where the hell did I park it? There it is. Now

I fumble the keys. Why am I so nervous?
Everything will be fine, right? Please, God.

Oh, shit. This isn't because of Gaga, is it?
Some kind of reaction to kitten dander?

Saint Mary's isn't far. I find a parking place
right near the ER. See? God's watching out

for us. He always does. But by the time
I find Mom and Gram inside, the doctor

has already broken the news. Mom's face
is whiter than the walls, and her hands tremble

> in her lap. Gram pulls me aside. *They're
> doing more tests. But Dr. Malik believes*

> *that Shelby's heart is giving out. It doesn't
> look good, honey.* She tries to hug me, but

I push her away. "No, damn it! He could
be wrong, right? She's rallied back before."

Please, God, no. All that stuff I said about
a dignified death? I didn't mean *now.*

> *He could be wrong. We'll know more
> soon. Nothing we can do but wait.*

It's a very long two hours, butt wrestling
hard plastic chairs. An hour in, Dad calls

> Gram's cell. She gets up and moves away
> from Mom, but I hear her say, *Chris, you need*

> *to catch the first plane home.* Unspoken words
> float like dandelion spores: *Before it's too late.*

Despite Our Hopes and Prayers

The tests support Dr. Malik's diagnosis.
By the time he comes to confirm, Dad
is on his way to the airport for a flight
home and Aunt Andrea and Alex are here

        to hear him say, *Shelby's time is short.*
        A week at the outside. We can keep
        her here, but I suggest you take her
        home. She'll want to be close to you.

Mom nods, but doesn't cry. I think
her tears are all used up. She doesn't
speak, either. Maybe her words are all
used up, too. Aunt Andrea asks about

        hospice care. She doesn't seem to
        notice the obvious male interest in
        Dr. Malik's eyes when he looks at her,
        says, *I'll contact them right away.*

When they wheel Shelby out, we all
try to act cheerful. But the performance
is noticeably forced. Though we smile
and banter and joke, our sadness is palpable.

Shelby

Sadness

I've heard that word before,
on TV and DVDs. They always
say, "Be happy, not sad." I know
what happy is, but I

don't

understand what sad means.
It must be how you feel, like
when you can't find your smile.
I hear Daddy tell Mommy, "Don't

cry,"

and that means when your eyes get
wet and I think that's something
like sad. Sometimes I feel lonely.
And sometimes I feel bored. But

for

most of the time, I feel happy.
Especially when people I love
are all around me, close to

me.

Like now. I only wish they could
be happy, too. I only wish
they could find their smiles.

I know the saying is cliché, but that's how
I feel tonight. Like everything's just right.
My first week at high school was a cruise.

I found all my classes, no tardies. Figured
out how get to my locker between them.
Most of my teachers are ace. And, except

maybe for World History, I think this year
will be pretty easy. With the workouts
I did all summer, even PE seems okay.

Better yet, the new clothes Cassie
bought me are stylish, and with my
new haircut and makeup, I almost feel hot.

I even got "the look" from some guys.
Okay, they were all freshmen, and
ninth-grade boys are mostly dweebs.

But, hey, it's a good start. And tonight
I'm going to the rib cook-off in Sparks.
It happens every Labor Day weekend,

and it's one of my favorite events.
Looks like I'm going with Brianna.
Her mom just pulled her car over at

> my bus stop. *Hey, Harley. Your mom*
> *asked me to pick you up. She . . . had*
> *to help your aunt Marissa do something.*

I'd call that vague. "Isn't she coming
to the cook-off tonight? It's her birthday,
and we were going to celebrate it there."

> *She said she'd try. I know she wants*
> *to. I guess this is important, though.*
> Okay, that's kind of weird, but whatever.

Trace is riding shotgun. He doesn't
even look at me when I get in the backseat
with Bri. "Do you have any idea

what's going on?" I whisper to Bri.
Something about this feels like a secret.
One everyone here knows, but me.

Even If That's True

No one's confessing. I call Mom,
>hoping for an explanation, but all
>I get is her voice mail, so I leave

a simple, "Happy birthday. Don't
>forget about the rib cook-off."
>I hope she calls back, but whatever.

>We stop by Bri's house for a few.
>>*I want to change,* says her mom,
>>who's wearing workout clothes.

>She eyes my short skirt. *It will*
>>*probably cool off when the sun*
>>*goes down. You can borrow*

>*a pair of Bri's jeans if you want.*
>>*Looks like they just might fit you.*
>>*By the way, you're looking great.*

"Thanks for noticing." I have to
>admit, I like when someone notices.
>Even if that person happens to be

the mom of a friend who refuses
       to acknowledge the very same
       thing. Maybe she's jealous. Or

maybe she's still a little miffed
       that I told about Mikayla. When
       we go to her room, she asks me,

              in short little bursts, *So, do you*
                     want to borrow jeans? Sweats?
                     Something? Now it's she who

is checking out the height
       of my skirt on my thighs. "Nah.
       That's okay. Maybe a sweater,

just in case." She goes to her closet,
       digs through it for a sweater that
       will be baggy on me. Doesn't mean

I have to wear it. She tosses it.
       "Thanks. Hey. You're not mad
       at me about anything, are you?"

She Sighs

Sits on her bed. Her voice, when
she answers, is very, very quiet.

> *No. It's just, I'm worried about*
> *some stuff. That's all. Not your fault.*

"You mean, like Mikayla? Because
I'm really sorry I told. I just thought . . ."

> *It's okay. Someone had to tell. I should*
> *have told, but I was scared. I'm worried*
>
> *about her, but also about Mom. Tomorrow*
> *she and Mikki are going to meet Sarah Hill.*

"Who's that?" Is she important?
I've never heard the name before.

> *She's Mom's biological mother. Mik found*
> *her on Facebook. I don't know if she's why,*
>
> *but lately Mom's been kind of weird.*
> *Distracted, I guess. Like she's here, but not.*
>
> *I don't know if it's because of Sarah Hill,*
> *or Mikayla, or something else, but . . .*

Her voice trails off and it hits me
that lately we haven't really talked.

"Well, come on, Bri. If she just found
her biological mother, she's probably

freaking out. I mean, wouldn't you?"
I can't imagine not knowing who

> my parents were. Bri just kind of nods.
> *I guess so. But Mom and Dad are always*

> *fighting lately. He even stayed gone*
> *all night last week. That never happens.*

Not a good sign. Even as little as
I was, I remember my parents fighting.

Look how they ended up. But I'm not
going to say that to Bri. "They're just

stressed because of Mikayla, I bet."
But now she shakes her head.

> *That's not it. Believe it or not, Dad*
> *still doesn't know she's pregnant.*

Too Many Secrets

In this house, but I'm not going to say
that, either. It's time to go, we're told,
so I can leave all the things I didn't say
behind us. Unvoiced words echo loudly.

But Bri doesn't seem to notice, and
neither does her mom. Mrs. Carlisle
has poured herself into really tight jeans.
She looks amazing in them, too.

We pile back into the car, in the same
configuration. "Isn't Mikayla going?
Or Mr. Carlisle?" I didn't see any sign
of either of them, come to think of it.

> *Mikayla went with Dylan. And Jace*
> *is working late on a case tonight.*
> *So it's just the four of us, unless your*
> *mother can find a way to join us.*

Up pop questions that I won't ask.
What are Mikayla and Dylan going to do?
Who works late on a three-day weekend?
What in the world is going on with my mom?

Like Fourth of July

The entire Victorian Square area
        is blocked off. Foot traffic only.
                But unlike the Fourth, the streets
                        tonight are filled with the delicious

smell of cooking ribs. Barbecue
        chefs come from all over, trying
                to win money for their special
                        recipes. And we get to taste test.

I've been saving up calories
        for days. My mouth waters
                at the smell of hickory smoke,
                        lifting into the early evening.

Trace spots a friend and off
        he goes. Mrs. Carlisle yells
                to meet back at the car at ten.
                        Then she decides to check out

the band. Boy, do heads turn
        to follow her butt bounce.
                Bri acts disgusted. As for me,
                        I really want to give it a try.

The Difference

Between tight jeans
and a short skirt is, when
it comes to butt bounce
you've got to be a lot
more careful in the skirt,

at least if you don't really
want your butt to come
bouncing all the way out
from underneath it. Glad
I'm wearing panties, and

      Bri's glad, too. *What* are
      you doing, Harley? People
      are staring. You remind me
      of my sister. Not especially
      a good thing. But she smiles.

I don't point out that I'm
actually imitating her mom.
"Like, who? Any cute boys?"
I do give my skirt a tug down
in back. No panty peeks.

*Those guys are definitely
checking us out. They're kind
of cute, I guess.* She nods
toward two boys hanging
out on a small patch of grass.

One is familiar. I met him
with Chad on the Fourth. Lucas.
Yeah, that's it. His eyes go
all up and down me, which is
awesome and creepy at once.

"Don't look now, but they're
coming this way. The tall one
is a friend of Chad's." Which
means he's probably a stoner,
too. Definitely not Bri's type.

> Not my type, either, right?
> And does Bri really have
> a type? Her voice is edgy
> when she says, *What do
> you think they want, Harl?*

Good Question

One just about to get answered.
Lucas is cuter than I remembered
him, and his friend isn't bad, either.

It's a volley:

Hey. Remember me?

"Of course. Hi, Lucas."

This here is Kurt.

"This is Brianna."

Good to see you again.

"You, too. What's up?"

Not much. Where's Chad?

"I don't have a clue."

Cool. Wanna hang?

I glance at Bri, who shrugs.
And just like that we're walking
around with a couple of older guys.

It doesn't seem to bother them
that we are a little younger. For
once, I don't feel inferior to Bri,

who has somehow been paired
with Kurt, leaving Lucas with me.
Which is more than okay. It's rockin'.

Lucas

Rockin'

This sweet little thing
has a rockin' bod. And
the best thing about it
is, I'm betting it's

                              virgin

territory. She's pure
as snowmelt, despite
all the ass waving going
on, and unmarked

                              girls

are a raging turn-on.
Me and Kurt got two right
here. Pretty, tight and
looking for love, which we

                              aren't

exactly offering. But they
don't know that. The game
now is to see how

                              easy

we can make them, how far
they'll let us take them
on promises meant to be
broken. Such potential is hard

                              to find.

It's Hard

To pretend everything's fine
when clearly I have changed.
Not outwardly. Not yet. I don't
look any different than I did
before summer started. I still

                         fit into my size-five clothes
                  have the same haircut
            wear the same makeup
       accentuate myself with
Dylan. We still walk hand

in hand or arm around waist as if
love isn't enough to connect us.
We are who people at school
picture when they think "couple."
But I don't smile as much. Don't

                    laugh nearly as easily. Don't
              stick my tongue down Dylan's
         throat in total defiance of the
     no-making-out-on-campus rule.
Not like I did last year. I don't.

It's Even Harder

Hanging out with friends
like we used to—Dylan and I.
Our regular crowd is fast.

Weekends are all about partying.
Tonight, for instance, before
the rib cook-off we dropped by

Clay's. Emily and Audrey were
there, and this guy named Chad,
who happens to be the guy my cousin's

been gushing about all summer.
Anyway, they were all getting buzzed
on some excellent weed and when

the blunt came around to me, what
could I do but take it? If I didn't,
they'd want to know why not. I've

never turned it down before. And,
okay, the truth is, I didn't want to
turn it down. Not even for my baby.

I Can't Not

Think of it as a baby. I'm ten weeks
pregnant, give or take a few days.

The doctor said I really need to make
my decision right away. Mom made

me an appointment with her ob-gyn.
I couldn't stomach the thought of a visit

to Planned Parenthood, so I went to
Dr. Ortega instead. She was nice enough,

I guess, but not exactly sympathetic.
She bombarded me with questions.

> *Are you sure who the father is?*
> *Does he know? Have the two of*
>
> *you discussed options? You're*
> *not planning on marriage, right?*

Yes. Yes. Yes. And what the . . . ?
Marriage? It's not even on the table.

No one has said a thing about it.
But why not? I mean, at least as

a possibility. When Sarah Hill got
pregnant with Mom, abortion was

out of the question. Ditto raising
a kid alone. So it must have come

down to two things—adoption
or a shotgun wedding. Things

> sure have changed in forty years.
> *A kiss for your thoughts.* Dylan

interrupts my reverie. "I was just
thinking about marriage. Oh, don't

look so scared. The doctor asked
if we were planning on it. I said no."

His relief is obvious. Unreasonably,
that makes me mad. "For some people

that *is* an option, you know. Not so
long ago, one of the only options."

> *But we can't. I mean, how could we?*
> *I don't even have a job or anything.*

He's Whining Now

And that really irritates me. But I
           back off. What's the point of fighting?
"I know. I'm sorry. Let's just try

to have fun tonight, okay?" It's dark
           by the time we get to Sparks and park.
"God, that smells good. I'm starving."

We head straight for the food booths,
           find a few that offer free samples,
and take advantage of those. We are

                    finishing our fourth mini-plate when
                        a nasal voice falls over our shoulders.
                  Hey, Dylan. What's up? Kristy Lopez,

Tyler in tow. Poor Ty looks uneasy,
           but not nearly as uncomfortable as
Dylan, who says, *Not much. What are*

you guys up to? He does me the favor
           of not staring up at her boobs, which
she's totally hanging over the top of him.

Okay, That's a Pisser

But things get worse immediately.

Ty: *Eating ribs, same as you.*

Kristy: *Are you coming tomorrow?*

Dylan, shrugging: *Not sure yet.*

Me: "Coming tomorrow where?"

Dylan, face flaring red: *Tahoe.*

Ty: *There's a barbecue and kegger.*

Kristy: *At Camp Rich. Didn't you know?*

Me, giving Dylan the evil eye. "No."

Dylan, lying: *Thought I told you.*

Me: "I'm going to Vegas tomorrow."

Ty: *Too bad. Should be killer.*

Kristy: *But Dylan could come, right?*

Seething

That's what I am, and it shows.
"Dylan can do whatever he wants."

                     Hissed with enough venom
                     for Ty to tell Kristy, *We should go.*

               Her smile says way too much.
               Hope we see you tomorrow.

          Dylan is a sharp-toothed rat,
          in a trap. *Yeah, well, we'll see.*

Ty and Kristy take off and I stand.
"Will you please take me home?"

             Look, I'm sorry. I didn't mention
             it because I didn't plan to go.

Whatever. "Don't lie to me, Dylan.
God, that's one thing I can't take."

             Suddenly, he's angry. *The universe*
             does not revolve around you, you know.

"I know. Obviously, it revolves
around you. Can we go now?"

We Don't Speak

Most of the way home. It's a very
long half hour, simmering silently.
As we turn up the road to my house,

> Dylan is the first one to speak.
> *I won't go tomorrow, okay?*
> *I should have told you, but I knew*
>
> *you'd get mad that Kristy invited*
> *me. I swear, I don't know what's*
> *up with that girl. It's like she knows . . .*

"You didn't tell her! You didn't
tell anyone, right?" What would I
do if people found out? Or will they?

> *I haven't told anyone.* He pauses,
> thinking. *Does this mean you've*
> *decided to have the abortion?*

"Dr. Ortega made an appointment with
the clinic for next Friday after school.
But that doesn't mean I will keep it."

I think you should, but you know
how I feel. I'll take you, if you want.
God, Mik, I just want everything back

like it was. I love you so much. . . .
He makes the sharp turn into our
driveway. *I hate it when we fight.*

"Me, too." I'm sick of all the arguing
going on around here. No need to
mention my parents, though. "And

I love you, too. And I'll call you
from Vegas, okay?" He parks, comes
around to open my door, and when

I get out, he kisses me so sweetly
I can barely remember why I was so
angry. Oh yeah, Kristy. "I really don't

want you to go to the party. Okay?"
He promises he won't, but something
in his voice makes me worry that he will.

I Try Not to Stress

About that as I let myself into
        our totally dark house. No one
                home? Surely Dad can't still be
                        working? I turn on lots of lights,

leave them burning as I get ready
        for bed, thinking about nasally
                bitches and sharp-toothed rats.
                        Ack! Maybe he's right. Terminating

would make everything go back
        like it was. Dylan and I would
                be the perfect couple again.
                        We would graduate high school,

head off to college together and
        without major complications.
                Perfect. Except. Except there
                        is something growing inside me.

And while I'd love to believe it's
        a blob of cells, not a life or a soul,
                that is bullshit. Dylan can choose
                        whomever. I choose to let my baby

        live.

As I Lie in Bed

Waiting for sleep to come
I know I have made the right
decision. It's only the first
of many more to come.

How—and when—do I out
myself, confess to Dad,
my grandparents,
my friends?

Do I stay in school?
If I do, for how long?
Should I move to a charter
or some other special
program?

Will I keep my baby?
How can I support it?
Would Mom and Dad help?
Would Dylan? I don't
think he would.

But is adoption the answer?
After carrying it
for nine months, feeling
it grow inside me,
becoming more and more
a part of me,

could I give my baby away?

Dylan

More and More

I realize that keeping
a relationship alive isn't an
easy thing. It takes more than

love,

more than great sex.
It takes seeing eye to eye
on pretty much everything.
Not difficult, when it

is

a laundry list of small
things you need to agree
on—what movie to see
or radio station to listen to.
But something as major as

a

pregnancy, unplanned and
unwanted? A lack of consensus
there, and your rock-solid
devotion becomes

fragile

as delicate crystal, and as sharp
when it shatters. It will slice
you to the bone. And you
barely feel a

thing.

Shelby has always been that.

> Frail.
> Fragile.
> Easily broken.

But now she is something else.

> Sheer.
> Gossamer.
> Ethereal.

She's like some mythical creature.

> Elf.
> Fairy.
> Sprite.

Trying to outfly the coming storm.

> Downpour.
> Tornado.
> Hurricane.

But it's catching up to her fast.

There's Nothing I Can Do

Except watch her lose ground.
        Nothing anyone can do, but
                ease her passing. I try to help.

I empty the trash can in her room.
        Don't want her to have to smell
                diapers. Don't want Mom to smell

them either. She won't leave
        Shelby's bedside. Dad hovers
                there, too, singing lullabies and

old Beatles songs. Gram spends
        all her time in the kitchen cooking
                chili and soup and other stuff

no one has an appetite for. I eat
        it, if only to make her happy.
                But I also escape the house often.

Alex comes and gets me, says I
        shouldn't drive in my condition.
                Like hollow and drunk are synonymous.

He'll Be Here Soon

I sit on my bed, petting Gaga,
who has claimed my pillow
for herself like a regular queen.
I guess I don't mind sharing it.

"I'm glad I don't have to hide
you anymore." Gram discovered
her while I was at school. Mom
insisted I go the last couple of days.

> *What good will it do for you to*
> *stay here and stress?* she asked.

So I went to school and stressed
instead. And yesterday Gram
heard Gaga mewing. Asking
for attention. She's kind of an

attention hog. When I got home,
I found Gram in my room,
scooping the litter box while
Gaga purred on my pillow.

> *I think it's time someone here had*
> *a pet,* Gram said. *Good for the soul.*

I Don't Know About That

But I do know it's nice having
something to comfort me at night.

Something alive to chase away
all thoughts of death that haunt me

while I try to sleep. I was eleven
when Grandma died—plowed down

while crossing the street. I don't think
there was a whole lot left of her, because

they kept the casket closed. I remember
sitting at the funeral, wondering what

that coffin concealed. Had nightmares
about it popping open to let me see inside.

I'm sure Gaga's snuggles are about her
need for affection, but when I lie in bed,

praying I don't have death nightmares,
it sure seems like she tries to make me feel

better. Maybe that's what Gram meant
about her being good for my soul.

Someone's at the Front Door

The sound of the bell reverberates
in the hallway, followed by the slight
clip-clip of Gram's footsteps. Alex?
But when I go to see, it isn't him.
It's Mom's friend, Drew. Gram

steps back from the door and from
here I can see Drew's genuine smile.
Leah. You look amazing. He gives
her a giant hug. *So sorry we have to
meet again under these circumstances.*

Gram pulls away, assesses Drew,
scalp to toenails. *How many years
has it been? Thirty?* Now she looks
at the stuffed Barney he's carrying.
That was so thoughtful of you.

The doorbell rings again. Gram
lets Alex in before showing Drew
the way to Shelby's room. He waves
at me as he starts up the hallway.
I'd like to know him better. He's cool.

Alex Trails Them

Until they disappear behind
Shelby's door. I can hear a flurry
of greetings. What's unusual

is how cordial Dad sounds.
He can't stand having Drew
around. Alex reaches my side,

> gives me a quick kiss. *Who*
> *was that with your grandma?*
> I take his hand, pull him into

my room before I answer.
"Drew is Mom's best friend,
and he used to be her boyfriend."

> *Really? Before or after your dad?*
> He smiles at his own lame joke,
> jumps onto my bed next to Gaga.

"He was her first boyfriend.
In Oregon, when she was a kid.
They all lived on a commune

together. Gram. Gramps. Mom.
Aunt Andrea. And assorted others,
including Drew and his parents."

> *Sounds, um, interesting, to say*
> *the very least. And did they all*
> *move to Reno together, too?*

"Right. No, the story goes Gram
told Gramps she was finished
with the open marriage thing and

he had the choice to come with
her or stay behind. He chose
his family and northern Nevada.

Drew moved to Tahoe a few years
ago, after he got divorced. Mom won't
say so, but I think he wanted to be close

just in case something happened
between Dad and her." I don't mention
that something almost did. Still might.

Alex Thinks It's Romantic

I guess it is, and not so very long
ago, I might have encouraged Mom
to send Dad packing. Now I think
they need each other in a profound

way. Of course, that could change
after . . . Weird, but I haven't really
allowed myself to think much about
after. I hear Mom in the hall, talking

to Gram. In the hall! I poke my head
around my door. "What's going on?"
Neither looks panicky, so it can't be
anything major. Mom looks at me

> with dark-circled eyes. *Drew chased*
> *us out. He said I stink. . . .* She sniffs
> her armpits, runs a hand through
> her limp hair. *Okay, he's right.*

Gram jumps in. *Actually, he said*
he was hoping to watch a Barney
rerun and for your mom to take
a nice, hot bath. He's a dear, isn't he?

Considering

Mom has barely left Shelby's room
to even take a piss, Drew *is* a dear.
"You deserve a hot bath, Mom."

But she shakes her head. *I agreed
to a quick shower. At least I'll smell
better. And I'll grab a bite to eat.*

I made a nice shepherd's pie, says
Gram. *Tell Alex there's plenty, and
it's ready.* The ladies part ways, Mom

to the shower and Gram to the kitchen,
which is starting to leak some amazing
scent. "Yo! Alex! You hungry?"

I have no idea what shepherd's pie is,
but my stomach's growling. I haven't
eaten a whole lot the past couple of days.

Food is probably a good idea, and maybe,
for just a half hour or so, sharing the dinner
table can make us feel something like normal.

Alex

Sharing the Table

Breaking bread in the literal
sense, passing butter and salt,
midst meaningless conversation,
we are immersed in

                              living.

But as hard as everyone
tries to appreciate Drew's gift
of time, the small talk shrinks
all the way to minuscule

                              and

then dissipates completely.
Nice while it lasted—
a half-hour vacation from
the crushing wait for

                              death.

It's hard being here, where
I'm reminded of fate's
cruel nature and my fears

                              are

intensified. But Shane needs
me, so I come and stay or
take him away for a while.
Love and sacrifice are

                              inextricable.

Love Is Weird

Last weekend I still thought
        I was in love with Chad.

But then he went and made
        it clear he considers me

his little sister and kissing
        me would be sort of like

incest. He's full of it, but
        whatever. Anyway, I was still

all crazy for him right up
        until last night. Now the only

guy I can think about is Lucas.
        He's totally amazing. And we

already kissed! I was so scared
        I'd mess it up, I almost pulled

away when he tried. Instead,
        I went ahead, and it was perfect.

The Perfect Kiss

Is
not too rough
not too sweet
not too slobbery
not chapped.

It's
a gentle joining
an even building
a total melting
together. Hot.

It's
a tilt of the head,
a slick slide of lips
a sublime exploration
tongue touching tongue.

And now
I know the perfect
kiss isn't between
Chad and me. It's
between me and Lucas.

And, for Once

Bri and I are on the same page.
She and Kurt made out too.
I spent last night at her house
and we talked instead of sleeping.

"Lucas's really cute, don't you think?"

> *Yeah, but not as cute as Kurt.*

"Did Kurt kiss better than Chad did?"

> *Lots!* But she didn't give details.

"I wish Lucas went to Carson."

> *Yeah, but at least he's got a car.*

"I know, right? That's so awesome."

> *Will your mom let you ride with him?*

"Probably not. But Dad might."

Dad Is Pretty Distracted

He and Cassie got engaged.
They're shopping for a ring today.
I guess I'm happy for them.

Actually, I'm pretty happy all
the way around today. Saturday,
and Mom just picked me up to take

> me back to the rib cook-off. *Sorry*
> *I couldn't get there last night.*
> *We'll make up for it today, though.*

"No problem. We had fun, even
without you." More fun than she wants
to know about. But I can't *not* tell her

about Lucas. What if he calls? What
if we happen to see him today? "So,
uh . . . guess what?" She seems to be

> about a million miles away
> because it takes several seconds
> before she finally says, *What?*

I Almost Chicken Out

But she's my mom. She should know.
In fact, she should be happy for me.

"I, uh . . . I'm kind of going out
with someone." Again, the slight

> delay before the news sinks in.
> *Going out? What does that mean?*

"You know. Seeing each other."
A slight exaggeration, but still.

> *Seeing each other? Since when?*
> *And who are you talking about? Chad?*

"No, not Chad. His name is Lucas,
and we just got together." I don't

say where, or how, and I don't tell
her he has a car. "He's really nice,

Mom. You'll like him. Can you
believe I've got a boyfriend?"

> *No. I mean, yes. I mean, of course*
> *I can believe it. I just hope you'll be . . .*

"Careful? I will, Mom. I remember
everything you've told me about sex

and why I should wait. I don't plan
to have sex with Lucas. I'm too young,

and anyway, he and I just met. You
have to fall in love to have sex, right?"

> *Actually, you don't. A lot of people*
> *who aren't in love have sex. But I*

> *promise it's a lot better with someone*
> *you love. I'm glad you understand that.*

I haven't even considered sex.
Kissing is as far as I've fantasized

about going. Now I've done that,
though. When will I want to do more?

"More"

Is pretty much everywhere
as Mom and I walk around
the cook-off, checking out
craft booths, listening to music
and, of course, munching ribs.

It's like I never really noticed
how guys slip their arms around
their girls' shoulders, then let
their hands wander, or how some
girls even encourage that.

It's like I totally missed how
some girls walk their fingers
up their boyfriends' thighs,
all the way to where they must
be touching very personal body

parts, or how that makes those
guys kiss them—not romantically,
but more kind of crazy. It's hot!
And I'm glad Mom doesn't notice
me noticing, or thinking it's hot.

Mom Isn't Noticing Much

She's here, but not.
       Talk about distracted!
       Finally, I have to ask, "Hey,
Mom. Are you okay?"

            She looks at me with dopey
                eyes. Sorry. Lots on my mind
                right now, I guess. Is it okay
         if we go soon? I should get

         back to Aunt Missy's. She thinks
            a minute, then says, *Maybe*
            I could drop you off at your
         dad's? Something strange

is going on. But, like, what?
       "Dad and Cassie aren't home.
       They're shopping for rings
and stuff. What's up, anyway?"

         Shelby's gotten very sick, so Mom
                and I have been trying to help
                Missy take care of her. She thinks
         for a minute, then makes a call.

Jace? It's Andrea. Can I drop
                Harley off? I want to get back
                to Marissa's. Three beats. *Really?*
That would be great. Twenty minutes?

"Let me guess. I'm going back
        to Bri's for the night?" Hey,
        wonder if we can figure out
a way to see Lucas and Kurt.

                And maybe tomorrow, too,
                depending on how things
                go. She collects her purse.
                You don't mind, do you?

"Nope. It's okay." On the short
        walk to the car, the wheels in
        my brain are turning. I don't
want to call Lucas. Too forward.

I bet I can find him on Facebook.
        I can't use my account. Mom
        checks up on me there. But Mrs.
Carlisle never snoops. We'll use Bri's.

Bri's Dad Agreed

To meet us halfway so Mom doesn't
have to drive all the way to Washoe
Valley. By the time we reach South

Meadows, they're already there.
Mr. Carlisle gets out of his car, comes
over to ours. The look on his face

is a mixture of concern and—what?
Compassion, maybe. As I open
the car door, he gives Mom a gentle

> smile. *You okay?* He waits for her
> small shrug. *Let me know if you need*
> *anything. I'm just a phone call away.*

What the heck is going on? I join
Bri in the cushy leather backseat
of her dad's awesome Audi. Before

> I seal myself in, I catch the end
> of something Mom is saying.
> *. . . help with the arrangements.*

Wonder What They're Arranging

Guess I'll find out sooner or later.
Meanwhile, I've got my own

arrangements to worry about.
When we get to Bri's, we go straight

to her room, turn on her computer
and bring up Facebook. It doesn't take

long to find Lucas's page. I message
him: "Last night was fun. Hope you

had fun, too. Looks like I'm spending
the weekend with Brianna. If you can

come out to Washoe Valley, it would
be great to see you. Kurt, too." I think

that's good enough. Oh, except I give
him my cell number again. "Call any time."

Now, I guess, it's a waiting game. Patience
isn't my best thing. Hope it doesn't take long.

Lucas
The Waiting Game

Must be played correctly
to get the desired results.
Call too quickly, the

anxious

state you're hoping for
won't have time to build.
But wait too long, most

girls

will get annoyed,
give up on you. Of course,
the younger ones

are

usually more patient,
and the longer you extend
the play, the

easier

it is to win the game.
I think it's time to put
round two in motion.

Two Small Carry-Ons

That's all Mom and I are taking
      to Vegas. It's just an overnight
      trip—nineteen hours start to finish.

            Dad drops us at the Southwest
                  check-in. *Take care of your mom,*
                  he tells me. Like anyone could.

            Then he says to her, *Keep your*
                  head, and don't expect too much.
                  Lecture, lecture, lecture. God!

      But she takes it well. *No worries.*
            I've got things pretty much in
            perspective. She must. She doesn't

seem nervous or worried at all.
      I'm a wreck. If this goes wrong,
      I'd have to say it's totally my fault.

            Okay. That airport cop is giving
                  me the evil eye, says Dad. *Better*
                  go. Love you. Mom says she loves

him too, and gives him a kiss.
        She must be mad about him
        lecturing her. Despite the mutual

declaration, there didn't seem
        to be a whole lot of love in that
        kiss. Which makes me wonder

if I'll ever kiss Dylan and not be
        overwhelmed with love. I trail
        Mom through security. Notice how

the cute TSA guy totally checks
        her out. Bet he'd like to give her
        a pat-down. And why does he ignore

me completely? Am I giving off
        pregnant vibes? Why do I care?
        Safely beyond the metal detector,

        Mom says, *We've got an hour
                before our flight. Want some
                lunch?* Lunch? Is she cracked?

I Decline

But she's determined to leave
me sitting here alone by the gate.

> *Back in a few. If you change*
> *your mind, I'll be at the bar.*

I get it now. She's not hungry.
She's "thirsty." "Think that's a good

idea? You don't want to be drunk
when you meet her, do you?"

I seriously think she's an alcoholic.
She must be reading my mind,

> because she half shouts, *First of all . . .*
> Heads turn our direction. She lowers

> her voice. *I don't plan to get drunk.*
> *And I don't think you have the right*

> *to tell me how to live my life, or how*
> *to meet my mother. I'm a grown-up, Mikayla.*

Act like it, then. "Maybe you are.
But sometimes lately, I wonder."

I Expect an Angry Retort

Instead, she smiles. *Sometimes
I wonder too. Anyway, being
a grown-up isn't all that much*

*fun. You might consider that
before you decide to become one
at seventeen.* And off she goes.

I want to javelin insults at her.
She and Dad don't seem to think
we hear them when they fight.

But no door in the world is thick
enough to insulate their vicious talk.
The other night I heard Dad scream

at Mom about fucking off on him.
He never uses that word, or at least
he never had before. I don't know

if Mom is messing around, but I do
know she's different. And I'm scared
that might mean they'll get divorced.

Are All Relationships Cursed?

Must they all sputter to a bad end,
dismal failures? I've read that it's
not human nature to stay faithful.
That people are little more than

animals with libidos incapable
of single-mate satisfaction. But
that can't be right. I don't need
anyone but Dylan. And I'm sure

he feels the same way about me.
Or at least, he did. He's been
cool lately. But that's because of
the baby, not because he's seeing

someone else. Right? Suddenly,
inside my head, I hear Kristy's
plugged-nose voice asking Dylan
if he was going to the lake today.

He promised he wouldn't. Vowed
he wouldn't. What good are vows if
the vowers don't take them seriously?
God, Dylan, please don't go.

Mom Gets Back

Just as they call our flight. We line
       up like kids going to recess. Mom

stands behind me, leaking warm breath
       tinted with tomato juice and vodka.

Bloody Marys for lunch is my guess.
       And now, for no reason I can fathom,

       she says, *Anytime you want to talk,*
          I'm here for you, okay? We shuffle

down the Jetway, onto the plane. Talk?
       About what? Relationships? Infidelity?

Stinking Tahoe barbecues? I'm actually
       relieved when, ten minutes past takeoff,

Mom slips into uneasy sleep. Her head
       tips to one side. A small moan escapes,

and her arms and legs twitch slightly.
       Dreaming. I hate to think about what.

Las Vegas Is Insane

The taxi drives slowly along
the strip. The driver couldn't
hurry if he wanted to. Saturday
traffic is ridiculous, and so are
the crowds cruising sidewalks,
casino to casino. "God, Mom.
Disgusting." Billboards and
signboards and giant outside
televisions advertise bodies.
Come view them. Come screw
them. Flesh, everywhere you
look. Boobs. Butts. Girls. Guys.

We pull into the Venetian, where
Mom has booked our room. It's
fabulous. Beautiful. Fake Italy.
Marble. Pillars. Crystal. Chandeliers.
Our room is a suite. "God, Mom . . .
A sunken living room, and did
you see the bathroom? Can we
stay an extra day?" Our house
is nice and all, but this is amazing.
Mom goes to call Sarah Hill, and
it hits me why we're here. I tuck
all the craziness inside. I'll save
it for another day. A different day.

As We Wait

For them to get here, Mom finally
looks nervous. It doesn't take long,
thank goodness, or she'd be a wreck.

When they knock, she jumps a little.
Oh my God. There's no doubt that
Sarah is Mom's mother. The resemblance

      is crazy, right down to her shaking
      hands, one of which lights gently
      on Mom's cheek. *I was afraid*

      this day might never come. I'm happy
      we can know each other. She and Mom
      stand there, searching for something

in each other's eyes. Tia—*Aunt* Tia—
comes straight into the living room
without a word. She glances at me

and I see that she's afraid. Of what,
I'm not sure. But I try to break the ice.
"Hi. I'm Mikayla. Awesome to meet you."

It's an Awkward Few Seconds

Of silence. But then Mom breaks
the inertia. *Come on,* she tells Sarah.

*Your granddaughter can't wait to meet
you. And we have some catching up to do.*

And now there's a wave of motion.
Hugs and greetings and sitting

and smiling, all of us doing our best
to relax in a very uncomfortable

situation. I bet Mom wants a Bloody
Mary. I bet Tia wants one, too. She's got

an edge. Looking at her really closely,
she's not a whole lot older than I am.

Midtwenties, maybe. And pretty. Not
as pretty as Mom, but almost. Even

though they don't look that much alike,
they both look like Sarah. Especially

their eyes, which are almost turquoise.
Weird, what genetics can accomplish.

Now the Catching Up Begins

What they learn about us:
    Dad is a high-powered lawyer
    who keeps us well in a house
    on a hill in northern Nevada.

        Mom's a loser. Okay, housewife
        with three kids, workout queen
        and wannabe romance writer.

            I am a high school senior.
            Dating an amazing guy.
            (We omit the pregnant part.)

What we learn about them:
    Sarah's a preschool teacher,
    twice divorced and dating
    a "hot electrician." Turns
    out she fancies herself a poet.

        Tia's a social worker, married
        to a prison guard. She's a good
        Christian who loves sports.
        And (yikes!) is writing a novel.

Overdosing on Small Talk

I kind of space out—fall
asleep with my eyes open.
They're talking about writing.
Poetry. Short stories. E-book
versus print publishing.

Blah, blah, blah. What I really
want to know right now is,
"Wasn't it hard to give a baby
up for adoption?" How can
you give a piece of you away?

> Sarah doesn't blink. *Not at
> first. No one encouraged me
> to keep her, and I just couldn't
> see doing it on my own.*

Okay, I get that she didn't
have a support system. Still,
"You said not at first. What
about later?" Did you miss her?

> *Later I regretted my decision.*
> She turns toward Mom. *I'm sorry
> I wasn't stronger.* The whole truth.

Tia

The Whole Truth

Is like a big old spoonful
of cough syrup. Hard to
gag down, but necessary.
I had absolutely

no

clue that I had a sister
somewhere. You'd think
Mom would want me
to have that kind of

information,

if only to avoid a surprise
of this magnitude. I came
here, convinced it was
a scam, and it still

might be,

but what's become crystal
clear is that she and I
are related. What I don't
know is if that's good or

a really bad thing.

Shane
Bad Things

Happen to good people.
        Isn't that what they say?

What I'm confused about
        is why. Hey, all-powerful Dude

in the sky! Why? I asked
        Mom why God let Shelby live

at all, if this was the most
        He was going to allow her.

      I can't speak for God, she said.
              But I have thought long and hard

      about this. Shelby has given us
              a glimpse of human perfection,

      because inside that flawed
              body is a spirit untouched

      by greed or artifice or hatred.
              Shelby is the essence of love.

And so maybe the reason for
        her short time here is to show

us how we might love better.
        My first thought was "sermon."

But later I noticed Dad join
        Mom on the deck, watching

the city light up against
        a falling curtain of night.

He put his arm around her
        shoulder. Said something

I couldn't hear. And then
        they kissed. Gently at first,

then with passion, something
        I thought was long dead to them.

So maybe Mom was right.
        Maybe Shelby's mission

                was to teach us to love better.

It Is Early Morning

The light through the glass
is pallid. Weak, and yet enough
to wake me here on the couch,
where Gram and I talked long into
the night with Aunt Andrea.

Planning for after. Yes, there will
be an after. Calls to make:

                   the funeral home
                   relatives
                   friends
                   acquaintances

Beyond that, there is Dad's request
that Shelby's room be emptied,

                   boxed
                   scrubbed
                   painted
                   carpet replaced

All these things whirl around in
my head. And then I hear,

                   no
                   no
                   sobbing
                   weeping.

In the Recliner

Aunt Andrea stirs from her dreams.

Gram comes from the kitchen.

None of us hurries. We know there

is no reason, and Mom and Dad

deserve a few private minutes

of mourning. I don't have to look

through her door to know Shelby

is gone. It's like her energy was sucked

from her room, leaving us all in

a vacuum. Conflicting emotions

tug-of-war inside my head, my heart.

     Shock.   Certainty.
          Grief.   Relief.

Joy at her escape to freedom.   Anger at what might have been.

Gram Goes to Make the First Call

This early on a holiday morning,
an answering service person is
the first one to hear that Shelby

has died. The funeral parlor
director is doing his Labor Day
thing. It will take a while for

someone to come collect my
sister's shell. Meanwhile, Mom
refuses to let go of her hand.

> *Why is she getting so cool?*
> *I don't want her to be cold.*
> *I have to keep her warm.*

I want to help Mom, but have no
idea how. I want to put my arm
around Dad, cry into his shoulder.

But we haven't shared that kind
of intimacy since I was a little boy.
And anyway, he's propping up Mom.

Death Is Awkward

Despite all the talking, all the planning,
no one really knows what to *do*. I glance

around the room at all the specialized
equipment we won't need anymore.

For years, it's been the heartbeat
of this house. It has been silenced.

> The hush is stunning. Finally, Gram
> asks, *Did you note the time of death?*

We were instructed to write it down
for the death certificate. Mom shakes

> her head, but Dad says, *Six thirty-eight
> a.m.* None of us asks if he's sure. What

does it really matter, anyway? I want
to call Alex, but it's so very early.

I can't do anything more in here, though,
so I go into the living room. Outside

the sliding glass doors, storm clouds
simmer up, black over the hills. Fitting.

It Is Ten A.M.

Before they arrive with a gurney.
Shelb's last trip in a stander of sorts.

                    I smile,

thinking about the times
Alex and I pushed her back
and forth between us.

                    I cry,

remembering the cruel words
"retard" and "alien."

                    I wonder

for not exactly the first time
how much Shelby was aware
of everything around her.

                    I wish

she could have told us,
helped us understand. If

                    I knew

for sure, I would sleep
better tonight.

Alex Shows Up

Just as they wheel Shelby out
of the house. I didn't even call
him. It's like he just knew. Mom
is still holding on to Shelby's

> hand. *Please don't let her be cold.*
> *Please? Promise me.* Dad has to
> pull her away. *Let them go now,*
> *Missy. They'll take good care of her.*

I can't stomach the thought
of what will come next for Shelby.
Thank God Alex is here. Dad leads
Mom past me and off toward

their bedroom. I hope she sleeps.
She needs to fall down into some dark
quiet place. Somewhere warm. Alex
waits for the corpse carriers to load

Shelbs into a plain white unmarked
van. Guess they save the hearse
for the actual funeral. As they drive
away it hits me. I didn't say goodbye.

It Isn't Until

Alex and I go inside and pass
the bedroom emptied of her,
body and spirit, that it really
sinks in that she will not ever
be coming home. She is dead.

And all that talk about dignified
death was total bullshit. I didn't
want her to die. Period. What
I really wanted was for her to live
whole. Well. Capable. Happy.

But that was not in my power,
nor in the power of any human—
no doctor. No surgeon. No researcher.
All we could do was try to make her
comfortable. To allow her a few

joyful hours beyond the many
she spent lying in bed. Mom tried
to give me a reason why a true
omnipotent God would create
something so broken, and send

her to us for such a short season.
But I really don't understand it.
If there is a God and He did this,
I don't think I like him very much.
Hey, God. Are you listening?

The door to my room is open.
But Gaga is in her usual spot
on my pillow. Did she not know
she could venture out into the hall—
into the larger world? Or was

she afraid to? Shelby never had
the chance to venture out into
the larger world, at least not on
her own. Did she miss being able
to? Would she have been afraid to?

Suddenly, it strikes me that I don't
know how she felt about stuff.
I could tell when she was happy.
But was she ever sad? Scared?
Did she even know I loved her?

My Eyes Sting

No, goddamn it, I can't. Men don't cry,
not even gay men. Right? Alex, who has

totally let me get mired in my musings,
notices my gay slipping out. He opens

      his arms, entices me into them. *Go*
      ahead and cry. I'm so sorry, Shane.

I want to shout, "What the fuck for?
It's not like *you* did anything." But my tears

won't let me. I'm sad. Pressed down
by sorrow. I'm angry. Pissed at God,

if there is one, and the way things are.
I'm scared. Confused by the whys.

Why are we here? Is there, really, some
intelligent design? Why do we cry for

someone who leaves us if there's some
Grand Pearly Gate in the sky? Why worry

about how we build our lives if the ultimate
ending for all is death, a single breath away?

Alex

Death

Of course I think about it.
But death as a worry is not
exclusive to people with HIV.

Who

but a total innocent
hasn't considered their final
breath? And who really

knows

what that means? Philosophers
muse on it, but find no answers.
Ministers preach propaganda—

what

a person must do on earth
to reach some mythical heaven.
Seems to me religion's true motivation

lies

within the offering plate.
I wish I had answers, wish
I could offer Shane solace

beyond

the comfort of my arms.
But until we get there, we won't know
for sure what's on the other side.

I Wish

People would stop treating me
like a little kid. I'll be fourteen
in a couple of weeks. I'm not a child.

Even my mother, who claims
to know me better than anyone
else in the universe, did not respect

me enough to tell me the reason
she was so distracted last weekend
was because my cousin was dying.

She never said a word until after
Shelby died, and when she finally told
me, I lost my temper. "I had the right

to know," I pretty much yelled. "I had
the right to say goodbye. God, Mom.
I'm not a baby. I understand that

people die. Why do adults try to hide
the ugly stuff from their kids? People
die. People fall out of love and get

divorced. Or they fall out of love
and stay together when it's obvious
they shouldn't, like Bri's mom and

dad. All they do is fight. It's stupid."
They had a whopper when Mrs. Carlisle
got back from Vegas. I didn't give

       details, but Mom acted all shocked
       anyway. *How do you know they fight?*
       She and Bri's mom are tight. How could

she *not* know? "I've got ears, Mom,
and so does Bri. Her dad thinks her
mom is sleeping around. And guess

what else. He still doesn't know
Mikayla is pregnant. Don't you think
someone should tell him before

baggy shirts can't hide it anymore?
Especially since she's going to keep
the baby." Mom just sat there, gawking.

Which Made Me Even Angrier

If Gram hadn't called right then,
        I might have said something really
                mean. Like, is her head up her butt

or something? Of course, later
        I felt bad about how mad I got.
                Everyone in the family is kind of in

shock. I guess I knew Shelby
        wasn't going to live a long time.
                But she was only four. Little kids

shouldn't die! I wasn't, like,
        close to her, even though she was
                my cousin. Even if she hadn't been

sick, she was a lot younger
        than me, so we wouldn't have
                hung out together. She *was* sick,

though. Visiting her was kind of
        creepy, and the smell gagged me.
                But now I feel sort of guilty that

we didn't do it more. I bet
        Mom feels the same way.
                She's sitting next to me, staring

at the coffin. Shelby is inside,
        or something that looks sort of
                like her. She's so still and white

she could be made of wax.
        Her hair is curled in ringlets,
                and she's smiling in her deep,

forever sleep. Did she die
        smiling? Or did someone mold
                her lips that way? Is she real?

People are still coming in as
        the music starts to play. I wave
                to Bri, who just got here with

her family. As usual, her dad
        and mom are miles apart, even
                though they sit side by side.

If Mom Can't See That

She's totally blind, and she's def
checking them out. When she turns
back around, she looks sad. But
everyone looks pretty sad, especially

when the minister starts to talk
about how Shelby is home now,
and whole in God's arms. So weird,
thinking about how some energy inside

you might escape when your body
dies. That it might go someplace,
become something different. An angel.
A whole other person. I don't know.

But I'm sure there's nothing left inside
the Shelby-looking thing in the casket.
I've never seen a dead person before.
Now people get up to talk about her.

> Gramps goes first. He calls her
> *a little blossom who nourished*
> *us with the nectar of her laughter.*
> *Our lives are enriched because of her.*

Gramps is a poet. Who knew?
Now Gram says a few words,
and Mom does, too. And then
Shane's boyfriend, Alex, stands.

> *I've only known the Trask family*
> *a few months. But I am grateful*
> *for the short time I had with Shelby.*
> *She brought light into my life, and*
>
> *wherever she is now, it is a brighter*
> *place because she's there. I miss you,*
> *Shelbs, I . . .* But his throat knots
> up. He can't go on, so he returns

to his seat beside Shane, whose face
is in his hands. Almost everyone
here is crying, the one huge exception
being Aunt Marissa. She looks like a marble

statue—hard, white, unmoving. In fact,
she could be dead, too, except every now
and again she blinks dry eyes. Maybe you
only have to die *inside* to turn into a zombie.

After the Words

And Disney Channel music are finished,
the casket is closed. Shane, Alex, Gramps
and Uncle Chris carry it to the hearse

> and we form a car parade to follow it to
> the cemetery. *Will you please ride with*
> *Gram and Marissa?* Mom asks me. *I want*

> *to talk privately with Gramps.* She offers
> no other explanation, leaving me totally
> wondering, again, what's up with her.

More too-adult-for-me-to-know-about
stuff, no doubt. But what can I do except
say, "Sure." I sit in the back with Gram.

All of us wall ourselves up into invisible
boxes of silence. It's a fifteen-minute
creep-along ride, and I steal a few to text

Lucas. FUNERALS SUCK. CAN I C U
TOMORROW? I have no idea how I'll
sneak away, but I'll think of something.

In the past week, we've seen each other
three times—the day after the rib cook-off,
when he and Kurt came out to Washoe Valley

and picked up Bri and me at the 7-Eleven; and
twice after school. I'm glad he has a car.
Each time, we found a private place to park.

He keeps trying to get me stoned, but
so far I've been good. What I've been bad
about is making out. He's the best kisser

in the world. The last time I even let him
go to second base. Amazing! But the days
I don't see him just seem so long. Especially

since they've been all about death. I need
a big injection of life. It will have to wait
for a while, though. Right now, I get out

of the car, follow the people procession
to the gravesite where what's left of Shelby
will be left to decay beneath Nevada sand.

A Gentle Slant

Of September sun spotlights
the casket as they lower it

into the ground. At the cemetery's
edges, the rabbit brush is blooming.

The air is thick with its pollen and
its bittersweet scent mixes with the perfume

of Gram's citrusy shampoo. Together,
they smell like rotting oranges. The coffin

hits dirt with a soft *whump*. I watch
them pull the canvas straps out of the hole.

The minister says some final words,
invites us to take a single purple rose

from the vase beside the grave, toss
it inside. *Tink. Tink. Tink.* They hit

the casket lid. My ears go hypersensitive.
A jet landing. A dove moaning.

Sniffling. Distant traffic. A train passing
nearby. Music. A symphony of death.

After the Dirge

We go to party. The wake is at
my house. Whoopee. I think
it's weird that people celebrate
dying. Is that something I'll get
when I'm allowed to be grown-up?

Gram and Gramps spent all day
yesterday cooking. I ride home
with them, ahead of the rest, so we
can start putting food out on the long
table Mom borrowed. Everything,

> from the tablecloth to the napkins
> to the centerpiece flowers, is purple
> and pink. Shelby's favorite colors.
> *It was a nice ceremony,* says Gram.
> *Don't you think so?* Gramps and I

mutter agreement. I mean, how nice
can a funeral be? People start arriving
within a half hour. Oh, good. There's
Bri, with Trace, Mikayla and their dad.
Mrs. Carlisle isn't with them. Not into wakes?

Bri and I Load Plates

Leave Trace and Mikayla surrounded
by talkative adults, go back into my room
to eat. I take the time to check my cell.

No text messages. No voice mails.
"Wonder what's up with Lucas," I mumble
around a bite of Gram's homemade pizza.

> *Mm-mm-mmh,* is the best Bri can do.
> Then she swallows. But before she can
> comment on Lucas, she notices something

outside my window. I can see her eyes
following movement. It's her dad and
my mom, on the patio. They are alone,

and caught up in some conversation.
Mom's lips move and now he looks
kind of sad. He leans toward her,

but she steps away. Shakes her head.
Whatever he said, I see Mom's clear
resolution. "What the heck is that about?"

> Bri shakes her head. *I have no idea.*

Brianna

I Have No Idea

What's going on anymore.
Everything feels tenuous,
like standing at the ocean's
edge, the licking waves

                              eroding

the sand from beneath
my feet. My best friend
is turning herself into
somebody new, steadfastly

                              changing,

and maybe not for the better.
My sister is clinging to
some weird fantasy, make-
believing she is

                              slipping

toward happily ever after.
And my parents have become
an unknown equation. Two,
divided by x, and the farther

                              apart

they push from each other,
the likelier they will never
bounce back.

Mikayla

Divided

That's how I've felt ever since
        I found out I was pregnant. Torn
        in two, one half insisting on the easy

solution, the other on doing the right
        thing. When I got home from Vegas
        and told Dylan I had decided to keep

        the baby, he gave me an ultimatum—
                It's me or it, Mik. I love you. But if
                you keep it, you will lose me. And

        don't expect any help from me.
                Each word struck like a jagged blade,
                piercing skin, flesh and heart.

I can't imagine life without Dylan,
        and I changed my mind again. I totally
        planned to keep the appointment.

I would have let Dylan drive me
        to the clinic. But fate intervened
        and I went to a funeral instead.

I Didn't Know Shelby

Didn't even really know she existed,
or what her life was about. Our only

relationship was my sister being friends
with her cousin, and my mom with her aunt.

A long, elastic thread. But when she died
and that cord snapped, it was a sharp reminder

of the value of life. She was only four. Not
much bigger than a baby doll, and that's how

she looked in her frilly white burial dress,
her hair all curled in ringlets. A sleeping doll.

So much sadness at her passing, though it
wasn't unexpected. How could you carry

a baby for nine months, dreams building,
only to have hope crushed by a heartbreaking

diagnosis? How could you live knowing
your child's time with you would be so short?

So I Was at the Funeral Today

It was not my first, so I knew
the minister would talk about

                                        dying

how it's really a beginning, and
how Christ is key to conquering

                                        death

and through him, one day we
would be reconnected with our

                                        dead.

Then the eulogies, personal
stories about Shelby's

                        living

and how her spirit added
layers of hope to every

                        life

she touched. And I wished
I'd known her while she was

                        alive.

And Hearing About

How those four short years
        meant so much to those who

shared them, I knew without
        a doubt that my baby deserves

the chance to bring his or her light
        into this world. It can't be up to me

to snuff it out. Making this decision
        has been a tug-of-war. Or maybe

more like a teeter-totter ride.
        Back and forth. Up and down.

Either way, I've thumped to
        the ground, and now that I have,

things can only get harder, but
        I won't change my mind again.

First I've got to tell two people—
        the baby's father. And mine.

I Don't Know Why Mom

Didn't come to the wake. She said
she had a headache, but that's not
a very good excuse. I hope she's home
when I get there. No use putting this off

any longer, and I need her support.
Oh, good. Her Jeep's in the driveway.
As Dad puts his car into park, I say,
"Hey, Dad. I need to talk to you.

It's important." Trace and Bri both
look at me, eyes asking if I'm going
to confess. I nod an acknowledgment.
If they want to listen in, fine. I go

inside and find Mom on her computer.
The glass beside it is almost empty,
a small puddle of red wine in the bottom.
"Mom?" Reluctantly, she draws her attention

away from the screen, refocuses it on me.
"I'm going to tell Dad about the baby.
I need you to be there, okay?" She starts
to say something. Stops. Gets out of her chair.

We Find Dad in the Kitchen

Pouring himself a drink. Death
and alcohol seem to partner well.
I could use one myself. Oh, wait.
Seeing Mom trail in behind me,

> Dad has to know something is up.
> *Okay, Mikayla. What's so important?*

I notice Trace and Bri, hovering
in the background. But what the hell?
It's now or never. "I . . . um . . ."
Come on. Straight out. "I'm pregnant."

> He stares, like I told him in Swahili.
> Then he takes a gulp of his drink. *Oh.*

Something of an anticlimax.
"Uh, Dad. Did you hear me? I said
I'm pregnant and . . ."

> *I heard you.* His voice is steady, but hard-
> edged. *What do you want me to say?*

I don't know what I want him
to say, or where to go from here.
Except, "I'm going to keep the baby."

Trace and Bri

Have crept closer, obviously anxious
to know how this will go. Dad notices,

and now the anger switch flips to on.
His eyes rotate. Trace. Bri. Mom. Me.

> *All of you knew? All of you, crotch-deep*
> *in this conspiracy?* Unreasonably, he turns

> on Mom. *How dare you keep this from me?*
> *One lie on top of another, huh? Bitch.*

Wow. Mom tries to defend herself.
We wanted to wait until Mikayla

decided what to do. We weren't trying
to hide it from you. Actually, we were.

> And Dad, of course, knows it. *Really.*
> *So, would you have told me if she had*

> an abortion? Two beats. *That's what I*
> *thought. How far along are you?*

I try to hold his gaze. Fail. Look past
him, to the far wall. "Twelve weeks."

*And Dylan is the father? He waits for
my nod. What does he have to say?*

"He wants me to have an abortion.
But I'm not going to kill this baby."

> *Goddammit, Mikayla! How can you
> have a baby? You're not even eighteen.*
>
> *How will you finish high school? What
> about college? Is Dylan planning on*
>
> *supporting you? Or do you expect me
> to? What the fuck is wrong with you?*

*Take it easy, Jace, Mom intervenes.
This is not the end of the world. We can—*

> *We? Who's we, Holly? You and me?
> We're not even sure there is a you and me,*
>
> *right? And now we're supposed to throw
> a baby into the mix? Are you insane?*

He slams his drink on the counter. Shards
of booze-flavored glass spray the granite.

He leaves the mess, storms from the room.
Bri and Trace scramble to get out of his way.

Good thing. He probably would have
crashed right through them. "Well, that

went pretty well, don't you think?"
The joke thuds. I grab a sponge, start to

clean up the glass. Mom comes over
to help. There's a big chunk of something

stuck in the silence. Some huge piece
of information I'm not privy to, but I

think I need to be. "What's going on
between you and Dad?" Whatever it

is makes Mom sad. "Nothing major.
Just a rough patch." The lie settles

into the space between us. Shimmers,
like the slivers of glass we sweep away.

Dissolve

One bad scene, into the next. I call
Dylan, ask if I can see him. He agrees
to meet me at Emily's, and as I drive
over there it occurs to me that I don't
have to sneak around anymore.

It's dark by the time we hook up.
I leave my car, get into his, slide close
for a kiss that feels awkward. "Can
we go somewhere?" I touch his thigh,
the way I know he likes. "I want you."

> *Rock Creek?* I agree and he starts
> to drive to one of our favorite parking
> spots. *So how was the funeral?* It's
> the kind of question you ask when
> you don't know what else to say.

"Sad." I know he wants to ask if
I have rescheduled my appointment,
but I don't want to tell him until
I have the chance to touch him. Kiss
him. Make him remember our love.

We Are Barely Parked

And I am all over him

        because I want him
        because I need him
        because I love him

can't bear the thought of

        losing him
        going on without him
        seeing him with someone else

I cover his mouth with mine

        give him my kiss
        open his lips
        with the tip of my tongue

And now we are naked

        skin rubbing skin
        bone against bone
        flesh into flesh

I tell him I love him

        a murmur
        a scream
        a moan

Right at this moment there is

        no baby
        no worry
        no one but the two of us.

Dylan

At This Moment

I

have never loved her
more. She has possessed
me, this demon girl,
infiltrated me, and I

don't

know how to exorcise her.
If I found the right words,
some damning incantation,
would I even

want
to

use them, command our hearts
apart? More than lust connects
us, so why doesn't she understand
how much there is to

lose

if she pursues this ridiculous
plan? I refuse to be dragged
along. And, love or no love,
that will mean leaving

her

behind.

The Plan

To eradicate every reminder of Shelby
while we were all at the funeral
seems to have gone like clockwork.

Alex and I arrive home before everyone
else, and I go straight for the bedroom
I used to avoid. Emptied. No furniture.

No TV. No VCR. Lung assist machine?
Gone. Donated to a family who needs
one but can't afford it. One small measure

of good. Thank you, Shelby, wherever
you are. You *are* there somewhere, right?
What a fucking joke. I snort a half laugh.

      Alex looks at me with curious eyes.
      What's so funny? Good question.
      He probably thinks I've lost

it, and maybe I have. "Nothing, really.
Just pondering the Great Beyond.
You know, the Giant Void, and all that."

Now he looks at me, surprised. *Giant*
void as in space? Or as in the place
you used to call heaven?

"What's the difference? It's all a huge
bowl of nothing, isn't it? And just what
the fuck is the point of any of it?"

> *That isn't you talking, Shane. I really*
> *think you need to give it some time.*
> *Do you want me to stay or should I go?*

"I think I want to be alone for a while."
We exit the immediate void. Alex tries
to kiss me goodbye, but I'm not

> in the mood. *Call me if you need me,*
> he says, starting toward the front door.
> When he's almost there, he turns back

> to me. *Just so you know, your unshakable*
> *faith, despite everything, is a very big part*
> *of why I fell in love with you. It's who you are.*

It's Who I Was

I watch him leave, go to my room,
turn on my computer. Enter "Death"

into the search engine. Holy crap.
Pages and pages of definitions

and theories and obituaries and stories
about people dying. Death pictures.

Death videos, including YouTube vids
labeled "gruesome." What kind of freaks

post those? And who the fuck wants
to watch them? Oh my God. There

are more than a dozen beheadings.
Car wrecks. Executions. Maybe I do

want to watch them. See if I can find
any evidence at all of souls, fleeing.

Morbid curiosity is getting the best
of me. I believe I need to see one, and

am just about to click on it when I hear
familiar voices coming through the front

door. Footsteps follow, some moving
toward the kitchen, others up the hall.

Suddenly, there is screaming. A high,
sharp keen. Mom? I run toward the sound

and almost trip over Gaga, scrambling
for haven under my bed. Dad and Gramps

hurry from the other direction. We all know
where we'll find Mom. Her siren wail

echoes in the emptiness of Shelby's room.
No! No! No! How could you? Bastards!

We don't try to stop her. It isn't anger
she's screeching. It's pain, and we can't

make it go away. She paces the perimeter,
mascaraed tears striping her face. When

she sees us, she raises the volume. *Who
did this? Whose idea was it? Christian?*

It was Dad's idea, but it is Gramps
who says, *We thought it would be best.*

Mom turns on him. *Oh, you did?*
You thought it would be best to wipe

my daughter from my life, scrub away
the last five years as if they never happened?

How dare you? Her voice rises, approaches
hysterical. *How dare any of you assume*

what's best for me? How . . . how . . .
And now she breaks down completely,

throws herself onto the floor where
the carpet is darker from Shelby's bed

having covered it all these years. Dad
and Gramps and I exchange silent

questions. Should one of us go to her,
urge her to her feet? Finally, Dad shakes

his head. We back out of the room, leave
Mom to her tear-drenched memories.

I Go Back to My Room

Sit in front of my computer,
try not to look at morbid pictures.
But some force more powerful
than curiosity draws a mouse click.
I spend the next two hours examining
death in its many forms.

Peaceful.
Accidental.
Purposeful.
Brutal.

I look at faces.

Contorted.
Aborted.
Bloated.
Beheaded.

I study mourners.

Distraught.
Resigned.
Curious.
Furious.

And nowhere do I see a sign of God.

So I Do a Search for "God"

I find God on Twitter. God TV.
             Five Steps to Hearing God.
                          Fifty Reasons There Is No God.

Scientific evidence proving God.
                     Stephen Hawking disclaiming
                               them. God Hates Shrimp—

a rather funny gay parody
               dissing some people's Bible
                        beliefs. Westboro Baptist

Church's God Hates Fags.
               God's Yellow Pages. God Tube.
                          God in Islam. God in America.

There is so much God—or
               lack thereof—that it's damn
                        hard to wade through it all.

But the more I wade, the more
               I realize that no one really
                        has a clue if God is or isn't.

I Realize Something Else, Too

If there is no God, it doesn't matter
what the fuck I do. All
that self-righteous

whiny crap is for
cowards, really. *I have to
do what's right* is synonymous

with *I'm scared to do what's wrong.*
Is that how I've lived for
sixteen years—afraid?

Screw that. If I don't
have to worry about pleasing
some Pearly Gatekeeper, I'm damn

sure going to live large. First I have
to find the courage I somehow
missed. I close my door,

open my window. Smoke
half of a fatty. Grab my keys,
step into the hall, listen for voices.

I don't hear Mom at all. Gramps and
Dad are talking on the deck.
I make the kitchen

undetected, reach
up into the cupboard, where
I know Dad keeps his booze stash.

I've never had a taste for alcohol.
Too hard to get buzzed on
without getting busted.

Plus, I hate what it's done
to my father. But screw it. This
is a special day. Vodka, right. You can't

smell it as bad. I take a big gulp. Yech.
Still, I take another. And one
more. Enough. I don't want

to get wasted. Just brave.
I don't tell anyone I'm leaving, but
get into my car and head toward the freeway.

I want to go fast and I do, windows open
to let any idea of God out. Holy
shit. Ninety mph is flying.

Alex

Any Idea

Of Shane reconsidering,
at least right away, goes up
in figurative smoke when
he shows up at my door

                                   wasted

and unannounced. My good
Catholic family is loudly sharing
our old-fashioned Friday fish
dinner and it takes a few

                                   minutes

for us to recognize the doorbell.
I volunteer to answer it and
my first thought when I see
Shane is how did he get here? He

                                   can't

have driven over, right? Not in
this shape—hair wind-mussed,
eyes freaky wide, and smelling
like weed and booze. He must

                                   be

out of his mind, and I won't
let him in like this. I lead him
to my car, shove him inside,
praying the Shane I love can be

                                   reclaimed.

Praying

Is something I've never done.
It's as foreign to me as Somalia,
as is the concept of God. Gramps

was raised Jewish, and Gram
a Protestant, whatever that is.
Gram told me that when they met,

they embarked on a "search for
deeper meaning," trying paganism
and Buddhism and Wicca, winding up

mostly agnostic. Mom never took
me to church, never tried to provide
me with faith. Dad, well, Dad pretty

much only believes in himself, plus
a small measure of Cassie thrown
in. So I think it's really kind of weird

that Dad and Cassie will say, "I do"
in a church. What's even weirder,
and a little creepy, is it's the same

church where Shelby's funeral was,
almost a month ago. Since then,
I turned fourteen. We celebrated

with a sleepover—me, Bri and a couple
of girls I've made friends with at Carson
High. I think Bri is a little hurt about

that, but she doesn't go to Carson, and
I can't walk around all by myself,
looking like a total loser. Serena is quiet

and smart. A lot like Bri, in fact. But
Chloe is just this side of crazy. She'll
do anything for attention. And when

she gets it, I get it, too. For my birthday,
she brought an R-rated DVD. Lots of
nakedness and sex. Bri was humiliated,

       not that she didn't watch. Serena
       pretended it was cool. Chloe whooped,
       Uh-huh! That's what I'm talking about.

I Have to Admit

A couple of scenes embarrassed
       me, too. Is that what it takes to

be an adult? Later, I asked Bri,
       "Do you think our parents do stuff

like that?" I really can't picture
       Mom naked and rubbing against

       some naked man. Bri thought
              a second. *I guess they used to.*

"Things are bad between them,
       huh?" I probably shouldn't know

       half the stuff I do, including
              her answer, *They pretend it's okay.*

       But we'd have to be stupid not
              to know what's going on. I think . . .

       Her face kind of collapsed in on
              itself. *They're talking about divorce.*

I Hate How Relationships

Are so fragile. How they
                crack
                        shatter
                                fall to pieces.
And the hammer is
                time
                        distance
                                moving forward.
Why can't people grow
                closer
                        tighter
                                welded together?
Instead they go
                looking
                        for the next
                                frail connection.
There must be a way to
                stay
                        in love
                                no matter what.

Case in Point

My fickle mother.
Here she meets Robin,
who I really think she liked
a lot. But when he went back to
Vegas, where he lives, she cut things
off completely. I know it's hard to maintain
a long-distance relationship, but why not
try to nurture a connection? They
hadn't spoken since he left, and
he called the other night when
we were eating dinner. She
answered but was cold

as January. Freezing, frigid
cold. Seemed like she wasn't
saying something she wanted to.
So maybe that's part of the problem.
Lack of communication. Why can't people
just open up and talk about what bothers them?
Now she's dating one of Shelby's doctors.
She says it's not serious, and until it
is, she won't bring him home for
a home-cooked introduction.
Is it me she doesn't want to
disappoint? Or is it him?

I Don't Want to Think

About it tonight, so I won't.
Tonight I'm going out with Lucas,
just the two of us. He's picking me up
as soon as Dad and Cassie leave.

They're having a joint bachelor/
bachelorette party. Not sure what
that is, but if it involves strippers,
it could be interesting. Or gross.

Dad comes out of his room,
dressed up for a change—slacks
(who knew he had them?) and
a button-down shirt. "Wow. Snazzy."

> He smiles. *I know, right? Your old*
> *man still cleans up pretty good.*
> *You don't mind hanging out here*
> *alone? Chad will be back later.*

I shake my head. "No problem.
Plenty to keep me occupied."
Hope he doesn't find out just
how much. "You guys have fun."

Now Cassie appears in a tight
pink dress that doesn't hide a whole
lot. *Okay, I'm ready. Don't wait up.*
We'll probably be late. She takes

Dad's hand and off they go.
I text Lucas that the coast is clear,
then go to the bathroom. A little
more makeup is required, now

that it won't draw too much attention
from anyone but Lucas. I also change
into a skirt and clingy long-sleeved tee.
I'm going for the "wowza" look.

Not quite as sexy as Cassie, but
enough, I hope, to make Lucas never
want to let go of me. I'll do just about
anything to keep him hanging on.

He Makes Me Wait

Almost an hour. I throw open
the passenger door. "What took
so long?" But the "what" slams into

>   me like a booze-flavored wave.
>   *Do you want to get in or not?*
>   Oh God. I've made him mad.

"Of course I do. Sorry. It's just
I should probably be back by eleven
and I want to be with you as much

as I can." I plop down on the seat,
hike my skirt a bit, some weird
apology, for what I'm not sure.

>   *That's better,* he says, pulling
>   me to him for a kiss. He tastes
>   of weed and alcohol, but I don't

care, and I give him as good as
he gives me. His spare hand lands
on my exposed thigh, starts to creep.

I leave it there, but say, "Not here.
I think the neighbors are spies."
He laughs, thank goodness.

> *Okay. Let's go someplace private.*
> It isn't far to a little turnout along
> the river. Half of me wants to be here.

The other half is whispering,
"This isn't good. This can't be good.
You know what he's after, right?"

Scenes from my birthday movie
start flashing in my head. And then
I hear Mom warning, "You're not

ready for sex. You're not old enough."
And I wonder if I am. And I think, really,
I'm not. I'm still not that kind of girl.

Yet, I Let Him Kiss Me

And it's the kind of kiss that makes
goose bumps break out all over my body.

He pulls me into his lap, licks down
my neck, to the curve of my shirt.

> *Take it off*, he says, and as if he has
> hypnotized me, I do exactly as I'm told.

Quickly, his hands work the hooks
of my bra and before I can even think

> to say no, my entire upper body
> is bared. *That's it, my pretty little girl.*

He moves to kiss my nipples, and
though I want to say no, I can't. It feels

good. Great. Amazing. Beneath my skirt,
I feel him grow hard against the thin

barrier of my panties. I like how that
feels, too. But I'm still not ready. "Stop."

His mouth is around my nipple
and he mumbles, *Why?* All innocent.

Now his lips move an inch or so
higher and he starts to suck, softly

at first, then harder. It is crazy good
and it makes me moan but when

he tries to slide down my panties
I know I can't. Not yet. "I . . . I have

my period." It's a lie, but he can't
know that, and it's better than saying

       I'm too young. He stiffens. Stops.
       Then he says, *We can do something*

       else then. He lifts me up, undoes
       his zipper and this is no movie

when he frees his erection and shows
me exactly how to use my mouth

to get him off. I wish I could say
I don't like it. But somehow I do.

Lucas

Getting Off

Is easy. You don't even need
two to make it happen. The proper
grip with a slippery fist, whoopee,
there it goes. But man does not live
by ejaculation alone. There's

the

whole pursue-and-conquer
thing to consider, which is why
loose girls aren't all that much

fun.

Okay, maybe I'm a bit warped
that way, but hard-to-get
turns me on. Besides, I kind
of like playing teacher, which

is

why I'm so patient with this
little girl, who will so be worth
the wait. Oh yes, I plan on

winning

a major jackpot, taking her all
the way for the very first time.
If that means patience, okay
by me. It's only part of

the game.

Patience

That's what Dr. Ortega says to have
now, at sixteen weeks pregnant.

Well into my second trimester, the risk
of miscarriage has largely passed and

my baby is approximately the size
of an avocado, with ears and toenails

and a beating heart. The heart part
is true. I've heard it. As for the rest,

I'll have to take her word for it until
after my ultrasound. It's a whole month

away. At twenty weeks, we can find out
if it's a boy or a girl. Meanwhile, I have

some decisions to make. Mom and I are
going to talk to my counselor, Mr. Taylor.

We're in the office, waiting. And, though
I'm not showing yet, I feel like everyone

knows why we're here. The secretary
keeps giving me one of those looks

that says, *Hello? Haven't you heard
about birth control?* I try to return

a look that yells, "What the fuck
business is it of yours?" But I fail

miserably, turn my eyes toward
the checkerboard linoleum floor.

How does she know, anyway? Aren't
counselors supposed to keep stuff

like this quiet? I'm not showing yet.
At least, I don't think I am. I stare

down at my belly. Push my shirt flat.
Nope. Not yet. So why do I suspect

that everyone passing through—teachers,
students, some who I know and many

I don't, are completely aware of me
and why I'm here? My face goes hot.

I Am Semi-Saved

By Mr. Taylor's appearance at his
door. *Mikayla? Mrs. Carlisle? Please
come in.* Suddenly, I want to run.

But I don't. Instead, I follow Mom
inside his clean, starched office.
The man is totally anal. Even his desk

is clean. We settle into hard plastic
chairs, most certainly designed to deny
comfort. *Tell me what I can do for you.*

Mom looks at me and, okay, it's my
place to speak up. But I've lost my voice.
Lost my confidence. This confession

is all about judgment. Mom speaks
for me. *Um . . . well . . .* Then, straight
out, *Mikayla is pregnant. We need to*

*know what options she has regarding
her schooling. She wants to graduate,
of course.* She turns to me. *Right?*

Now they're both staring at me.
"Well, of course I want to graduate.
Why would that have changed?"

Mr. Taylor's jaw stiffens. *Ahem.*
Well . . . uh . . . congratulations
or sorry, depending. He shuffles

the two pieces of paper on his desk.
Ahem. You do have options. You can
stay in school as long as it's viable.

He studies me with creeping eyes.
When are you due? When I tell him
mid-March, he nods. *We have a good*

virtual academy available. Really,
the question becomes when to move
you into it. I'm not sure how you feel

about everyone here knowing you're
pregnant. If you don't care, I'd suggest
moving at the semester break. If you do . . .

Do I Care?

I still don't know, and I've thought
          about it a lot. "I . . . I haven't figured
that out yet. I have time to decide."

                    Some time, Mr. Taylor replies. *But*
          it will go faster than you think.
                    I assume Dylan Douglas is the father?

Now any sense of embarrassment
          segues to anger. "Of course he is!
Why would you think anything else?"

                    Calm down, Mikayla. I'm not judging
          you, and it wouldn't be the first
                    time a fling resulted in unwanted

                    pregnancy. . . . His pause can only be
          translated as, *It* is *an unwanted*
                    pregnancy, right? Which pisses me

off even more. "It was just a mistake,
          and it's Dylan's baby, if that's your
concern. Why is it important, anyway?"

Mom starts to interfere, but Mr.
Taylor lifts a hand. *Look. I don't*
know where Dylan stands on this,

but the fact is, he might not want
the rest of the school to know
about the baby, either. He has a right—

"Bullshit! It's my baby and my life
and, hey, if Dylan is concerned
about how his friends feel, well,

he should have thought about that
before he convinced me the rhythm
method would work fine one or two

times. What is it with men, always
cheerleading for the guys in this
situation? That's totally fucked up!"

Mikayla Jean! huffs Mom, as if
she never heard me swear before.
You apologize to Mr. Taylor right now.

As If!

Mom glares at me, and Mr. T. looks
like "fuck" is a foreign four-letter word.

"Did I offend you? You know, I really
don't care. And I don't care who else

I might offend, either. This is a baby,
not some kind of a burden. And, while

it might have taken two of us to create
this baby, the only opinion that matters

here is mine. I'll stay in school for now,
unless you want to suspend me for f-bomb

usage. If so, write me up. If not, I'll see
you bright and early tomorrow morning."

> I don't wait for an answer, but as I go,
> I hear Mom apologize for me. *I'm very*
>
> *sorry. She's a bit emotional. . . .* Her voice,
> and his response, fade into the ether.

When I Pass Through

The office this time, I tip my head high,
        meet everyone's look with a straight-on

glare. Apologize? When hell freezes
        solid. The last bell rings as I swing into

the long corridor, now swarming with
        kids. I wind my way through them and

nobody gives me a sideways glance.
        How will I feel when that changes?

When everyone stares at me? I turn
        down the hallway toward my locker.

Skid to a halt when I see Dylan shoulder
        to shoulder with Kristy Lopez. She reaches

her own locker, and when she stops to
        open it, the way he watches her is almost

protective. Simmering anger boils
        into fury. I stomp right up to them. "Can

I talk to you, Dylan? Or, are you too
        busy to give me a couple of minutes?"

Kristy Smiles Triumph

And suddenly I understand
that I have lost Dylan. Still,
he follows me outside.

I turn into him.
Fall against him.
Look up at him.
Imploring him.
So in love with him.

"Talk to me, Dylan."

> *What do you want me
> to say? I told you what
> would happen if you
> decided to keep the baby.*

"You never said you'd
leave me. Never said
you'd go back to her."

> *I am not going to be
> a father, Mikki.*

Anger and sadness melt
into one. "Yes, you are."

I Gentle My Hands

Against his cheeks. Find sadness
in his eyes, too. "Even if you never
once see this baby, you will be its
father, Dylan. You can't change that."

> *So what do you want from me?*
> *I have no way to pay child support.*

"I'm not asking you for money.
I'm asking you to stay in love
with me. Begging you, in fact.
How can I do this without you?"

> He pushes my hands away. *You*
> *figure that out. It's all on you.*

He pivots, and I watch him walk
away. "You said you loved me!"
I call after him. "You promised.
Love doesn't just die, Dylan."

> He turns back long enough to say,
> *Maybe not. But sometimes people kill it.*

Stunned

Stung, as if I just disturbed a hive
of yellow jackets, I stumble
to my car, slide under the steering
wheel and rest my head against it.
All my earlier bravado fades
into a black mist. I let myself sob

until a knock on my window coaxes me
out of the dark cloud. Mom. I lower
the glass. "What do you want?"

I just want to know if you're okay.

"Do I look okay?" It slips out softly.
I don't want to yell. I want someone
to hear me. "Dylan just broke up with me."

Do you want to talk about it?

I nod, and she says she'll drive me
home. I scoot over and she takes
the wheel. I want to talk about it more
than anything, but as we're backing up,
I notice Dylan walking Kristy to his car.
My voice drowns in a downpour of tears.

Kristy
I Want to Talk

To Dylan about why he has
made this one-eighty.
When summer started
he and Mikayla were

                              inseparable,

twisted together so tightly
I thought they'd smother.
But now, it seems their

                         indivisible

days were numbered. Part
of me is gleeful, gratеful for
another chance. But I also
need to know what made his

                         incessant

devotion to her dissolve, sugar
into vinegar. Clearly, he loved
her, and I thought he loved me
once. How can I believe that

                         emotion

is something he's capable
of giving? What made him
pull away? And will it
happen again?

I Pulled Away

From Tara. Shoved Alex to one side,
and it's lonely in my minuscule corner

of the universe. At school, I suppose
I'm learning something. I ace every quiz,

every test. But why? Even if I work my ass
off to impress some Ivy League scout, even

if I graduate *cum laude*, build an amazing
career, eventually I'll die. So what the fuck

is the point? On the plus side, when I am
accosted in the hallways, assaulted

by under-the-breath insults, I just smile.
Those pricks aren't any more immortal

than I am. And if I'm lucky I will live
to read their obituaries before someone

I know reads mine. That thought stops
me cold. Goddamn. I'm only sixteen.

It's Not Like People Close to Me

Haven't noticed. They have,
and every one of them offers
pretty much the same advice.

> Various teachers: *Shane, I know*
> *this is a difficult time. I think*
> *you should talk to a counselor.*

> Counselor: *Shane, I'm sure it has*
> *been hard to come to grips with*
> *this. If you need to talk, I'm here.*

> Dad: *Shane, we are all working*
> *through this the best we can. It*
> *might be good to talk to your mom.*

> Mom: *Shane, it will get easier.*
> *It hasn't yet. Not for you. Not for*
> *me. But you have to talk to me.*

Everyone wants me to talk. To
tell them how I feel. They won't
want to hear I feel nothing at all.

I'm Staring into My Locker

Lost in the thick smoke of voices
        surrounding me when suddenly
                someone taps my shoulder.

    Hey, soldier. Tara. *Are you going*
        to keep ignoring me forever?
                Because I kind of miss you.

"Soldier?" I have to smile at that.
      I turn, and for one millisecond,
           seeing her face makes everything

just like it was. And then, *psst!*
    everything is back, just like it is.
        "I miss you, too," I have to admit.

    Good. Because I don't want to eat
        lunch alone. Let's go somewhere.
                You owe me a ride in your car.

A small measure of guilt turns
      my face red. "I guess I do. Come
           on." She follows me to the parking

lot and when I stop next to
the Sportage, she whistles. *Sexy.*
Almost as sexy as its driver.

So Tara. "Whatever. Get in."
We only have a half hour.
"What do you want for lunch?"

She shrugs. *Conversation.*
I want to know what's up
with you. Are you okay?

Shit. "Sure. I'm great, in fact.
Life is totally awesome."
I swing the car toward

McCarran Boulevard. Punch it.
Easy. Are you mad because
I'm worried about you?

Gah! If I hear that one more
time . . . "Jesus H. Christ!
Everybody's worried about me!"

The Lord's Name in Vain Thing

Doesn't faze her.
But what she says
totally takes me down.

> *I'm not everybody.*
> *I'm your best friend,*
> *or at least, I was.*

Damn. "You still are.
I'm sorry. But please
don't worry about me."

> *Okay, I'll try not to. But*
> *only if you converse with*
> *me. Tell me about Alex.*

I've only talked about
him in text messages,
and I'd really like to

go into detail, except
for one thing. "Uh, we
might have broken up."

Unexpectedly, She Freaks

What? And you never mentioned
it to me? I saw you at the funeral,

and the two of you looked pretty
close. When did this happen?

"It hasn't officially happened.
I just haven't seen him in a couple

of weeks. Okay, it was my fault.
I kind of showed up at his house,

drunk. . . ." I tell her how he refused
to let me in. How he insisted on driving

me home. How he yelled at me for
daring to get behind the wheel in

the condition I was in. "He told me
not to call until I 'waded through

my personal hell and vanquished
my demons.' That hasn't happened yet."

I have no idea where I'm driving,
so I circle back toward school. Tara

stays quiet for a minute. Then she says,
And you can't understand why people

are worried about you? Shane, in all
the years I've known you, you have never

been even close to as happy as when you
were with Alex. You can't throw that away.

A giant wad of choking sadness collects
in my throat. "I kn-know," I spit out.

Suddenly, I am hungry for him, so when
she says, *Promise me you'll call him?*

it isn't hard to agree. And, when we
reach Reno High and I park the car,

I don't wait to text Alex. DON'T KNOW
IF I'VE VANQUISHED MY DEMONS. BUT

I DO KNOW I LOVE YOU AND NEED TO SEE
YOU RIGHT AWAY. PLEASE FORGIVE ME.

Then I reach over and give Tara a kiss.
"Thank you. And thanks for being you."

Gram and Gramps

Have moved into a small apartment
while they continue to look for a place
to buy. They left their travel trailer
parked next to our house and I've

made it my haven when I want to be
alone. Tonight, for the first time, it
will be a haven for Alex and me. While
I wait for him, I try to calm my nerves

with the help of some nitro-weed.
I have to admit, I'm anxious to see
him, and with each green inhale
my anxiety grows. So much for stress

reduction. It seems to take forever,
and when he finally knocks softly
on the door, I open it so quickly
he jumps back a little. "Sorry."

> I let him in and he sniffs the air.
> *Wow. It's a little, uh, thick in here.*
> I want him to grab me, pull me to
> him. Instead, he studies me carefully.

That shouldn't bother me, but it
does. "What? Did I grow another
nose or something?" He grins,
and a barrier falls. When I reach

for him, he comes to me. And now we
are kissing. It's the kind of kiss
that means it's been way too long.
A sudden longing floods my body—

a torrent of deep, lust-drenched
need, flowing through my veins.
"Make love to me." Heart pounding,
I tug him backward, toward the small bed.

He wants me just as much. The proof
is obvious, despite two layers of jeans
between us. Yet, he hesitates. *Is this
the only reason you wanted to see me?*

"No, goddamn it! I love you and
I've missed you, and maybe it's part
of the reason because I'm sick of
not feeling. Make me feel something!"

I Yank My T-Shirt

Over my head, put his hands
on my chest, over my thrashing
heart. "This is the most alive

I've been in weeks. Please. I don't
want to be dead inside anymore."
He slides his hands around me,

drops them to my thighs, lifts
and carries me to the bed. Now
water becomes fire coursing

through me, consuming, filling
the emptiness inside me with flame.
I fall back against the small, hard

mattress, rushing my zipper as Alex
removes his own clothes. I open
my arms and he comes to me, kisses

      my mouth. My neck. Down my chest.
      Then he looks up at me with those
      sea green eyes, and swears, *I love you,*

before kissing me in the most intimate
way of all. His mouth urges me to
quench conflagration, but I don't want

to. "No! Not yet." Too soon. And not
enough of him. I could go all night.
Besides, "This has to be good for you, too."

> He pushes up over me, stares down
> at me. *Do you have a condom?*
> *I didn't bring one. Didn't think . . .*

"I . . . no . . ." Shit. But, you know,
"I don't care. You can withdraw.
What are the odds? Please . . ."

> His eyes flash terror. *No fucking way!*
> *I would never take a chance like that.*
> *I'm okay. Let me take care of you.*

I do. And it's good. And when
we lay woven together afterward,
it comes to me that I might not want

to be dead inside, but maybe a sliver
of me wouldn't mind being dead. Period.

Tara

A Sliver

That's all I could find
left of the Shane who's
been better than a brother
for more than eight years.

                              Is there a way

to reinfuse my forever
friend with the humor I so
love him for? Did Shelby
take it with her? Can she
beam it back? I want

                              to make him

laugh again, and for him
to make me laugh, about
everything or nothing at
all. I want to watch him
walk straight-spined,

                              like he

always has, despite gay-
phobic commentary; to hear
his acerbic comebacks. I want
him to be the totally flawed,
totally perfect Shane he

                              used to be.

Totally Changed

That's what I am.
      A girl transformed
           by a boy she's not
                even in love with.
                      I definitely don't feel
about Lucas the way
      I did about Chad, like
           every minute away
                from him is an hour
                    too long. He's not even
all that nice to me. He
      never tells me I'm cute
           or smart or good at
                anything. Never asks
                    about school or Mom or
Bri or what I like to do
      for fun. He mostly just
           wants "favors." So why
                am I willing to do almost
                    anything he tells me to?

"Almost," Meaning

I still won't go all the way.
He probably thinks this has been
a world-record period—ten days
and counting. I've done a lot

of other stuff, though. Stuff
I never thought I would, not even
with a guy I *did* love. I guess I do
it because he wants to do it with me.

Me. Not some other girl. Me.
Chloe says I should enjoy it.
Not the attention. "It." The kissing
and licking and touching and rubbing.

I do like it. It feels good. I totally
get the lust part. But wouldn't lust
feel even better with a little love
involved? Bri thinks I'm stupid.

> *No way! With him? Why, Harley?*
> That's what she said when I told her
> about the first time I did it with my mouth.
> *You could get a disease like that!*

I actually never thought about
that, but I don't think Lucas
has any diseases. Not that I could
ask him. That would make him mad.

But I for sure can't get a disease,
or pregnant, doing what he wants
me to do right now. Mom's still
at work. I'm alone in my room.

Lucas texts instructions. GET NAKED
AND LIE DOWN ON YOUR BED. He gives
me time to comply, and I have to
admit I get a little thrill, thinking

about what might come next. Soft
October sunlight filters in through
the window, spills across my skin,
warming it just enough to let me

stay uncovered. I keep my panties
on. As far as he knows, I'm still
on my period. PLAY WITH YOUR
NIPPLE. GET IT HARD. I WANT A PIC.

I Try to Make It Sexy

Like the girl in that movie. I'm not
sure I can accomplish that with a cell

phone camera, but I give it my best
shot, then hit send before I chicken

out. I wait for another text. It doesn't
take long. *BEAUTIFUL! THIS IS AWESOME.*

*AND NOW I WANT ANOTHER ONE. TOUCH
YOURSELF. YOU KNOW WHERE. LET ME SEE.*

He called me beautiful. That's a first.
Am I beautiful? I look at the photo

I sent him. Is that really me? I look . . .
good. Leaning back against my pillow,

my stomach goes all the way flat, but
my boobs don't. For sure they grew

over the summer. I cup them gently, and
they overflow the bowls of my hands.

Wow. How did that happen? Suddenly,
my cell buzzes. *WELL? I'M WAITING.*

Part of me wants to keep him waiting.
The other part doesn't want him mad.

I let one hand slide to the crotch
of my panties, pull the lacy material

just a little to one side. I keep my fingers
covering the most personal part, take

a quick picture that I hope will do.
While I wait for his response, I leave

my hand where it is, just above a soft
pulsing between my legs. I have never

touched myself there before, not the way
he wants me to. But now I do. Just to see.

Just to know. I move my middle finger
slowly along the slick strip, discover

the nub hiding beneath my pubic bone—
the source of the building throb.

My Cell Buzzes

But I ignore it for the moment.
This is something I need to know
more about. Something I must learn.

Unbidden, my finger starts to move
faster and, unbidden, my body rocks
against it. It's like I've been possessed

by something—someone—I have no
control over. I can't stop. Wouldn't
even if I thought I could. So I give

myself up to the woman inside me.
Let her move my hand. Teach
me what to do. She is instinct, pure

or filthy, and I listen to her, follow
her direction. Some urgency begins,
grows like surf moving toward high

tide. Breaks that can't be harnessed
or slowed or stopped. That swell
into a tidal wave, and with it a crash—

and a bolt of understanding.

If There Ever Was an Eve

This must be how she felt
right after she first figured
out what orgasm meant.

Enlightened.
                    Embarrassed.

Excited to try it again.
I will. But not now. Why
don't they teach you *this*

in school? That you really
don't need someone else
to make you feel this good?

Satisfied.
                    Contented.

I mean, they sort of mention
it, but not as a means to an end.
And some people even call it a sin.

No making that element happy,
I guess. Ask me, self-pleasure
could be the key to abstinence.

Listen to Me

Like I've suddenly become
        an expert on self-pleasure.

I put on my clothes. Go wash
        my hands. And when I get back

to my room, I finally check
        my cell for Lucas's text message.

        AWESOME. BUT NEXT TIME I WANT
                TO SEE EVERYTHING. GOT IT?

I'm not quite that brave. *I'LL*
        THINK ABOUT IT. WILL I SEE

YOU THIS WEEKEND? It's only
        Wednesday. Friday seems like

such a long way away.
        His return text takes a while.

Tit for tat, right? I made him
        wait while I . . . My face sizzles,

        white hot. Finally, the buzz.
                ARE YOU OVER YOUR PERIOD?

Guess I'll Have to Be

Sooner or later. Problem is, it's going
to start for real at some point soon.

What can I use for an excuse then?
Or should I just come clean, admit

I wasn't ready and couldn't think
of another way out? The problem

with lies is they start to pile up, one
on top of another, until it's hard to find

your way out from under the heap.
I wish I could talk to Bri about it.

But she'd just lecture me. Mom? Yeah,
right. She still thinks I'm her little angel.

Can't believe she hasn't noticed my
wings are long gone. Chloe? Maybe, but

I know what she'll say—*No excuses.*
No apologies. Just live in the moment.

One other person comes to mind.
I dial her number. Hope she's home.

She is. "Hey, Cassie. I, uh, wanted
to talk to you. I'm kind of seeing this guy. . . ."

> *Boy problems? Already? School*
> *has barely started. Okay, what's up?*

"Well, um . . . See, he's sort of pushing
me to have . . . you know. And I'm not . . ."

> *Ready? I would think not, especially*
> *if you just started dating. You remember . . .*

Someone—Dad? Chad?—interrupts,
says something I can't quite make out.

> *Okay, Cassie says to him. Now, to me, Your*
> *dad says to tell any guy who bothers you*
>
> *he'll have to answer to your father. Listen.*
> *I have to run. We'll talk Saturday, okay?*

It's Not

But I say, "Okay." We're going
shopping for my bridesmaid's dress.
Guess it will wait till then. Meanwhile,
maybe biology homework (regeneration)
will take my mind off Lucas

         and   scattered   notions

of   lies   excuses

      periods   invented   pending

      sexting   pics   nipples

touching   that   place   until . . .

A door slams and Mom calls
out that she needs help unloading
the groceries. I close my notebook,
stash every deviant thought and try to
regenerate some hint of angel wings.

Chloe

Deviant

Some people seem to think
"deviant" is my middle name.
Okay, I may be the kind of girl
who truly believes

life

is totally much more amazing
when you straddle its edges.
First, always, is self-preservation,
but once you get a handle
on the challenges that

presents,

you can take control. And
isn't that really the point?
To choose your path, veering
around anyone who insists
you're wrong, from the

endless

shortcuts and switchbacks
along the straight and narrow
way. To avoid the tried-and-true
in favor of imagine-this

possibilities.

Straight

I've gone completely straight
for my baby, and that makes
being pregnant even harder.

No booze, no weed, no pills
except for prenatal vitamins.
Nothing to take my mind off

my slowly expanding belly
or how lonely I am without Dylan.
Wednesday is Halloween, and as

October fades into November,
the ever-shortening days seem
to grow longer. And the snap-cool

nights are longer yet. You'd think
I'd be really tired, but apparently
that isn't so until the last trimester.

At twenty weeks, I'm halfway
there and at my next doctor's
appointment, I'll have the ultrasound

that will show if the baby is a boy
or a girl. Halfway there, and so far
I haven't told anyone. Not Emily.

Not Audrey. None of my teachers,
though I'm pretty sure a couple
of them know, which means

apparently there is no counselor-
student privilege. Before long, though,
the baggy shirts I've taken to wearing

won't hide my belly bulge. I might
as well spill to my friends first.
Find out if they are, in fact, friends.

Today being Nevada Day, it's a no-
school Monday, so I wait until after
eleven to call Emily. "What's up?"

> Not much. Going to the carnival
> in Carson later. Want to come?

Rides? Don't think so. "Nah.
Been to one carnival, you've been
to pretty much all of them, you know?"

I Almost Invent an Excuse

To hang up. I used to feel close
to Em, but recent distractions

have lodged us apart. She only
asked about Dylan once and I kind

of went off. Okay, totally went off.
We haven't talked much since.

"Listen. First, I apologize about
the Dylan thing. I was just so pissed."

> *Hey. It's okay. I would be pissed, too.*
> *Can't believe he broke up with you.*

"There's more. I . . . I'm pregnant.
That's why he broke up with me."

> *Silence. One-one thousand. Two . . .*
> *Wow. I'm kind of speechless. What . . .*

"I'm keeping the baby. Dylan wanted
me to get an abortion. But I couldn't."

> *Wow. But how . . . ? I mean, I thought*
> *you were getting on birth control.*

"I was going to. But I hadn't made
the appointment, and we were out

one night and he didn't bring
a rubber and he swore it would

be fine. That he'd pull out. And he
did, but not soon enough, I guess."

> *Wow. I'm sorry. Or, I'm happy for*
> *you. I don't know. What should I be?*

Good question. "Don't be sorry.
Not about the baby. You can be

sorry about Dylan if you want."
Just please don't say *wow* again.

We talk for a while, and by the time
we hang up, I'm glad I told her.

I can't do this alone. I really need
support from my family and friends.

Courage Bolstered

Now I want to fess up to everyone
else I think should know. I send
an email to Sarah Hill, ask her to share
my good news with Aunt Tia. If I keep

thinking of it as good news, will that
make it less scary? I'll have to tell
my other grandparents in person.
I go find Mom, who is in the guest

room, which is now her bedroom.
She told Trace, Bri and me it's because
Dad snores, but we know that's bullshit.
My parents are on the verge of divorce.

And I'm partially to blame. Mom
defended me, which only drove
Dad further away. They barely talk
at all, and when they do, every word

is hard-edged and hurtful. Dad stays
at work later and later. Mom runs.
Lifts. Spends hours at her computer,
writing. Building her own career.

I Knock on the Door

And her terse *Come in* says I've
interrupted her train of thought.

But I can't stop now. "I wanted
you to know that I emailed Sarah
and told her about the baby."

Mom turns to me. *That's good.*
But, by the way, she already knows.

How? "You told her? Because
that really wasn't your place."
Anger crackles like lightning.

I didn't tell her. She guessed. Maybe
she's psychic, or maybe it had to do
with all those questions you asked.

"Oh. Sorry." A day for apologies.
And confessions. "I want to tell
Grandma and Grandpa Carlisle."

She considers. *Talk to your father*
first. He should go with you.

Dad took Trace and Bri to the Nevada
Day parade. And, "I don't want to wait.
Will you come with me? Please?"

I wait for her to refuse. Instead,
she says, *Okay. If they're home. But
I would not anticipate it going well.*

She calls. They're home. Expecting
us, but most definitely not what I have
to tell them. It's a short drive, with

butterflies dancing around in my
stomach. Wait. That's not butterflies.
"Mom. I just felt the baby move. I think

it was the baby, anyway." Alive and
kicking, as the old saying goes, even
if this is a whole different context.

Mom actually smiles. *Babies
have a way of doing that. Just wait
until she starts doing push-ups.*

She?

I kind of thought it might be
        a boy. Masculine like its daddy.
        She. What if it's a girl like me?
Thinking in such concrete terms

makes me even more determined
        to admit to the world I'm pregnant.
        We arrive at my grandparents'
monstrous home. Why do they need

such a big place for the two of
        them? Some people, I'm sure, find
        it beautiful, with its marble floors
and giant columns, outside and in.

It reminds me of a mausoleum.
        Not that I've ever admitted such
        a thing to anyone. Not even Mom,
who I'm pretty sure feels the same,

if not about the house, about
        the people who live inside it. I love
        my grandparents. But they've never
exactly been affectionate to Mom.

Curly and Larry

Announce our arrival with gruff
Newfoundland barks. The dogs
are big and slobbery, but puppies
at heart. I want a dog someday.

Mom says they're too much work,
and maybe they are. But I want one
anyway. Just not a hundred-fifty-
pound behemoth like these two.

> Grandma Carlisle opens the door
> before we reach it. She scopes out
> Mom's running shorts. Scowls. *Come
> on in, then. Henry! They're here.*

She leads us into the family room.
The living room is reserved for special
guests—ones who won't stain the white
carpet and furniture. Grandpa appears

> like a magician's assistant, from thin
> air, it seems. He waves us to the leather
> sofa. *Make yourselves at home. Can
> I get you something to drink?* Pretty sure

Mom would like something *strong*
to drink, and I would, too. A giant
glass of alcoholic courage. But both
of us shake our heads. "No thanks."

Grandma gets right to the point.
*Okay, then. Tell us. What is this
important news?* She looks at Mom,
who looks at me with a silent *It's*

not my place. And she's right.
I clear my throat. "Ahem. I don't
know how to say this except to come
straight out with it. I'm pregnant."

Grandpa turns the color of pickled
beets. Grandma goes more toward
blanched almonds. Their heads rotate—
toward each other. Away. Toward Mom.

Away. But neither can quite look
at me. "I'm five months along, and
I have decided to keep the baby
and I wanted you two to know."

Sixty Seconds

To the barrage. At me:

> graduation
> > college
> prepaid college!!

> marriage
> > child support
> stepping up to the plate!

> programs
> > staying home
> what will the neighbors think?

Unbelievably, at Mom:

> supervision
> > or lack of
> where the hell were you?

> moral fiber
> > or lack of
> chip off the ol' block.

And now I blow it.
"How dare you blame Mom?
This isn't her fault. It's mine."

Emily
Fault

Is easy enough to assign.
It's Dylan's fault for taking
the easy way out. It's Mikki's
fault for going along. The only

                                      innocent

is the baby, who has no choice
at all. And here, friendship
becomes murky. I kind of want
to yell at her. I mean, I might be

                                        guilty

of casual sex. Maybe even with
a friend's boyfriend. But, damn,
at least I'm smart about it.
The last thing I want is an infant

                                        who

needs a blood test to determine
paternity. Mikki knows who
the father is. But is it fair to push
him into that role because she

                                        decides

to play mommy? Should I be
mad at him, like a good friend
might, when I think he's right
to walk away, leave her behind?

A Good Friend

Listens to what you have to say.
And then tells it like it is, or at least
how it appears to be. Today Mom's
good friend, Drew, is here. Right now,

he's listening. I know, because I'm
on the floor by my door, eavesdropping.
They're in Shelby's room, which has
been transformed into an office/sitting

room with mauve walls and flouncy
white curtains and plush new carpeting.
The furniture is white wicker—
desk, love seat and rocking chair.

> If you ask me, Mom spends way
> too much time in there. Not sure
> what she does, except read. *I can't
> quite let go of Shelby yet,* I hear Mom

> say. *I have no clue how long it will
> take, or if I'll ever get over her
> completely. I know I have to do
> something. Get out of the house.*

Get a job. Something. I just don't
know what or when or how to pull
myself away. I feel like she's still
here. Still needing me. It's strange.

Come on, Drew. Tell it like it is.
It's not strange, Missy. She was
the biggest part of your life for
the past five years. Take all the time

you need. He pauses, and then,
How are things with Chris? Is he
living up to his end of the bargain?
Dad's attentiveness to Mom has

waned a bit. But will she admit
that to Drew? *Up to a point, I guess.*
He still works really long hours.
Still travels a lot, too. I'm not sure . . .

Is he still in the guest room?
Okay, that was direct. Asking it
like it is, if not telling it. I'm pretty
sure Drew won't want to hear

Mom's answer, which is not quick
to come. *No. I told him if we are to
have any chance at all, we need
to try and be husband and wife again.*

This pause is even longer. Gaga,
who has been roaming the house,
comes through the door, shimmies
into my lap, purring for attention.

Finally, Mom says, *I'm not sure
it's working. I mean, the sex is fine.
But I can't say it's like it used to be
before . . . her. I don't know. Maybe*

*it's me. I keep picturing them together.
Wondering if he's thinking about her
when he's with me. It's painful.
But my choices are limited right now.*

I understand, says Drew. I can
imagine the hurt look in his eyes.
He totally loves Mom. *Just know
you'll always have a place with me.*

Way Too Much Information

All the way around. It's not like
I didn't know about Dad's affair,
but I really don't need the details.
I am about to get up, move away
from the door, when I hear Drew

        ask, *And how about Shane?*
        How's he doing? Good question,

      one I want to hear Mom answer.
      On the surface, okay. He seems to be
      doing well in school. He and Alex
      are still going strong. But to tell you
      the truth, I'm worried about him.

      It's like he's collapsing inward,
      imploding, but without the "bang."
      Christian says it's his way of grieving
      and he'll get over it eventually.
      I hope he's right. I really do.

Oh, great. Now I'm a source of worry
for Mom, too. Like she needs more.

I Am Such a Loser

A fucking, no-good piece of crap.
All I do is feel sorry for myself.

What about Mom?
What about Dad?
And Gram and Gramps
and everyone else
who cared about Shelby?

What the hell is wrong with me?
I should be over this by now.

But I'm a mess.
A basket case.
I want to eat.
Want to sleep.
Want to fuck all day
like a Viagra poster boy.

And I can't do any of those things.
Because, as much as I want to,

Food just won't stay down.
When I sleep, I have nightmares.
And I can't fuck because
when I try all I do is cry.

Poor Alex

He wants to help, but doesn't know
        how, and I have no answers for him.

Still, I call him because I have no
        one else to call. He's at work, so I

get his voice mail. "Please come
        over as soon as you can. I need you."

Meanwhile, I gently put Gaga
        on my pillow, scratch her head

the way she likes. Then I sneak
        past Mom and Drew, who are all

wrapped up in each other and
        conversation about Dad and me.

I detour through the kitchen.
        Reach up to raid the alcohol stash.

Grab the first bottle—like booze
        roulette—and come away with what?

Absinthe. What the hell is that?
　　　　Guess I'll find out the hard way.

I close the back door quietly. Head
　　　　to the trailer, where my weed is stashed.

I roll a big fatty, light it up and take
　　　　a swig from the bottle. Whoa, Joe!

Absinthe is strong, and it comes
　　　　out my nose in a giant licorice-

flavored spray. Licorice and skunk,
　　　　a heady combination. One that tastes

better when not exhaled in a snort
　　　　from the nostrils. I look at the bottle.

Seventy percent alcohol. Holy
　　　　crap. On a mostly empty stomach,

I'm feeling dizzy already. Dizzy
　　　　and happy. And if a little makes me

happy, a lot should make me
　　　　ecstatic, right? One way to know.

The Bottle

Is a third gone when I happen
to notice the price tag. Sixty-four
ninety-nine. Yowza! I just drank

twenty-two dollars' worth of Absinthe.
And, you know, I'm close to ecstatic.
Except now I think about Mom,

all the crap she's going through.
And damn if she isn't worried
about me. I am plunging south

again when someone tries to open
the door. Good thing I locked it.
"Who's there?" Anxiety ripples.

Did someone smell the weed
and call the cops? A shimmer
of fear threatens my buzz. But

> then, *It's me, Shane. You asked
> me to come over, remember?*
> Alex. Shit. Duh. My fingers

don't want to work. That makes
me laugh, which only makes it
totally impossible to open the door.

"Hang on. I'm trying. Jus' wait
right there." Stupid. Where else
would he wait? And my speech

is a little blurred around the edges.
Finally, success. Alex stands on
the step, looking half-amused,

half-concerned. Ah, shit. *Um . . .*
Are you okay? He pushes inside.
Sniffs. *What* are *you drinking?*

"Absinthe. Ever tried it?
It's wicked, man." I offer
the bottle. He takes a tiny sip.

Grimaces. *Wicked is right.*
How much of that have you had?
My shrugs says too much. *All this?*

I Swear, If He Says

He's worried about me,
I'll go play in traffic.
> But all he says is, *Bet*
> *you'll have a headache*
> *tomorrow morning.*

"Yeah, but maybe I'll
actually sleep tonight."
> *You're having trouble*
> *sleeping? Maybe you*
> *should go to a doctor.*
> *Self-medicating isn't*
> *always the best way to go.*

Please don't say you're
worried. "I'll think about it."
> He pulls me into his arms,
> and I'm almost positive
> he's going to say it. But
> instead, he kisses me.
> *Maybe I can help you*
> *fall asleep. Want to try?*

Oh, Yeah, I Do

And I think maybe just one more
little taste of wicked strong booze
will help me become the Viagra
poster boy instead of a weeping

fool. I take a swallow. He refuses
one and I really, really think he's
going to say it now. Wait. Wow.
Am I challenging him on some

subconscious level? Whatever.
I leave the bottle by the little sink,
follow Alex back to the lumpy
bed. Hungry. But not for food.

Starving for his body. Famished
for his love. We tangle together,
and I am grateful that he takes
control. I'm a wreck. But less

of a wreck than I am without
him. And he never says it, even
if he wants to. At this moment
there is no worry. But still, I cry.

Alex

Without Him

Life
>   might be easier. He is
>   a major complication.
>   Something important
>   to stress about. But what

would
>   my days be like, emptied
>   of him? Scrubbed
>   clean of his warped humor.
>   His energy. His presence. I

have
>   been in love before and,
>   doubtless, would love again.
>   But could I love like this—
>   overwhelmed, overboard,

no
>   holds barred? He tells me
>   he's fine, that this strange
>   condition is temporary.
>   Says not to worry. But there is

meaning
>   behind his silence. His binging.
>   His extraordinary need. How
>   weak is he? And how strong am I?

I Want to Be Strong

But I swear I'm such a wuss
when it comes to some stuff.

Especially, anything having
to do with Lucas. Pretty much

whatever he asks, I can't say no
to. Case in point. Tonight

is Halloween. Bri always comes
over. And we always trick-or-treat

together. But Lucas wants to see
me and he's bringing Kurt along.

>   Bri broke up with Kurt weeks ago.
>   *He keeps touching me in places*
>
>   *that I don't want him to touch,* she
>   explained. *He doesn't understand "no."*

I wanted to tell her to lighten
up. That getting touched in those

places is actually not so bad.
That she might even like it if

she just gave it a chance. But
I didn't. I wussed out there, too.

And when she asked about trick-
or-treating I told her I thought

we were getting kind of old for it.
Didn't want to hurt her feelings

and say I'd rather hang out with Lucas.
I'm setting Kurt and Chloe up. Pretty

sure she won't mind him touching
those places. Mom's driving me

       over to Chloe's house. *Don't you*
       want some dinner first? Or will

       your friend's parents feed you?
       Chloe lives alone with her dad, who

works swing shift. But all I say
is, "I'm good. I had some soup."

I Did Have to Lie

When Mom asked why Bri
wasn't coming tonight. "She's not
feeling so hot," I told her. Any other
year, Mom would have talked to

Mrs. Carlisle about it. They used
to be really tight. Something has
come between them. Not really
sure what it is, but they don't go

out like they used to, or even
just get together for coffee.
Which is okay for a short time, but
not for good. Mom doesn't have

a whole lot of friends. She can't
afford to lose her best one. Which
makes me rethink what I'm doing
tonight. I don't want to lose my best

friend, either. Still, plans are plans.
I'm not changing this one now.
I'll call Bri and we can do something
this weekend. I'll make it up to her.

But I Am Curious

We are almost to Chloe's when
I get the nerve to ask Mom, "Did
you and Mrs. Carlisle have a fight?"

> Mom squirms obvious discomfort.
> *Not at all. Holly is just going*
> *through some stuff right now.*

"You mean, like a midlife crisis?
That's what Bri says—that her mom
is going through a creepy midlife crisis."

> That makes Mom smile. *I don't*
> *know about "creepy." It's not*
> *uncommon for women of our age.*

"Did you . . . have you . . . are you
going through one, too? Is that why
you and Mrs. Carlisle don't talk much?"

> Her smile falls away. *Harley,*
> *honey, that's not it at all. Don't*
> *worry. Everything's okay. Okay?*

Something About Her Denial

Makes me think everything is *not*
      okay. But we've arrived at Chloe's.

       Will someone bring you home?
            Don't forget it's a school night.

"I have a ride home and I promise
      not to be out past eleven." I watch

Mom drive away before going to
      the door. Chloe answers in a French

maid's costume that shows off pretty much
      everything. "Wow. You're brave."

       Always good to make a great first
            impression. Kurt is worth impressing?

"Oh, yeah." Not as worthy as Lucas, who
      I really hope she doesn't impress as much

as I think she might. My vampire outfit
      is sexy, but not completely see-through.

I totally have to quit wussing out.
      "Can I go change?" She points to a hall

            bathroom. *Help yourself. Want*
               a beer? I'm going to have one.

"Your father lets you have beer?"
      I call from the far side of the bathroom

            door. *Sort of,* she calls back. *He buys*
               twenty-four packs. Doesn't miss them.

One beer couldn't hurt, right?
      "Okay. If you're sure." I only tasted

beer once. Mom thought she was
      teaching me a lesson, and I guess

it worked. The beer was the color
      of coffee. And it tasted like how cat

pee smells. I took a couple of big sips
      anyway. Haven't touched beer since.

This Beer Is Light

Colored, and its smell isn't obnoxious.
And, though I told Mom I had eaten,
that was another lie. Half the can
makes me fuzzy-headed. I've started

on the second half when the doorbell
rings. Chloe steps back to let the boys
in. Lucas, who is dressed in a black
duster, boots and cowboy hat, checks

       her out. Whistles. *Well, hello there.*
       You can clean my bedroom any
       time. Long as I'm in it! Now he looks
       at me. *You look pretty good, too.*

Wow. Nice. Guess I should make
the introductions. "That's Lucas.
And that's Kurt. And thish is Chloe."
My mouth is a little fuzzy, too.

       Lucas notices. *Wait a minute.*
       What's that in your hand? Miller
       Lite? I thought you didn't drink.
       You're just full of surprises, aren't you?

The Guys Want a Beer, Too

Chloe goes to the kitchen, and
I follow her. "Won't your dad miss
those?" The last thing I need is for

> her dad to tell my mom I've been
> drinking. But she says, *Nah. He never
> keeps track. Can't drink it all, though.*

"I can't drink any more than this
one. I can't miss school tomorrow.
I've got a history test." Chloe rolls

> her eyes. *I know. I'm in your class,
> remember? Don't worry. We won't
> get drunk on a beer or two.* She might

not, but I'm feeling pretty buzzed.
She hands me a can for Lucas, and
we go back to the boys, who down

> their beers in a couple of big swigs.
> Lucas drapes his arm around my shoulder.
> *Ready for a little Halloween fun?*

His hand drops down over my boob,
and his fingers obviously play
with my nipple and I'm worried

that he thinks this beer means I'm
going to have sex with him, right here,
right now. "Uh . . . What kind of fun?"

> *Seriously? Trick-or-treating,*
> *of course. Emphasis on the "tricks."*
> That makes me just a little nervous,

but I can't say no. Chloe stashes
the beer cans outside in the recycling
bin and we all pile into Lucas's car.

The first thing he does is light up
a pipe stuffed with pot. He passes it
to me, and for a change I go ahead

> and take a small puff before handing
> it over the seat to Kurt. Chloe giggles
> and inhales a big drag. *Good stuff,*

she says, trying not to blow any
of it out. I don't know if it's good
or not. But whether it's the weed or

the beer or the combination, I am
definitely woozy. Do people really
like feeling this way? In the back,

Chloe and Kurt seem to have hit
it off. They're sitting really close,
and she's laughing at some dumb

joke he's just spouted. Then they get
really quiet and I think they must
be kissing, not that I want to get all

voyeuristic or anything. I'm glad
when Lucas parks the car in an upscale
neighborhood where, I'm sure, the candy

is plentiful. "Hey. What are we putting
our candy in? Did you bring a bag
or a pillowcase or something?"

The Question

Makes Lucas and Kurt bust up.
We'll be collecting pillowcases
from, um, some volunteers, says Kurt.

I have no idea what he means
until we get out of the car. Chloe
and I follow the guys, who scope

out the action on the street. They
wait for the kids with parents along
to go by. But when they spot a group

of older kids walking unaccompanied,
they motion for us to hide behind
a tall, unlit hedge. As the kids

pass by, the guys jump and yell, *Boo!*
It scares the bejesus out of them.
Then the boys swipe their candy and run.

Nothing else to do but run, too.
It was mean, but it isn't the worst
trick Lucas and Kurt play tonight.

Chloe
The Worst Trick

The guys play tonight
isn't stealing candy from
middle schoolers. That's

                    funny,

really, especially the way
those kids yell to come back,
like we would. What's sort of

                    unfunny

is smashing jack-o'-lanterns
on pretty front porches and
squishing chocolate bars into

                    Depends,

and leaving them on the front
seats of unlocked cars. Still,
we laugh and go along. But

                    on

the far side of funny is when
Harley says she's going to be
sick, and Lucas asks Kurt, *Is*

                    your

phone handy? And when
she falls on her knees and
pukes up her guts, it's in full

                    view

of an active camera.

Funny

How fast word spreads
when the word that's spreading
is "pregnant." I told one friend

and by the next day pretty much
the whole school knew. Okay,
maybe that's a slight exaggeration.

Let's just say by the next day,
people who used to admire me
seemed to be looking down on me

or avoiding eye contact completely.
There were some notable exceptions.
Audrey marched straight up, gave

> me a big ol' hug. *I know it's hard.*
> *But you're doing the right thing. I wish*
> *I would have been as strong as you.*

She's the only person who has told
me I'm doing the right thing. It's good
to know someone is in my corner.

Still, I wasn't happy about Emily
opening her mouth. I caught
her at lunch. "Why did you tell?"

> You didn't say it was a secret,
> and I only told Margot. She's got
> a big mouth. I'm sorry, I guess.

"A huge mouth, apparently. But
whatevs." It was going to happen
eventually I've got to get used to it.

And it might not have been so bad
except I had to bump into Kristy.
I expected smugness. I got sympathy.

> Hey. I heard about the baby,
> she said, examining me for signs.
> I'm sorry about Dylan. He's a pussy.

Don't know if that means they're
together or not. And, really, what does
it matter? But I had to say something.

And What Slipped Out

Of my mouth was, "Yeah, he
        totally is." And in that moment,
        it hit me. Yeah, he totally is.

Weeks of hurt exploded in a flash
        of nuclear anger—a mushroom
        cloud stamped with the word "pussy."

He's nothing more than a fucking
        pussy, and who needs one of those
        for a father? Not my baby, for sure.

Except, it's still *our* baby. And why
        should he be able to deny that? No
        freaking way. He can't. He won't.

Goddamn it, what happened to my
        clear-cut life? Goals. Forward
        movement. Being in love. Swamped

with love. Six months ago I would
        have laughed in the face of anyone
        who claimed my love for Dylan—and

his reciprocal devotion—was all
        in my mind. It *was* real. It *is* real.
        I love him now more than ever.

Even if he is a pussy. Even if
        he is screwing Kristy. He can't love
        her. And how can he possibly not

love me? Just because there's
        a baby—half him, half me?
        How do I convince him to come

back? How can I make him see
        that the two of us can only be
        better when we become three?

I tried seducing him. It worked—
        for fifteen or twenty minutes. I tried
        cajoling him, which only got his back up.

I go for my ultrasound this afternoon.
        Will seeing a picture of our—his—
        baby make him understand the stakes?

I Sit Alone

In the waiting room. Other women
are also here solo, reading magazines

or checking their phones. The lucky
ones wait with their men, most

of whom look excited to be included.
They hold their partners' hands,

bounce them on their knees, as if
those hands are promises of what

will be in the aftermath of what has
already been. Some of the ladies

look ready to pop. Will I really get
that big? Have a giant balloon belly?

Right now, it's just a little pooch,
but it is noticeable and it's growing.

                    A nurse comes to the door. *Mikayla?*
                    I get up and follow her, excitement

building. I'm going to see my baby.
We go into a small room and the nurse

>   says, *There's a hospital gown.*
>   *Put it on, open in the front. You*
>
>   *can keep your undergarments*
>   *on. I'll be back in a few minutes.*

She closes the door and I do as
instructed, really wishing I could

go pee. They made me drink four
glasses of water. A full bladder

is supposed to make baby viewing
easier. I get back up on the padded

>   table, just as a knock comes on the door.
>   The tech pokes his head in. *All ready?*

"Sure." The guy is kind of cute, and
I'm most of the way naked, which

makes me a little uncomfortable,
even if he *has* seen it lots of times

before. The nurse returns and watches
as the tech rubs a cold gel substance

>> on my belly. *Okay,* he says. *This device*
>> *is called a transducer. It sends sound*

>> *waves into your body, where they reflect*
>> *off internal structures, including your baby.*

He moves the transducer around
my tummy, tells me to hold my breath

>> several times. *Now the sound waves*
>> *reflect back to the transducer, which*

>> *creates an on-screen image of your baby.*
>> *Look at all those fingers and toes. Ten*

>> *of each, I'd say. And . . . do you want*
>> *to know if it's a boy or a girl?*

"Yes. Please." It comes out a whisper
and when he says it's a girl, I start to cry.

Something About Knowing

She's a girl—that I can use the word
    "she" and contemplate pink dresses—
        makes everything completely real.

Dr. Ortega comes in to discuss what
    the ultrasound shows —a healthy
        little girl with all her parts in all

the right places. And while I keep
    nodding my head, I'm only half
        listening. I keep looking at the printout

they gave me of my daughter *in*
    utero at twenty-one weeks. I think
        she looks like a girl, and imagine

what she'll look like when she's born.
    Will she have dark hair like Dylan's?
        Blue eyes like mine? Will she have

perfect pitch and sing soprano, or
    will she pitch a perfect softball?
        She moves inside me—a dragonfly.

I Get Dressed

Take a totally necessary pee.
        Clutching the grainy photograph
of my baby, I am about to leave

               when someone says, *Hello.*
Mikayla, right? It's Mrs. Trask.
               I've only seen her a couple of times.

The last was at her daughter's wake.
        She is thin. Pale. Drawn. "Oh, hello.
Yes, I'm Mikayla. How are you?"

               She shrugs. *Okay. It's been a hard*
few weeks, but it's getting a little
               better. I miss her terribly, of course.

I can't even imagine having such
        a sick child, let alone dealing with
her death. "I'm so sorry about Shelby."

               Thank you. And . . . For the first time,
she notices my condition. *Looks*
               like congratulations are in order?

That makes me smile. "Depends
    on who you're asking. I just had
my ultrasound. It's—she's—a girl."

        I offer the printout like it's great
    treasure and she takes it the same
        way. *She is a girl. Wow. This reminds*

        me of when I got Shelby's ultrasound
    results. I so wanted a little girl,
        and I was nervous she'd be a boy.

        I tried for eleven years . . . She sputters
    a little, but continues, *It was the happiest*
        day of my life. Her eyes fill with tears,

        and she wipes them with one hand,
    returns the photo with the other. *Well,*
        congratulations. To you. And whoever.

I Drive Home

Caught in a tornado
of confusion. Life
isn't fair. Why me?
Why did I get pregnant
with a baby girl no one
wants? I mean, I think
I want her, but maybe
I don't. Not if I have to
raise her alone. Why me,

when women like Mrs.
Trask try for years to
get pregnant. Hope for
years to have a little girl.
And then they succeed,
only to lose that daughter
to a fatal illness? Total
suckage. I'm having a girl.

I have the pic to prove
it. But who can I share
it with? No one cares
but me. Not even her
daddy. Not my friends.
Not my parents or my
grandparents. Life isn't fair.

Kristy

Life Isn't Fair

I

have Dylan back. But look
at the circumstances. It wasn't
because he came to his senses,
decided what he felt for Mikayla
was more lust than love. He still

wanted

her when he dumped her. The only
reason he left was because
he knocked her up and, despite
his demands, she refused to take
the easy way out. I never expected

to

respect her. If circumstances
were different, I might even like
her, and learning the truth
has made me like Dylan a lot less.
It would be so much easier if I could

gloat.

Instead, on an almost cellular
level, I kind of want to get even
for her. "Pussy" doesn't cover it.
Dylan is a major asshole.

Shane
Ducking for Cover

Lately, that's what it feels like
       I'm doing. Hiding out. Getting by.
       Just barely. I'm faking my way

through school. Most of my teachers
       don't care. They're just hanging in there
       long enough to qualify for a pension.

But one or two have noticed
       how I show up for class physically,
       though I'm not really present at all.

Ms. Luther, my creative writing
       teacher, keeps using the *D* word.
       D, for depression. I suppose that has

a lot to do with the poetry I keep
       handing in. On time. As assigned.
       The problem is, she lets us choose

what we want to write about. Death
       figures prominently in mine. Death,
       externally, and death internally.

And Also Death as a Character

This is one of the poems she liked:

Death waits impatiently
outside my door. We are betrothed
and he wants to set a date.
It will be a marriage of shadow
and light, matrimony in sepia.

Death waltzes on my lawn —
a delicate dance meant for two.
But I'm not sure of the steps,
and I don't want to look like a fool.
So I watch from behind the glass.

Death calls to me in breathless
whispers. Coaxing. Coaxing.
His voice is soothing, and when
he hums, his song is a lullaby.
I close my eyes. And listen.

She Gave Me an A

On that one. But then she called me in
for a private talk. When I got there,

> copies of my poems were on her desk.
> *I'm mandated by law to report what I see*

> *as a possible — probable — problem.*
> *Beyond that, I like you, Shane, and*

> *I just want to make sure you're okay.*
> Yeah, yeah, I know she meant well.

That she's *worried* about me. But somehow
it just pisses me off. So, now I'm sitting

here, seething, waiting for my counselor,
Mr. Albert, to call me into his office. Apparently,

I'm not the only student with issues.
I've been here close to an hour. Finally,

> the door opens. Out comes one problem
> kid. And now it's my turn. *Come in, Shane.*

I'd really like to wipe that phony
smile from his face. Maybe with acid.

Except then he'd look like the Joker
or Two-Face or something. He motions

for me to sit in the big overstuffed
chair. Looks like I'm in here for

the long haul. He pulls a short stack
of papers from his desk. Leafs through.

>   *This is some interesting poetry,*
>   *Shane. Pretty good, but there seems*
>
>   *to be a common theme here. Do you*
>   *want to talk about it?* He heaves a sigh.

"Not really." I think I've disappointed
him. But what does he want me to say?

>   He sighs again. *Sometimes talking*
>   *about what's bothering you can help.*

A Slow Burn

Creeps out of my collar, up my neck.
My ears must be the color of cranberries.
"What's bothering me is that my little

sister died. She was only four. Now,
how can talking about that help?
No amount of talk can bring her back."

       Mr. Albert swallows and his Adam's
       apple dips really low. *I'm sorry about*
       your sister. He thinks a second, then

       adds, *Did you know that the death*
       of a loved one can result in depression?
       It's really very common. And treatable.

Great. Now they'll want to lock me
away in some crazy ward. "Look.
I'm sad about Shelby. Sad, and angry.

But I'm not depressed and I don't
need treatment. All I need is time, and
for people to quit worrying about me."

He's not quite ready to let it drop.
Okay, so tell me. Are you eating?
Sleeping? Do you hang out with

your friends? Or are you keeping
to yourself? Your schoolwork has
slipped a little. Trouble concentrating?

Jeez, man. Is he spying on me?
I try to joke my way out. "My
mom's cooking sucks and sleep

is overrated. Look, Mr. A., I swear
I'm okay. I'll study harder and bring
my grades up. Thanks for caring, though."

> *In my opinion, you are displaying*
> *classic symptoms of depression.*
> *I'm going to call your parents and*
>
> *give them the names of a couple*
> *of good therapists.* Now he smiles.
> *Just don't shoot the messenger.*

If I Only Had a Gun

But I don't and I wouldn't want
         to go to prison for offing an idiot.

Anyway, he's welcome to call
         the house. Dad is currently in China,

and Mom drove Gram to Davis,
         California, for some kind of medical

tests. They won't be home until
         tonight. "May I go now?" Ever so

polite. He nods, and as I leave,
         I hear him go straight to the phone,

no doubt to tell our voice mail
         about his concerns. Appreciate

your effort, Mr. A. Really, I do. But
         Mom and Dad won't get that message.

I Decide to Skip

My last class of the day. I was
called to the office. Waited an hour.
Was baited for another thirty minutes.
I think I deserve to go home. Besides,

> I really don't want to talk to Tara.
> I can just hear Mr. A.'s response
> to that. *Do you hang out with your
> friends? Or are you keeping to yourself?*

It's not that I want to keep to myself.
But Tara will know something's up,
and if I tell her what's going on,
she'll offer some sage advice. I've had

way too much of that for one day already.
The empty house welcomes me
with its silence. I check the answering
machine first thing. Yep. A red light

> blinks. The first message is from
> Mom. *We should be home by nine.
> Be sure to feed yourself, okay?* Damn.
> She's worried about my diet, too?

Message two: Good ol' Mr. Albert.
Blah-de-blah-de-blah-blah. Delete!
I'm feeling pretty smug, until
I get to the last message. From Alex.

Hey, S. Check your cell voice mail.
When was the last time I did? Absent-
minded. *Trouble concentrating.* That's
me. I dig for my cell. Find four calls,

one message, all from Alex. *Where
are you? Sorry I haven't called
for a couple of days, but I've been
pretty sick. Thought it was the flu,*

*but it isn't getting better. I'm going
in to see my doctor this afternoon.
I'll call when I have more info.
Love you. Miss you. Everything okay?*

God

He sounded like shit.
And he wants to know
if everything is okay
with me. I miss him,
too. Last time I saw
him we argued about

sports, of all stupid
things. I thought he
was mad at me, and
I've been nursing
personal anger. But
it's probably a good

thing we haven't been
together. I don't need
to get the flu or what-
ever he's got. Nothing
to do now but wait for
him to call me back.

Meanwhile, I go into
the kitchen, scrounge
for something to serve
as breakfast, lunch and
dinner. Frozen Chinese.
I'll even get my vegetables.

Beef Broccoli Consumed

I am considering Dad's alcohol stash when
Alex calls. "Hey. What did the doctor say?"

> *Well, turns out it's pneumonia. But not*
> *PCP. Pneumocystis pneumonia would*

indicate his T-cell count had dropped way
low. Something that shouldn't happen,

> considering his drug regimen. But there
> are exceptions to every rule. *So it's even*

> *more meds for a few days. And no kissing*
> *until the sputum is under control.* Lovely.

I tell him to get well and keep in touch.
Then I reach for one of Dad's bottles.

Something strong to help me forget that
while HIV may be manageable, it's also

unpredictable. I pour a teacup full of
bourbon. Think maybe I'll also borrow

one of Mom's antidepressants. Whiskey
and Prozac. Bet I'll sleep great tonight.

Alex

I Sleep Great

Most nights. Don't toss
and turn thinking about
my relationship with time.
What's the point of

worrying

about something I have
no power over? The old
adage, "Live every day as
if it might be your last"

doesn't

work for me. I have to
plan a future, or just hang
it up right now. While
there's no real way to

change

the final outcome, how
I live until I get there
is completely up to me.
And if there's

one thing

I want people to reflect
on when I'm gone, it's that
I faced my fate squarely,
never tried to run.

I'm Running

With a fast crowd and I'm not
sure how I got here. Only something
like three months ago I was a total
loser nerd. I wanted to change

that, but I never expected to go
this far. In Carson, I'm getting a rep,
and it's from hanging out with Chloe.
I like her. But I'm kind of scared

of her, too. She's fearless, especially
when it comes to risky behaviors.
The kind they warn us about in health
class. Doesn't stop her, and when

I'm with her, it doesn't really stop
me. I feel like a different person.
What's weird is nobody seems to
have noticed. Not Mom. Not Dad.

Not Cassie. Adults get so caught
up in their own problems, they lose
sight of their kids. Keep believing
we're angels when we're so not.

When I'm Busy Running

I think that's good. When I have
         time to consider the overall picture,

I still want someone to care enough
         to slow me down. The only one who

seems to anymore is Bri. I can't tell
         her everything. She already lectures

me. If she knew about the weed
         and stuff, she'd probably disown me.

She doesn't really like Lucas,
         so when we're together, like now,

I try not to talk about him too
         much. The problem is, I don't have

a lot of other stuff *to* talk about.
         "You're coming to the wedding, aren't

you? You'll die when you see me
         in my bridesmaid dress. It's totally rad."

What's so rad about it? Is it tie-dye
or something weird like that?

"Not that weird. It's scarlet. And short.
        And pretty low-cut. Cassie had to buy me

a strapless bra, with major push-up power
        to help me fill it out. I found cleavage!"

                She laughs. *You've always had a lot*
more of that than I do. Call me flat.

We are in her room, listening to
        Pink sing about how she wants to be

somebody else. "Do you ever feel
        like that? Like you have to change

everything about yourself to get
        where you want to be, or think you do?"

                Now she's quiet. Finally, she answers,
"Think you do" says a lot, you know?

It Does, and So Does Her Response

And I'm really glad that, despite
everything else going on in my life,
she is still here. Still my best friend.

We talk about her—now obviously—
pregnant sister, who plans to stay in
school until the semester break.

> *Dylan broke up with her. Can*
> *you believe it? And he's going out*
> *with his old girlfriend again. Jerk.*

I can believe it. "Boys are dogs."
But, sometimes, so are girls. Which
prompts, "What's up with your mom?"

> Bri shrugs. *I have no idea. She's*
> *here, but barely. I know she misses*
> *your mom, though. She needs a friend.*

Now I shrug. "My mom's a prude.
She needs to learn not to judge . . ."
Shit . . . Shoot. "No one should be judged."

I Don't Know

If that's true. I only know
I wouldn't want to be judged.
Especially not by my best
friend. Mrs. Carlisle isn't
perfect. But neither is Mom.

What's weird is, Bri is
more like my mom and
I am more like hers. Except,
am I, really? Because when
I'm here, goofing off with

Bri, I feel more like the real
me. The Harley who runs
with Lucas and Kurt and
Chloe is a fake. But I'm not
sure how to get rid of her.

If I did, would I get bored
and restless and angry because
everyone would treat me like
a child again? I'm afraid
it's too late to turn back now.

So, After Mom Picks Me Up

I'll be going to my dad's, who
allows me to go out on Saturday
night. Mom would probably croak
if she knew. But he and I made a pact

> not to tell her. *As long as you stay
> out of trouble, there's no reason
> for her to know,* is what he said.
> *But if you get in trouble, I do, too.*

I promised to be good, and so far
have managed to avoid any sort of
trouble, although Halloween was close.
Some busybody saw us smashing

pumpkins and called the cops.
Luckily, Chloe knew a couple
of alley shortcuts and we got away.
I thought I'd pee my pants. Instead,

> I heaved beer. Not attractive.
> Even worse, Kurt took a pic.
> When I asked him why, he said,
> *To commemorate the occasion.*

I had no idea what he meant
by that, but the next day when
I signed on to my Facebook,
I saw he had tagged me in a picture.

I couldn't believe he had posted
that one, with my name on it. You
couldn't see my face, but you could
pretty much guess what I was doing.

I untagged myself and called Lucas.
"Why would he do that?" I demanded.
"Tell him to take it down! Please?"
Lucas's first reaction was to laugh.

> *Ah, come on. It's just a joke.*
> *Where's your sense of humor?*

Kurt removed it eventually, and
no one I know has said anything
about it. But that was just so mean.
And Lucas thought it was funny.

It's Late Afternoon

When Mom gets to Bri's. She comes
into the kitchen, where Bri and I are

helping Mrs. Carlisle chop vegetables
for soup. My hands smell like celery

and onions. Weird, but I kind of like
it. *Looks like you've got some great*

helpers, Mom says. *Do you have a few*
minutes to catch up? It's been a while.

Bri's mom looks pleased. *Of course.*
It has been a while. Will you excuse us,

girls? The potatoes and carrots need
to be cut up. Something to drink, Andrea?

Mom declines and they go sit at the big
kitchen table in the dining area.

Bri and I keep busy with our knives,
but we both tune into the conversation

on the other side of the room. It is friend
to friend, unstrained, at least at first.

They Start with the Usual

How have you been stuff. Move
quickly to deeper sounding.

> Mrs. C.: *How is Marissa doing?*
> *Things still good with Chris and her?*

> Mom: *Stable, I guess. But she got*
> *the wild idea to look into in-vitro.*
> *She went through all kinds of tests.*
> *Ultimately, the doctors told her*
> *if she really wants another baby*
> *to consider adoption. I'm not sure*
> *how Chris feels about diapers and*
> *formula and sleepless nights.*

> Mrs. C.: *No kidding. I'm not sure how*
> *I feel about it, either. And it's coming.*

I notice Mikayla hovering silently
on the far side of the doorway.

> Mom: *So Mikayla's still set on keeping*
> *the baby? What about the father?*

Mrs. C.: *Dylan wants nothing to do with the baby or Mikayla. Yes, she's determined to raise the baby on her own. Although she won't really be doing that, will she? She'll start Nevada Virtual Academy in January, so she will be able to graduate. But after that . . . she has no concrete ideas about what to do after that.*

Mikayla backs away from the door,
and I'm the only one who has seen her.

Mrs. C.: *Harley says your ex is getting married. Is that a good or bad thing?*

Mom: *Good, I guess. I didn't care much for Cassandra at first. But overall, I think she's been a plus for Steve. Not that I'd care, except Harley's relationship with him has improved. Can you believe they invited me to the wedding? I wouldn't even consider it, except Harley insists I come, to see her in her dress.*

She looks over at me and winks.
I just keep peeling potatoes.

> Mom lowers her voice, but not
> enough so we can't hear. *How's Jace?*

> Mrs. C.: *Working a lot. Trying to
> avoid decisions. Confrontations.
> It's been pretty tense around here.*

She doesn't elaborate and I wonder
if she would if Bri and I weren't here.

> Mrs. C.: *What about you? Still dating
> that doctor?* Total subject change.

> Mom: *Actually, yes. In fact . . .* She looks
> at me again. *He's escorting me to Steve's
> wedding. And I just invited him to join
> us for Thanksgiving at Marissa's. Mom
> and Dad will be there, so I'm kind of
> introducing him to the family. Is that okay?*

The question was to me. I shrug.
"If he makes you happy, I'm happy."

Brianna

Is She Happy?

I swear, Harley used to be
the happiest person ever.
Always smiling. Always joking.
Never worrying about

what

the next day might bring.
Now, she's so serious,
not nearly as much fun.
And though she says nothing

has happened

to change her, I know that
nothing is named Lucas.
Yet when I asked her if she's
in love with him, much

to my

surprise, she said not really.
So why does she need to be
with him all the time? Why
does she choose him over her

best friend?

Mikayla
Sometimes You Choose, You Lose

Maybe that's just the way of things.
I mean, forever, I was a winner.

> Popular.
> Ace boyfriend.
> Great grades.
> Decent home.

On my way. Today, I am a loser.

> Lost friends.
> Lost boyfriend.
> Declining grades.
> Declining home life,

with parents who can't get along.

Most of it came from bad choices.

> Wrong friends.
> Wrong boyfriend.
> Wrong night,
> wrong time of the month

not to insist on a condom.
I can't fix my parents, of course.

But I can rethink becoming a parent myself.

I Suppose, Sooner or Later

Pretty much everyone who is on
their way hits a dead end at some
point. Has to backtrack. Detour.
Choose an alternate route.

But how many people nose into
a brick wall and have to stay
there, no foreseeable way out?
Because that's where I am now.

I can see no way out for nineteen
years, give or take. I'm not quite
eighteen myself yet. How can I
dedicate more years to my baby

than I have experienced? I'm not
afraid of changing diapers or losing
sleep for late-night feedings. I'm scared
I don't have the tools to teach her

what she needs to know. I'm scared
I won't be able to give her necessary
things. I'm scared of messing her up
because I'm pretty messed up myself.

Still, Every Day

With her inside me, growing
            into a real baby, becoming
                        more and more human,

makes her more and more
            my child. Every time she
                        moves, kicking and pushing

and turning somersaults
            against the swelling balloon
                        of my belly, our connection

deepens. I've started to think
            about names. Amanda. Jasmine.
                        Claire. I'm looking into Lamaze

classes. Mom says I'm nuts,
            that they invented epidurals
                        for a very good reason. But I kind

of want to go natural if I can.
            To give the baby the best possible
                        start. Because after that, who knows?

Dad Being a Lawyer

He insists that Dylan must take
responsibility for child support,
whether or not he wants to.

>   *Once the baby is born, you must*
>   *establish paternity. Dylan can*
>   *volunteer to take the test, but if*
>
>   *he refuses you can get a court*
>   *order to make him. Dylan is*
>   *the only possible father, right?*

I should be insulted, I guess.
But on the other hand, it's a fair
question, and one that will be

asked by more people than Dad.
Dylan totally is the baby's father.
I've done my homework, too.

Dad is right. Dylan can't just
decide he's completely out of
the picture. Even if he never sees

his daughter, he has to help take
care of her financially. The question
really is: Will I make him step up?

But what if he did see her, and what
if he fell in love with her? Would
he remember falling in love with me,

and would he love me again?
March is too far away to find out.
I haven't even had the chance

to tell him we're having a girl.
He avoids me at school, and he
won't take my calls, and I'm not

about to deliver that news via
voice mail. But he can't keep away
from me forever. One way or

another, Dylan Douglas will see
the ultrasound pics of his baby
girl. And today will be the day.

Mom Always Says

When I set my mind on something
I am a force to be reckoned with.

Today I will be gravity—subtle,
but powerful and undeniable.

I see Dylan walking with friends
a few times, and once with Kristy.

But I need to find him alone, and
it finally happens right before fifth

period. He's at his locker pulling
out books. My approach is silent.

"Hey." I keep my voice gentle,
and when he looks at me, I'm sure

there's a hint of love in his eyes.
"I wanted to show you something."

> *I don't want to be late for trig.*
> His tone is harsh. *What is it?*

Carefully, I extract the printout
from my notebook. "Our daughter."

He studies it for a second, then shakes
his head, as if to clear it of confusion.

> I don't know what you want me
> to say, Mikki. It barely even looks
>
> like a baby. And it doesn't change
> a thing. I've got to go now.

"Please, Dylan. You're her daddy.
She's going to need you in her life."

I touch his hand. "I need you in my life.
But she is what's important." He jerks

> his arm away. *Not to me, she's not.*
> *Now, leave me the fuck alone, Mikki.*

He slams his locker and practically
runs down the hallway. My eyes sting

acid tears. "I am so going to make you pay!"
The words echo in the empty corridor.

My Last Class

Of the day is home ec.
A no-brainer elective.
I know how to cook.
But sometimes you need
an extra few credits.

> In the Thanksgiving spirit,
> we are experimenting with
> stuffing. *I hope next week*
> *you'll volunteer to make*
> *something a little different*
>
> *for your family's holiday*
> *meal,* says Mrs. Brennan.
> *And I hope every single one*
> *of you has something special*
> *to be grateful for.* She gives

me a knowing glance, and
I'm halfway to giving her
something special to suspend
me for when someone comes
up behind me, lays a hand

on my shoulder. *We haven't
talked in a while. Maybe we
should.* Tyler. I turn and look
up into his eyes. *I don't know
if you want to. But I'd like to.*

No one has been this nice
to me in weeks, and even
though there is a prohibition
against male/female touching
on campus, I slide my arms

around him. Lay my ear
against his heartbeat. And cry.
A soak-through-the-shirt-all-
the-way-to-the-chest-hair
kind of tears. Mrs. Brennan

doesn't say a word and neither
does Ty, or anyone else here.
They just let me weep into
the onion-celery-sausage-
sage-scented air. Thanksgiving.

I Think I'm Having

An out-of-body experience.

I am not holding myself upright.

Ty is. Ty, who I've known for

years. Ty, who has dated friends.

And enemies. Ty, who has never

touched me before, at least not

in any significant way. Yet, at this

moment, he supports my weight.

The weight of my muscles, bones.

The weight of my psyche, which

hangs heavily. The slight weight

of my baby. The weight of my weight.

That Weight

Is oppressive. And yet, knowing
somebody cares enough to prop me
up makes me believe I can come out
okay on the other side. Just maybe.

I tell him I'm sorry.
                    He says not to worry.
I beg him to understand.
                    He promises to do his best.

And, considering how many people
make promises they can't keep,
doing his best is all I can ask for.
Plus, in the haven of his arms

I find some slender ray
                    of hope that on the far
horizon a ghost girl lingers.
                    Mikayla Jean Carlisle,

as worthy as she ever was of fairy-tale
love. And why did that train of thought
even wind up on the same page
with me, anchored in Tyler's harbor?

Tyler
Fairy-Tale Love

Isn't something to aspire to.
At least, not if you dig down
beyond Disneyfied retellings.

                                        Original

versions are pretty sick. Take
Sleeping Beauty. The cartoon
portrays Prince Charming's love
as pure, but as first written,

                                        sin

drives a randy married king
to rape a comatose beauty,
leaving her pregnant with twins.
When the queen finds out, she

                                        is

rightly quite pissed, and orders
the castle chef to cook the kids
for dinner. Instead, he tells
the king, who decides

                                        a

nubile, fertile fox is preferable
to a murderous hag. Guess who
winds up roasted, sliced and

                                        given

a prominent place on the table?

There Are a Dozen Place Settings

On our Thanksgiving table.
That, in itself, is remarkable.
The guest list is kind of crazy:

Mom and Dad
Gram and Gramps
Aunt Andrea and Dr. Malik
Steve and Cassandra
Harley, Chad and me
(Plus Shelby!)

It was Gram's idea to include her.
An outsider could not understand
the meaning of that gesture. Shelby:

Never nibbled turkey skin
Never tasted pecan pie
(Did their magical perfumes
mean anything at all to a nose
completely uninfluenced
by a food-virgin tongue?)

I wish, just one time, I would have
touched some tiny taste of ambrosia
to her lips, some forbidden pleasure:

New York cheesecake
Crème brûlée
Pineapple sorbet
Hot fudge sundae
(With vanilla bean Häagen-Dazs
and homemade whipped cream)

And I wish, on more than one occasion,
she could have sat upright at our dining
room table, one of a family of four. Shelby:

Comfortable in a velvet chair
Holding her own silver fork
Over one of Mom's good china plates
Wiping her mouth with a linen napkin
Talking about her favorite Disney show
(Or taking a drive with me)

I Fantasize About That

As the very much still alive
(at least in most ways) rest of the guest
list sits down to dinner. Even without
Shelby, it's a very strange cast of players.

All of whom pretend it's not. All
of whom, for whatever reasons, are grateful
to be able to pretend it's not. And that,
for my own reasons, includes me.

The dialogue, stilted at first, begins
to pick up speed as the food arrives.

> Gram (putting bowls on the table):
> *Sorry Alex couldn't join us. How is he?*

"He's feeling better, but thought he should
spend Thanksgiving with his family."

> Gramps (spooning candied yams):
> *Hey, now. We're his extended family.*

> Cassandra (passing the cranberry
> sauce): *Yay for extended families!*

Steve (slugging fine wine): *Yes.*
Thanks very much for the invite.

Chad (eyeing Dad's turkey slicing):
Ditto. Real food for a change.

Mom (quickly to avert a retort):
Everything set for your wedding?

Cassie (overjoyed): *I hope so! Only*
a week away. You are *all coming?*

Mom and Dad exchange curious
glances with Gram and Gramps.
I ask the question they're afraid to.
"Were we invited?" Pretty sure not.

Harley (panicked): *Oh my God.*
Didn't I mail your invitations?

Aunt Andrea: *Harley! How could . . . ?*
The doctor puts his hand on her arm.

Cassie: *You didn't? But you prom—*

Chad (guffawing): *Way to go, Harl!*

It Is Dad Who Comes to the Rescue

He bangs down the carving knife,
like a judge wielding his gavel. *Okay,*
everyone, let's fill our plates and say
grace. We will all be at the wedding.

The relief, at least on the far end
of the table, is palpable. The food
goes around at dizzying speed, a blur
of, as Chad called it, real food.

Now Dad motions for everyone
to link hands. *Heavenly Father.*
Bless this table and all who sit here
surrounded by your presence.

Allow us to abandon our mourning
in favor of coming celebration.
Forgive our mistakes and please
let those who have been hurt by them

find the grace to forgive them, too.
We are thankful for this bounty,
each other, and you. In Christ's
name we pray. Amen. Echoed amens.

Waves of Food

And drifts of conversation make me
a little woozy. No one seems to notice
that I pick at my food, much like
Cassandra does. She probably wants
to make sure she can fit in her size-skinny
wedding dress, which I will,
apparently, see if Dad has his way.

> Eventually nothing much besides
> gravy is left on the dinner plates.
> *Gentlemen,* says Gramps. *Why
> don't we clear so the ladies can
> bring out the pie. I've had a peek.
> Hope you all saved lots of room.*

There are a few groans and several
*yum*s and with all the guys helping,
the dirties disappear quickly. I stash
a few bites of leftover turkey for Gaga,
who I had to leave shut up in my room.
Earlier, I caught her on the counter
sniffing the cooling fowl. Feline!

I take it to her, a peace offering, and
by the time I get back to the table,

it is covered with pies. Lemon. Cherry.
Pecan. Apple. And the requisite pumpkin.
The girls are busy cutting and taking
orders. I ask for a small slice of cherry.

Soon, everyone has a piece, even
Cassandra, who managed the thinnest
wedge of apple I have ever seen.
Now Gramps says, *I think the chefs
of this fabulous feast deserve a toast.*
He pops a bottle of champagne,
then another. Mom and Dad find
crystal flutes in the hutch, Steve
helps fill them. Gramps glances
around the table. *How about the kids?*

Generously (foolishly?), the parents
nod okay. Interestingly enough, it
is Harley who grabs a glass first.
Chad and I follow, and everyone
raises a toast to Mom and Gram
and Andrea, who brought the veggies
and the lemon pie. I sip the sparkly
slowly. No use calling attention
to myself. Besides, in my room I have
something stronger stashed for later.

It's Really Sort of Surprising

That my parents haven't missed
the alcohol that keeps vanishing
from the kitchen cabinet. To be

sure, there was a lot—bottles bought
and bottles gifted over the years.
I keep pulling them forward,

but sooner or later you'd think
someone would notice. Maybe
they will. And maybe that's what

I'm hoping for, that Mom or Dad
will notice and care enough to say
something. Tonight was nice, I guess.

But you have to wonder where
this small sense of family retreats
to when it isn't a holiday. I'm sure

part of the problem used to be Shelby.
Doesn't seem fair that it took her
dying to bring us closer again.

Post Pie

The guests retire to the living
room. Gramps opens the piano
and this time decides to sing
amped-up Christmas carols.

> *The season is almost upon us,*
> he says. *But before we begin,*
> *Leah and I have an announcement.*

He looks at Gram, who says, *We*
made an offer on a little house
and five acres in Pleasant Valley.
It's a short sale and they're anxious.
We hope to be in before Christmas.

> *It's a sweet little place,* adds Gramps.
> *We like it because it's halfway between*
> *Reno and Carson. Equidistant to our*
> *girls and our brilliant grandkids.*

"Brilliant, huh? I don't know for
sure, Harley," I say, "but I think
he's fishing for help with the moving."

> Gramps smiles. *Not only brilliant,*
> *but intuitive. Andrea, pick a song.*

She Asks for "White Christmas"

And, though Gramps does his best
        to rock it out, it's hard to get past
sounding too much like Bing Crosby.

I move stealthily toward the back
        of the room. "I'm going to check
on Gaga," I explain to no one at all.

        I am halfway down the hall when
      footsteps fall in behind me. *Who's*
        Gaga? asks Harley, with Chad in tow.

Damn. Almost got away. "She's my
        kitten." Oops. Mistake. I should
have said my vicious Rottweiler.

        Really? I didn't know you had a cat.
    I thought . . . Oh. Well, can we meet
       her? I'm not much for caroling.

What can I do but let them in?
        Gaga is in her usual pillow palace,
purring and burping up turkey.

Harley plops down beside her.
*Oh, she's so adorable. Where
did you get her? I want a kitten!*

I tell her Alex could probably
pull one out from under a sagebrush
for her. And that reminds me,

"I need to call my boyfriend. Put
on some music if you want." Chad
goes over to my iPod dock as I reach

for my cell. I dial Alex, who answers
right away, but can't talk, except
to say, *I love you. See you tomorrow?*

After my too-quick goodbye, I notice
a text from Lucas. Probably wants to
sell me some weed. But, no. It's a pic.

Of a naked girl. *Look familiar?*
On closer inspection, she does. Oh,
my God. "Uh, Harley. Is this you?"

Chad
Naked Girl Pics

Delivered randomly
to my cell phone are generally
fine by me. Oh yes,

I

got this one, too, at pretty
much the same time, which
means it's a blanket send, I

think.

Last I heard, Harley and Lucas
were still a thing, which disturbs
me deeply. What does

she

see in him? I did try to warn
her that he is not the nicest
guy, and that he obviously

has

an agenda. She told me not
to worry, that she understands
his motivation, but that it's not

a problem

because she's got a handle
on things. I'd say she totally
underestimated him.

What Is His Problem?

How could Lucas do this to me?
Not only did he get me to take
those pictures, but he actually
sent one of them to people I know?

Including my cousin and almost
stepbrother? "Delete it! Now!
Please?" On second thought,
"Wait. Let me answer it."

I text him back: REALLY CUTE
PIC. THANKS FOR SHARING. DID
YOU KNOW THIS IS MY COUSIN?
How many people did the jerk

send this to? His whole address
book? Must be, otherwise why
would Shane have gotten it?
Holy cow. Did he send it to girls,

too? I'm fricking dying here.
Wait. He's friends with Chad.
I glance over at him, and his
expression tells me. "You, too?"

He nods. *Me, too. Sorry. Want
me to kick his ass?* He looks as
embarrassed as I feel—all purple
faced and fidgety. Poor guy.

Poor guy? What about me?
Unreasonably, laughter bubbles
out around the sob stuck in
my throat. Why am I laughing?

Shane and Chad exchange
terrified looks. "I'm crazy, aren't
I? But don't worry. I won't hurt
you. Pretty sure I won't, anyway.

Lucas, on the other hand . . .
well, if he turns up dead, you won't
testify against me, will you?" I need
to call him. Make him explain.

It's Thanksgiving, but he seems
to have an abundance of time
on his hands. "I have to talk to him.
Can you give me a few minutes?"

Shane Nods at Chad

Who follows him toward the door.
When it opens, comforting scents spill

in, and familiar voices, singing
"Little Drummer Boy." I could lie right

here in Shane's bed, close my eyes,
fall asleep with Gaga purring in my ear.

But that wouldn't change things. So
I go ahead and call Lucas, mostly hoping

he doesn't bother to pick up. He does.
"Uh . . . hi." Why do I want to chicken

out? "Hey. What's up with you sending
those pics around? Did I do something?"

> He doesn't even hesitate. *No, babe.*
> *It's just I'm so proud of you being mine.*
>
> *I wanted to show off my amazing girl.*
> *You're not really mad at me, are you?*

He Wanted to Show Me Off!

How can I possibly be mad about
that? Except, "You know you sent
them to some of my relatives, right?"

People who've seen you naked before?

"Uh, not really. Well, maybe when
I was a baby or something." Or worse,
when I was a chubby little kid.

They're probably impressed then.

At least Chad never saw me naked
and fat. "It was pretty embarrassing,
Lucas. Did you know Shane is my cousin?"

Gay Shane? Huh. Well, he won't care.

"I care." But I find myself caring less,
which is really weird. "Promise not
to do something like that again?"

Okay. So, when can we get together?

Just Like That

I forgive him. Just like that,
      I feel good about him wanting
            to show me off. Just like that,
                  I think of a way to see him.

Even though it's a holiday
      weekend, Mom has to work
            tomorrow. I'll tell her I want
                  to go home with Dad tonight.

Hey, maybe she'll even get
      lucky with Dr. Malik. Anthony.
            That's what he said to call him.
                  Sounds like it's getting serious.

It must be, because when I go
      back out to the living room,
            Mom is standing so close to
                  Anthony there isn't a hint of light

between them. I don't think
      she's missed me at all. Gramps
            is singing "So This Is Christmas,"
                  a fitting last song of the night.

Mom's All for My Plan

Considering how much she used to hassle
me about going over to Dad's,
I'd say that means
something. But I don't
care. If she gets a little, maybe
she'll lighten up. And, more importantly,

maybe she'll be more understanding
about me wanting to go out.
Everyone packs up
their dishes and bums
leftovers and thanks Aunt Missy
and Uncle Chris for their hospitality.

It *was* a really nice Thanksgiving, despite
the nasty cell phone surprise.
We pile into Cassie's
burping Volvo. It's a quiet
ride, everyone fighting an overdose
of L-tryptophan, champagne and sugar.

When We Get to the House

Dad and Cassie stay outside
to smoke. Chad and I carry
the stuff in from the car. Spare
turkey, as Dad called it, and
a plate of mixed pie slices.

> As we're putting the food in
> the fridge, Chad says, *What
> did Lucas have to say?*

I don't think he'd understand
the showing-me-off thing, or
why it's kind of okay. "He said
it was a joke. And he apologized."

> *Harley,* he huffs. *I'd be very
> careful of that guy. He reminds
> me of my dad, who always said
> all the mean crap he pulled was
> a joke. Right up until the day he—*

"Lucas isn't like that. He would never
hurt me. But thanks for worrying."
That reminds me, though. "You haven't
heard from your father, have you?"

Actually, I have. He showed up
here one day. Said he wanted to
get reacquainted. Even tried
to say he was sorry. I told him
to go fuck himself. Know what he
said? That Mom had poisoned
me toward him. That she lied.

I remember the day we saw him
at the mall. Will never forget
the panic in her eyes. "She didn't lie."

I know. When I was a kid, I had
horrible nightmares. He was in
every one of them. Eventually,
they stopped, but lately they've
come back again. I don't want
you to have nightmares, Harl.
Please think about what I said.

That's the most sincere he's ever
sounded. "Thanks, Chad. But don't
worry. I can take care of myself."

I Don't Exactly Have a Nightmare

But I do dream
that I am naked
on a sea-drenched
beach, my sun-licked
skin all golden brown
and ocean-beaded.

Lucas is there, selling
tickets. One dollar
for a look-see, pay-
per-view. I tell him
I'm worth twenty times
that. He laughs at me.

But when I get mad,
he comes over, brushes
my hair off my face,
runs his fingertips
down along my body.
The way I like him to.

And, even though I still
believe I'm worth twenty
a pop, pay-per-view,
I forgive him. And I give him . . .

I Carry That with Me All Day

Through Black Friday insanity.
Cassie is the shopaholic queen.
Fifty percent off anything sends
her into the outer atmosphere.
Black Friday must have been
invented just for her. And I go along!

Then home for football. And more
football. Chad and my dad cheering
and groaning on the couch. Together.
It's kind of a weird picture. But good,
I guess, in a guy bonding sort of way.
At least they have something in common.

It is all so domestic, so boring, that by
the time Lucas picks me up I practically
run to the door, ignoring the look Chad
gives me—the one that reminds me to be
careful. I jump in the car. "Where are we
going?" Not that I care, as long as it's away

> from here. There's something in Lucas's
> smile that makes me wonder if I should
> have listened to Chad. But when he says,
> *There's a party at Ariel's,* I stash all doubt.
> Don't know Ariel. But I'm ready to party.

Turns Out

Ariel is Kurt's big sister. She lives
in a little house in a dicey neighborhood.
Also turns out Ariel is gone for the weekend,
and the party consists of Kurt, Chloe, Lucas

and me. The place is thick with smoke when
we walk in the door, and Chloe's eyes are almost
as droopy as the love seat Lucas motions for me
to sit on. *I'll get us something to drink.* He pours

a splash of Coke into tumblers of Bacardi
151. We listen to music and swap Thanksgiving
stories. We smoke. And I am halfway through
my second drink when it hits me how hungry I am.

I've been up since six a.m., fueled only by
a small bowl of granola. But when I try to ask
if there's anything to eat, it comes out, "Istherany . . ."
Which cracks everyone up. So, forget food.

I drink instead. And suddenly the room kind
of spins. It must show, because Lucas asks,
Are you okay? Maybe you should lie down?
He leads me into a bedroom and . . .

Lucas

I Lead Her into the Bedroom

Barely get her onto the bed
when her lights snuff out.
If I happened to be

a gentleman,

or maybe a little less drunk
myself, the sight of her lying
there, skirt pulled up over
her thighs, panties teasing
a major throbbing boner,

would

maybe not tempt me to take
her this way. But she's a sweet
little piece of virgin meat, and
I've waited patiently. The first

turn

belongs to me, and this is a
prime chance to take it. I climb
up beside her, tug off the baby
blue lace, fling it

away.

Her breath is hot and her skin
is hot, and between her legs
it is wet and hot and the resistance
lasts only a moment.

I Have Resisted

Thinking about the possibility
of a new relationship. For almost
a year, Dylan was the only guy
on my mind. He was an obsession.

After I got pregnant, I believed
he was a necessity, even after he turned
his back, walked (no, ran) away.
Once it became diamond clear

that he wasn't coming back, I was
sure no one would want me. Not yet
eighteen, I felt used, and used up.
Worthless. Contemptible. Hollow.

Suddenly, there is a flicker—a single
candle—of hope that I can love
and be loved beyond Dylan. Why
Ty would choose to shine for me

now is a total mystery. It's not like
he can't get another girl—prettier,
more popular, and a whole lot less
preggo than me. Yet, here he is.

I've Known Him

For a long time. Since elementary
school. We've hung out together, dated
each other's friends. Best friends, even.

We've stood up for each other. Worried
about each other. Obviously cared very
much for each other. But we've never

hooked up. Timing, I guess. Or maybe
on some level we felt like our friendship
might not survive a romance. So, why now?

When I asked, he said simply,
Because you need me now. And
when I asked if he wouldn't be

afraid of what people thought,
he said, *If I was, what kind of person
would that make me?* I kissed him

then. I couldn't help it. And he
kissed me back, so sweetly I knew
he meant it when he said, *I love you.*

It Was a Surreal Moment

Because in that candid declaration,
there was no promise. But there
was limitless possibility, and that

is better because promises fuel
heartbreak. All around me, I see
tattered commitments. Vows in shreds.

And yet, this "maybe," when I need
it most, means everything to me.
I have a future without Dylan.

What's less certain is whether or not
a baby belongs there. This baby, anyway.
What can I hope to give her?

Christmas is coming and everywhere
there are advertisements for toys
and games and clothes and holiday

things for children. Pseudo Santa
surprises. Memories in the making.
But how would she remember me

if all I could give her were hand-
me-downs beneath a Charlie Brown
Christmas tree? She deserves more.

Why is it so hard to admit that?
Pride? Conceit? Selfishness?
I'd like to think it has everything

to do with watching Mom struggle
with not knowing where she came from.
The pain of searching for the connection

most people take for granted. When
I talked to Ty about it, he asked,
Is she happier now that she knows?

When I said I think maybe, he asked,
*Would her life really have been better
if her birth mother had kept her,*

and tried to raise her all on her own?
Tougher question. One I keep trying
to answer. For Mom. And for my baby.

One Thing I Do Know

Is that I'm currently eating for two.
And both of us are hungry right now.

Thanksgiving leftovers are calling.
As I pass by Mom's room on my way

to the kitchen, I notice the door isn't all
the way closed. She is talking on the phone.

> *Vegas sounds really fun, but I can't get
> away till after Christmas. It will probably*

> *be our last one together. I'm not looking
> forward to splitting holidays with Jace.*

Why do I have to hear these things?
It's not like I try to tune into conversations

not meant for my ears. The last time,
I happened to hear Mom and Andrea talking

about me, and about poor Mrs. Trask,
trying to replace little Shelby via in-vitro

fertilization. That must have been what
she was doing at Dr. Ortega's that day.

God, she looked so sad, and yet she tried
to be happy for me and . . .

I am reaching for the mayonnaise
when the proverbial lightbulb switches

all the way to bright. Would she . . . ?
Could I . . . ? If . . , Wow. Bread. Mayo.

Turkey. Cranberry sauce. Making a sandwich
is logical. Making a giant decision is emotional.

Relief. Fear. Sadness. Joy. Not that anything,
really, has been decided. But this is a possible

answer. Possibilities, again. Chew, chew, swallow.
Chew, chew, swallow. My stomach fills with food

and butterflies. I finish the sandwich. Wash it
down with water. Go knock on Mom's door.

It's Such an Adult Idea

Mom can hardly believe it came
from me. But after all the initial
"are you sure's" (no) and "have you
really thought about this's" (not
exactly), her relief is obvious.

Her relief. Which is weird, but
whatever. Guess she thought
a grandchild would put a crimp
in her lifestyle. The one she's
planning on after the holidays.

> *It just might work out, Mikki.*
> *Should we talk to your dad first?*

"What for? He doesn't want a baby
around here any more than you do."

> *It's not about not wanting her.*
> *It's about what's best for her.*
> *This could really be win-win, I think.*
> *But there would be legalities.*

"If we get that far, of course.
But let's talk to Mrs. Trask first."

Mom calls her friend, Andrea, who
happens to have a sister who lost
a little girl and wanted another and may
jump at the chance to adopt the one
growing inside me. Still a part of me.

While we wait for the phone calls
that will relay my offer, I go do some
online research about open adoption.
Had I done so first, I might not have
considered it a viable option. So many

stories, not all of them positive! Most
of the negative ones regard jealousy.
On both sides. Birth parents changing
their minds. Court battles. Back child
support. Yikes! Better get Dad involved.

But there are good stories, too. Adopted
kids who know the important details—
who and where they came from, and
why. Birth moms who see their children
grow. Healthy. Cared for. Loved.

The Call Comes

Sooner than I expected.
Mrs. Trask—Marissa, she says

to call her—can barely hold in
all the questions. One by one,

out they pop, incrementally
harder to answer.

> *When are you due?*
> *The baby is healthy, right?*

Very important to her, of course.
"Everything looks perfect."

> *What about the father? Will*
> *he want to be involved?*

That's a good one. "I don't think
so. In fact, I'm sure he won't."

> *Can we help out financially?*
> *Could I be in the delivery room?*

This is starting to feel very intimate.
How close will we become?

Now, the Ones

I don't have answers to yet.

>How often do you want to see her?
>What if the father changes his mind?
>How much do you want her to know about you?

And the biggest one of all.

>Are you positive this is the right decision?

All I can say is, "I've struggled
with this for months. This is the surest

I've felt about anything. We can decide
the details as we go along." Now she asks,

>Do you have any questions for me?

I know a lot about her already.
Big house. Nice car. Her husband

has money. But is that enough?
"How is your marriage? Solid?"

She Prefaces Her Answer

With an audible sigh. Then says,
You know we lost Shelby after
a long illness. It's hard to stay
close when each day brings
so much sadness. But the reality

is, Christian and I are tighter
now than we have been in years.
He asked his company to lighten
up on the travel and he just got a big
promotion that will keep him in Reno

most of the time. His income provides
nicely for all of us, so I don't have
to work. The baby will have a stable
home, I promise you that. Plus, Shane
will be a wonderful older brother.

That's a lot more than I can promise.
More than most people can.
She needs to talk to her husband.
I need to talk to Dad. We set up
a meeting for next week. And I call Ty.

Tyler

The Setup

She describes sounds
perfect. Maybe too perfect.

I

want to support her decision,
but the idea of a guilt-free giveaway
seems like pie in the sky. You

don't

carry a baby for nine months
without a lot of bonding going on.
I could nod and go along, except I

care

about her way too much to see
her hurt again. Or maybe
my reaction is totally selfish.

What

if I encourage this move and it
goes badly? Would she ever blame
me? I'm not usually one of those

people

who looks for the downside. So
maybe the best thing I can do
is stay positive and try not to over-

think.

Shane
Staying Positive

Has become impossible.
                              It's hard to put into words,
but I feel fractured, and
                              though the two halves of me
still function together,
                              sooner or later I know one
side or the other will peel
                              away. Pretty sure half a person
can't survive, but even if
                              it could, it shouldn't. The split

grows wider, wedged apart
                              by things I have no control
over. Things like the coming
                              holidays. They haven't been
important for years, but now
                              Gram and Gramps want to
celebrate in traditional style.
                              I don't feel like celebrating.
Christmas should have been
                              all about Shelby, who never
really had one. Why should
                              we celebrate without her now?

There's Also the Not Small Issue

Of the semester ending in a couple
of weeks. With it goes Alex, who will
graduate near the top of his class.

He spent last week visiting
Catholic colleges in California,
all of which would be happy to have him.

Loyola Marymount. Santa Clara U.
Thomas Aquinas. University of San
Francisco. San Diego U. His parents

would have preferred an East Coast
school. He insisted on staying out
west. For me, he says. But even

though California isn't all that far
away, it might as well be a thousand
miles from here. How often can I see

him? A few times a year? Our age
difference isn't big. I never really
thought about how much it meant

when it was just about having fun
over the summer. If I hadn't fallen
in love with him, it wouldn't matter

the slightest bit. But he has become
an integral part of me. Who am I
if I lose him? How can I go back

to being the Shane I was before
I met him? That's who I'd be. I've got
the rest of this year, plus my senior

year here. That's a lot of time apart.
And, while I'll be stuck hanging out
with Reno losers, he'll be meeting

interesting people from all across
the country. What chance does our
relationship have of surviving that?

As If That Isn't Enough

Mom has gone totally apeshit
delirious over the idea of another
baby. First, all these tests to see if
she could carry some Frankenstein
test tube creation to term. I breathed

a huge sigh of relief when the doctors
told her no, and I'm pretty sure Dad
did, too. He and Mom are struggling
to put their lives back together.
I'm enough of a distraction. A baby?

How about a job, Mom, or volunteer
work? Something that doesn't require
stealing every ounce of your energy
away from your family? She might
even have gone there, except along

comes the perfect solution. For Mom.
For Mikayla and her family. Maybe
even for the baby. But what about
Dad? What about me? We've lived
with a hollowed-out you for five years.

This Evening, Mom Is Hosting Tea

For the prospective (over)extended
family. She cleaned—and spot-cleaned—

> for days. Vacuumed and revacuumed
> carpets and furniture. *Will you please*
>
> *keep that cat in your room? I can't*
> *get rid of all these little white hairs.*

Washed windows to let sunlight
spill into even the darkest corners.

Set the table with Grandma's fine
china. Including Thanksgiving, it's only

the second time it has been used in
six or seven years. I'm pretty sure

the everyday stuff would do. Right
now, she's showing them Shelby's

room. Which, if everything goes as
expected, will soon be the nursery.

I've tried to keep out of it completely.
So I'm more than a little irritated

when Mom calls, *Shane! Will you please
come here and meet the Carlisles?*

Have I suddenly become a criterion?
Must I put my best foot forward?

Considering I haven't showered
in a couple of days, I hope not.

I also hope she doesn't expect me
to drink tea. Still, no use upsetting her.

Well, maybe just a little. I pick up Gaga,
cradle her in the V of my elbow, go to

play the dutiful son. They are gathered
at the table. Each sits stiffly behind a cup

puffing steam. It reminds me of *Alice's Adventures
in Wonderland*, with Mikayla as Alice

and Mom as the March Hare. I stifle
a snort as Mom makes the introductions.

First Impressions

Mikayla: Pretty, in a blond
                 bombshell sort of way.
                 Probably conceited
                 before life (or her boyfriend)
                 dealt her this hand.
                 But now, uncertain.

Mrs. Carlisle: A knockout, for a woman
                 her age. Workout junkie,
                 and that's obvious even
                 well-covered by a pricey
                 jogging suit. Anxious
                 to be anywhere but here.

Mr. Carlisle: All business. Defines
                 the word *attorney*. Smart,
                 but no match for his wife,
                 and maybe not his daughter.
                 Prepared. Textbook answers
                 at the ready. Anger, in the flesh.

The baby: Will be beautiful and smart.
                 And Mom will love her more
                 than these people's hearts can.
                 And maybe more than she loves me.

Conspicuously Absent

Is Dad who, Mom explains,
got hung up in a meeting,
but should be home any time.
When he arrives, he will, no

doubt, be subjected to a similar
inquisition to the one I'm under-
going now. I try to answer each
question the way Mom wants me to.

> Mr. Carlisle: *How do you feel*
> *about this situation, Shane?*

I don't think he wants me to say
I'm sorry his daughter got knocked
up, so I go for, "I think it's gre—"
But wait. It's not great. "Uh, good."

> Not what he was looking for.
> *I mean, about having a baby sister?*

Mom looks at me with such
expectancy that what can I say
but, "Awesome, I guess. I mean,
it's been a while since I had one."

Okay, that wasn't right, either.
But what do they want from
me? To hear that I'm not done
grieving the sister I lost?

Mrs. Carlisle says, *Babies are a lot
of work. Your mom will need help.*

This one's easy. "I don't mind
helping. I helped with Shelby,
so I'm okay with changing diapers.
Mom has to do the late-night feedings,

though." I remember them well.
"Look. I want Mom to be happy,
and if a baby will do that, fabulous.
Anyway, I love little kids. It's all good."

I must have done okay, because
they let me go, just about the time
Dad comes bopping in. Gaga and I
retreat to our cat-hair-covered sanctum.

I Turn On My Music

To swallow their hum, reach under
             my bed for the bottles that will drown
      the questions jumbled inside my head.
                I pop some anonymous pill--the pharm
          dealers at school aren't always so
savvy. I asked for antidepressants,
              have collected them for a couple
       of weeks. Sort of fun going for a ride
without knowing exactly where
              you'll end up. So I pop another.
        Wash it down with big swigs
           of Jägermeister. Goddamn it.
        I should feel all warm and fuzzy.
Instead, I just want to cry. Can't.
        What if they hear me? They might
              think I've gone all schizo. Change
         their minds about giving Mom
the baby, who does not need
              a crazy-ass big brother. I grab
         the bottles, head for the travel
     trailer. "You stay here, Gaga."
              She doesn't need to see me cry,
either. It's freezing inside, so I turn
         on the heater. And while I wait
     for it to get warm, I down
             three or four pills. Maybe more.

Jäger and Downers

Make me feel great. Make me feel
like shit. Make me go ahead and cry.
I spiral down into a whirlpool of tears.
And I like how it feels and I hate how
it feels and right now I really just want
to keep going down and never come up   for air.

I think this must be limbo. Too dark
to see and too heavy to move even
though it's cold and you want to get
warm but really what difference does
it make because you're going to be here
forever where it's hard to breathe   the air.

And I'm sort of scared and sort of happy
because I think pretty soon I won't care
anymore but before that happens I need
to call someone. Alex. Yes, Alex, because
I love him. Speed dial number one. Good.
My eyes are blurry. Something about   this air.

"Hey, ba . . ." No, not baby. "Hey, you,
I luhv ya. Jush wanna say that 'fore I shay
goo bye." And he's yelling something
but I can't make it out because I'm falling.
And I like how it feels falling toward   death.

Alex

I'm Yelling

No! You can't leave me.
Not now. Not ever. Not
like this. Oh my God.
Any God. Tell me what to do.

I

hear him say he's falling,
and there is no way for me
to catch him. I call his house.
No answer. Come on.

Can't

you hear the phone? You
must be home. Finally,
his dad picks up. "Hurry.
It's Shane. You're going to

lose

him." And suddenly I know,
"He's in the travel trailer.
Please. You have to hurry."
The phone drops. He's gone for

him

and I get dressed. Slowly.
Go to my car. Slowly. Drive
to his house under the limit.
Afraid of what I'll find.

Afraid, Angry, Ashamed

Violated. Altered. Changed
forever and I didn't even get

the chance to say okay. I might
have, but Lucas never bothered

to ask. Instead, he stole it from me.
It's supposed to be a memorable

experience. One you don't enjoy
lightly. He didn't let me enjoy it at all.

In fact, I barely remember anything
about it. Alcohol blackout, they call it.

Only it wasn't quite black enough
to erase the entire memory. Weight.

There was his weight pushing down
on me. Stabbing. I felt him stab inside

of me. Breathing. Booze and weed
and onion-sweat stink. His hair,

like a spider creeping over my face.
The horrible shudder that meant

he was done. And still I couldn't
move. Not even when he rolled

off me, skittered across the floor
and out the door. Leaving me there

like discarded trash. Something
used up and left behind to rot.

Your first time should be special.
Not something you can't quite

scrub away, no matter how hard
you try. Something that sticks to you

like tree sap. Stubborn. Indelible.
Marring your finish until you rust.

I'm Not Even Sure

How I got home. Who drove,
        or when I got in. Stumbled in

at my dad's, made my way
        to the couch and crashed there.

Good thing it was Dad's. Mom
        would have been up waiting,

knowing exactly what my messed-
        up clothes and hair and alcohol

breath meant. I was so buzzed
        I didn't even wash until morning.

Waking up was the hardest thing
        ever, sunlight assaulting my eyes

and something hammering on
        my skull and a pool of acid swishing

around in my stomach. I barely
        made the bathroom in time, though

it was mostly dry heaves.
        Heaving what remained of me.

The Best Part of All?

He dumped me the same day.
Not only that, but he dumped me
secondhand, through Chloe.

I was waiting for Mom to pick me
up, still fighting the pounding
in my head, when she texted me.

>   THIS IS REALLY MESSED UP
>   SO I'M SORRY, 'K? LUCAS SAYS
>   TO TELL YOU HE DOESN'T THINK
>
>   YOU TWO ARE SIMPATICO. STUPID
>   WAY OF SAYING HE WANTS TO
>   BREAK UP WITH YOU. SORRY.

Two apologies, and both from
her. Just about then, Chad wandered
in and sat next to me on the sofa.

>   Heard you come in pretty late
>   last night and I noticed you slept
>   on the couch. Everything okay?

"Wonderful. Amazing. Really
great." Then I showed him Chloe's
text. But I didn't tell him the rest.

I Mean, Who Could I Tell

Something like that to?

Dad?
Ha ha ha ha.

Cassie?
Too busy being positive about the wedding.

Chloe?
Already has a good idea, but I'm not about
to give her any details. Don't really trust her.

Bri?
It's just way too embarrassing. Maybe
one day, if I get drunk enough. Except
lately I've been thinking that getting
drunk—especially blackout drunk—stinks.

Which kind of leaves Mom.
Who is currently crazy about her doctor
boyfriend. Who happens to be what a boyfriend
should be. Handsome. Rich. Upwardly mobile.
And, most of all, respectful. Of her. And of me.

I wish I could tell her. But I don't know
how. Where would I even begin?

So I've Kept It All In

And it's eating me up.
One good thing. I started
my period today. I'll be bloated
for the wedding. But I won't be pregnant.

Speaking of that, seems
Aunt Marissa and Uncle Chris
might adopt Mikayla's baby. I hope
that works out. They're talking about it

now, I guess. Our families
connect in weird ways. Triangles,
kind of. I think it's awesome, but Mom
is worried that Aunt Marissa might be acting

impulsively. Mom's a fretter.
I really don't want to be the cause
of her anxiety. So I'm just sitting here
next to her, watching TV, acting like nothing's

bothering me. She's doing
the same thing. But I know she's
waiting to hear the latest from Aunt
Marissa. The phone is right next to her.

It's So Close, in Fact

That when it rings, she jumps.
Guess she was caught up in the movie
after all. But if I thought she was worried

       before, whatever she's hearing is making
       her pace. Did Mikayla decide to keep
       the baby after all? *Thanks for letting*

       me know. We'll be right there. She keeps
       her voice calm, but it trembles, and so do
       her hands. *Get your coat. And hurry.*

Okay, this is bad. But we're both
bundled up and getting into the car
before I ask, "What's wrong, Mom?"

       She puts the car into reverse, backs
       carefully onto the icy street. *It's Shane.*
       Oh, Jesus, how could he . . . ?

"How could he what?" Now I'm
getting scared. And just as it seems
like we need to drive light speed,

it starts to snow. Blizzard. The first
major storm of the year, and it's an early
arrival. "Where are we going, Mom?"

> Saint Mary's. Shane . . . well, they're
> not sure if it was intentional, but he
> may have attempted suicide.

> He's in critical condition. She swerves
> to avoid a coyote, and the Subaru fights
> to stay on the highway. Damn animals!

"Take it easy, Mom. Slow down.
Getting into an accident won't help."
She regains control, lightens her foot

> on the accelerator. I know. Sorry. I
> just want to be there for Missy. How
> could he be so selfish? Good question,

if he did try to kill himself. He wouldn't,
though, right? I just saw him at Thanksgiving.
I would have known something was wrong.

Right?

Snow Swirls

In the headlights are hypnotic.
It's like I can't look away, and
as I stare, questions materialize,
ghosts, dancing against the windshield.

Why did he do it, if he did?
Why didn't anyone see it coming?
Why would he hurt his parents even
more than they were already hurting?

What, exactly, happened to make
him choose today? Was it because
of his mom wanting another baby?
Why wouldn't he want her to have one?

Those are the easy ones. The next
ones are darker. Macabre, even.
How did he do it? Why didn't it
work? Will it work in the end?

Who found him? How did he look?
Was he fighting for life? Or so close
to death that he looked like a corpse
already? And am I sick to wonder?

The Waiting Room

Is crowded with family. Gramps
meets us at the door, worry creasing

> his eyes. *Missy's in shock,*
> he warns. *They've sedated her.*

Her face is the color of parchment,
and her eyes are empty. She leans against

Uncle Chris, who clenches and unclenches
his left fist. I've never seen him show

emotion, not even at Shelby's funeral. His
right hand clutches Aunt Marissa's like if

he let it go she might leave him, too. "Sit
down, Mom," I tell her. She looks unsteady

> but she shakes her head. *I want*
> *to talk to Gram.* Gram, who paces

from the far wall to the door, poking
her head out every time she reaches it.

I sit next to Gramps. "Where's Alex?
He knows, doesn't he?" He must.

> He knows. I guess Shane called
> him to say goodbye. Which is why
>
> they think it was a suicide attempt.
> Alex called Chris, who found Shane,
>
> unconscious in the travel trailer. It
> smelled like gas, but he had taken pills,
>
> too. Antidepressants, Jägermeister and
> carbon monoxide can be lethal all by
>
> themselves. Combine them . . . He shakes
> his head. They pumped his stomach,
>
> put him on oxygen. They're not sure if
> he'll make it, or if he'll be okay if he does.

Alex must be freaking out. "So, where
is Alex? Why isn't he here?"

> He's here. He went down to the chapel.
> He said he hasn't prayed in a while, but . . .

Alex

But Maybe It's Time

To try prayer again.
Gay and Catholic are hard
to reconcile. Figure in
molestation and HIV,

I

gave up on God a long time
ago. Then I found Shane, who
offered not only love, but real

hope

that there might be something
beyond this life. Even for me.
So here's the thing,

God.

I'm asking for a really big favor.
Maybe one I don't deserve.
But Shane does. He reopened
my heart to you. So if it

is

your will, please, please send
him back to us. We need his light—
your light, shining through him.
And if you're feeling especially

generous,

please give him back whole.

I'm Feeling Good

About my decision. The Trask house
is huge. Beautiful. She'll have a big
room. Plenty of toys. Pretty clothes.
Nice things. Lots of attention. Love.

I'm feeling awful about my decision.
Every time she moves inside me
tonight, it's like she's asking, *Why,
Mama? Why do you want to give me away?*

In theory, getting to see her every
now and again will allow me peace
of mind. But what if knowing she's
that close only makes me want

to see her more? I hate being torn
like this. Hate Dylan for making
me fall in love with him. Hate
my parents for glomming onto

this solution, going on and on about
what's best for me, best for the baby,
when what they're really concerned
about is what's best for them.

A Big Part of Me

Feels like "my" decision has more
to do with them than it does with me.

When the Trasks walked us out to
our car, Mrs. Trask hugged Mom,

as if *she* was the one giving up her baby.
Then Dad shook Mr. Trask's hand.

> Like they were closing a business deal
> or something. *My colleague will be in touch,*
>
> Dad said. *We need to spell out the details*
> *on paper.* Go, Dad. Let's sign the contract.

I'm not sure if my current reticence
has more to do with all that than the simple

idea that I might be making a mistake.
Why can't this just be easy? Is it ever?

Exhausted

By the mental wrestling match,
       I fall back on my bed, look
       over the rising hill of my belly.

Will it ever return to flat terrain,
       or will a small knoll always remain,
       no matter how many crunches I do—

a reminder of sweet summer love
       turned sour? Where is Dylan tonight?
       Has he, for even the smallest fraction

of a second, thought about me
       tonight at all? Does he ever feel regret?
       Just a minute ago, I hated him. Why

am I filled with such love for him
       now? How long does it take to fall
       back out of love? How much time

to blunt the sharp stab of pain?
       How many girls must I see him
       with before I don't care anymore?

Outside

Snow falls softly from the night
        sky. Beautiful. Beautiful, and
               early this year. It brings hope

of a white Christmas. Here
        in northern Nevada, the chances
               of late-December snow are what

some people (especially tourists)
        might call a crapshoot. Growing
               up, I would send wish lists to Santa,

and they always included snow,
        carpeting the ground, frosting
               windows and falling while we opened

our presents. When it happened,
        I knew he was real because who
               but Santa could create such magic?

But on off years, I wondered
        what I had done to displease
               him. Funny, how things work.

Why snow this year?

Bone Weary

Still, I can't sleep. Might as well
study. Trigonometry. Radical.
What will I ever need this shit
for, and why did I sign up for it?
Not like I need it to graduate,

or to get into UNR. That's where
I have always planned to go.
Why leave home, especially when
your boyfriend is going to stay put,
too? Except he's not my boyfriend

anymore. And if Mom and Dad stay
on their current path, who knows
where home might be next year?
I could go to college somewhere
else. Or skip it altogether. Travel

Europe with a backpack and
a college fund expense account.
Meet some amazing guy, sipping
cappuccino in Paris. The possibilities
are limitless. Except with a baby.

Dylan
A Baby

Was not in my plans, and
the weird thing is, this ugly mess
has opened an unforeseen door.

                                                  I

had it in my mind that I would
stay in Reno, go to UNR. Maybe
share an apartment with Mikki
or something. But since there

                                                will

be no Mikki, I decided to join
the Marines as soon as I turn
eighteen. Fuck it. I could use
a little adventure. Yes, there's

                                              always

the possibility of deployment
to some third world hellhole.
Maybe it would make me man up.
I'm pretty sure there will never

                                              be

another girl in my life quite like
Mikki. But if there is, I'll do things
differently. I never, ever again
want to feel so goddamn

                                            sorry.

Someone keeps saying that.
Over and over. I think it's . . .
"Mom?" I open my eyes.
Where the hell am I? Everything
is blizzard white. But it's warm.

And it stinks like alcohol. So
it must be, "Am I in the hospital?"

> Mom, who is sitting in a chair
> beside the bed I seem to be in,
> jumps to her feet, grabs my hand.
> *Shane? Oh, honey! Look at me.*

I try, but it's hard to focus
past whatever tubes they've stuck
in my nose, apparently to breathe
for me. "Wha-what happened?"

> The emotion in her eyes segues
> from relief to suspicion. *You don't*
> *remember?* When I shake my head,
> she goes rigid. *You . . . you . . . you*
> *tried to kill yourself. If not for Alex,*
> *we'd be planning another funeral.*

Kill Myself?

Did I try to kill myself? Wait.
Splats of memory—

Cold.
Really cold.
Snow falling as I slipped
across the icy driveway.
Jäger.
Pills, three or four.
Maybe more. I don't remember.
Lying on the bed,
waiting for the heater.
Something about air.
Sliding toward darkness.
Spinning.
Alex.
Yes, I called Alex, to . . .

To say goodbye.

But I didn't try to die.
Did I?

Why Would I?

Almost as soon as I think it,
Mom echoes the question.

> *Why, Shane? Why would you?*

Before I can respond, to tell her
I'm not sure why I would or if
I even did, she hits me with,

> *How could you be so selfish?*
> *How could you do that to me?*

Something detonates inside me.
Something hot and vile and raging.
"Why is everything about *you*,
Mom? What the fuck about me?
When was the last time you talked

to me, or really looked at me, or
even thought about me? Goddamn
it! For years, you were all about
Shelby, and I got that you had to be.

When she died, I thought maybe . . ."
My heart knocks in my chest and
I'm wheezing. But I can't stop now.

"I thought maybe you would pay
attention to me. But, no. Now, you want
a baby. A Shelby replacement. Only
better because the baby won't be sick.
She'll be cute and sweet and you can

dress her up and take her for walks
and show her off. . . ." I'm running out
of steam. But I manage to repeat,
"What the fuck about me, Mom?"

Tears drip onto my chest from eyes
that can't meet mine. She doesn't say
anything for a while. Then, finally,

> *I– I . . . I don't know what to say except*
> *I'm sorry. It's just, I've been so sad. . . .*

"Yeah, Mom. Me, too." That makes
her look at me. She shakes her head.
Slowly, as if understanding is settling in.

> *You're right. About everything.*
> *Maybe we should all get help. Together.*

That She's Willing

To admit she might need help
        is a giant step in the right
        direction. I've known I need help

for a while. I was just too proud
        or scared or straight-out stupid
        to ask for it. You can't conquer

every demon on your own.
        "Hey. I don't suppose Alex would
        happen to be around here somewhere?"

        She smiles. *Of course he is.*
            It's not regular visiting hours,
            but I'm happy to tell them he's your

        brother. As long as you don't kiss
            him when a nurse is in the room.
            It wouldn't seem too brotherly.

She goes to get him. It feels like
        we came a long way in a few minutes.
        But not nearly as far as we have to go.

Brianna

In a Few Minutes

The "Wedding March" will start.
Not played on the organ,
but a recorded version by the old
band Queen. According to

Harley,

it's rockin'. I'm pretty sure I prefer
it traditional. But, hey, not my choice.
For a church wedding, this one

is

condemned to be off the wall.
Harl says Cassandra's dress
is even shorter than hers is.
Of course, Harley's is scarlet.

Still,

red, white or silver (!), you sort of
expect a bride not to flash thigh
during her vows. I will do

my best

not to judge her, any more than
I look down on Harley for things
she's done. Whatever. I'll always
be here for her. That's what a real

friend

does.

Here I Am

Waiting in the church nursery
for the sanctuary to not-quite-fill.

Hoping the industrial strength
maxi pad will be enough to get

me through the ceremony. My period
has been ridiculous this time. Don't

know what that could have to do
with that night with Lucas, but it

must. Punishment, maybe? Whatever.
All I know is, I feel like a fake.

When I first tried on this dress,
I loved how it looked on me,

all mid-thigh short and scooped
to reveal my pushed-up boobage.

I wanted to look grown up, and I do.
But I'm not. And now I don't want to be.

Too Late, Harley

Some things you can't take back.
Some things you can't talk about.
I only used a little makeup today—
a soft brush of blush, a little mascara.

Cassie looked at me as if she expected
more. She didn't say anything. But I kind
of wish she would have. How is it possible
that the people who really know me don't

seem to suspect a thing? If they looked
deep enough into my eyes, how could
they not see a certain knowledge there?
That, and shame. Not so much because

I lost my virginity, but because I lost it
to someone so unimportant. Someone
who enjoyed hurting me, the whole
time saying he was proud of me.

Maybe it's good I'm bleeding like this.
Bleeding every trace of him out of me.
Except the memory. I'll never lose that.
So I'll work on losing the bitterness.

The Door Opens

It's Mom. She hasn't seen me
in the dress and she takes a good
long look at me in it now. Sighs.

> Wow. When did you grow into
> such a beautiful young woman?

Corny, but whatever, and it makes
me smile. I make my voice all
stuck-up. "I prefer 'goddess.'"

> More like "temptress" in that dress.
> But beautiful, either way. Listen . . .

Uh-oh. She's getting serious. *Brianna
is out there and before the two of you*

> *talk, I wanted you to know that Missy
> has decided against the adoption.*

"What? Why?" It was the perfect
solution. How could Aunt Marissa
change her mind? "Does Mikayla know?"

Calm down, Harley. Yes, Mikayla
knows, and she understands. Missy

thought long and hard about it.
In the end, she decided she needs to

concentrate on her marriage and
on her relationship with Shane.

Okay, I guess I understand, and
I'm glad she told me now. But,
"What's Mikayla going to do?"

    I really don't know, honey. She
    still has some time to decide.

The door opens again. Cassie, back
from a very long bathroom trip and still
adjusting the skirt of her short silver

    dress. *Phew! Must have been nerves.*
    Ready? Your dad's starting to pace.

Mom winks. *Break a leg. Just not*
while you're walking down the aisle.

All Decked Out

In charcoal tuxes, Dad and his best
man, Chad, stand at the altar, waiting.
Cassie gives a little nod and Queen
begins to play an electric-guitar-heavy
"Wedding March." Fifty or so people

stand to watch me precede Cassie
down the aisle. When we reach
the front, Dad and Cassie join
hands and the minister launches
a prayer, asking God to gather

the hearts and minds of this pool
of witnesses. For some reason,
that reminds me of this author
who came to our school. He talked
about how every word an author writes

causes ripples, like tossing a stone
into a pond. And you don't know where
they'll go, or who they'll touch, or when
they might come back to you. I think
everything you do is kind of like that, too.

Author's Note

This book is a companion to my novel *Triangles*. It explores the same family situations from the points-of-view of three of the *Triangles* teens. Though they view these issues—teen pregnancy, adoption, HIV, chronic illness—through different lenses, their hearts are inextricably linked to the other characters in *Triangles*.

It is my hope that Alex's story will serve as a reminder that HIV and AIDS have not gone away. Some estimated statistics, according to the U.S. government:

- More than one million people in the U.S. are living with HIV.
- One in five living with HIV is unaware of his/her infection.
- Every 9.5 minutes someone in the U.S. is infected with HIV—an estimated 56,300 people every year.
- More than 17,000 people in the U.S. die from AIDS every year.

Mikayla's story is not unique, either. According to a study by the Guttmacher Institute:

- The teen pregnancy rate in the U.S. is the highest of any industrialized nation.
- More than 725,000 teen pregnancies occur every year.
- 82% of these pregnancies are unplanned.
- Although the teen pregnancy rate dropped in the 1990s, in 2006 it actually increased 3%.
- In 2006, 58% of teen pregnancies ended in birth; 27% resulted in abortions.
- Only 66% of teen mothers get their high school diploma or GED by age 22. Only 2% attain a college degree by age 30.

Sex is an important part of life, but please consider delaying it until you are in a committed relationship. And please remember that an unplanned pregnancy or sexually transmitted disease will change your life forever. Be smart.

Acknowledgments

Special thanks to my friend, Juan Guerrero, whose personal story inspired the character of Alex. And also to amazing author Bruce Coville, whose talk about words causing unexpected ripples inspired the last poem in this book. Finally, a huge nod to my friend Tracy Clark, an up-and-coming author to watch out for. Sometimes it takes neutral eyes to see the way to end a book. Thanks for being my eyes, Tra.